THE WORLD EVE LEFT US

THE WORLD EVE LEFT US

Boston Teran

HIGH TOP
PUBLISHING llc

To the little deaf girl with her battered camera
who lived in that basement apartment.

ACKNOWLEDGMENTS

To Deirdre Stephanie and the late, great Brutarian . . . to G.G. and L.S . . . .
Mz. El . . . . Roxy and the kids . . . and finally, to my steadfast friend and ally,
and a master at navigating the madness, Donald V. Allen

PROLOGUE

THE LETTER

Dear Reader,

I have helped to cover up a murder. I have helped to perpetuate a lie. I have done what my life, the law, my religion and my profession disavow. I am all the happier for it.

But, I have been asked now to help tell you the truth, to chronicle the story behind that truth, to detail the women's lives that led to that moment of truth.

If it had been left to me I would have told you nothing. I am, unfortunately, only a minor player in this drama, who knew of all this only after the third victim had been accounted for. If fate had tested me, I wonder, would I have had the courage to fire the gun?

· · ·

When Natalie finished the brief letter she added it, as a preface of sorts, to the edited manuscript, which she was preparing to send back to the publisher.

On her desk were the photographs Eve had taken on the streets of the Bronx, which would become part of that living record that would, in the end, expose the truth in all its tender and violent detail.

Natalie turned off the desk lamps. She looked out the window of her tenth-story, CO-OP City apartment and across the Hudson River Parkway to the wildlife refuge sanctuary. It was a silhouette of peace against the moonlight. A windblown solace of high reeds past which headlights flared then vanished. Yet even that held secrets.

She glanced at the photos, at the manuscript. She wondered, when the truth was known, how would it be judged?

TWO MOMENTS IN TIME

Chapter 1

August 26, 1975

54 YEAR OLD BRONX SHOPKEEPER
GUNS DOWN DRUG DEALER

Franconia Kuhl, aged 54, a longtime shop owner and resident of West Farms walked into Precinct 48 and surrendered herself to authorities for the murder of Bobby "B.Lo" Lopez.

Mr. Lopez, aged 28, had served sentences for the possession and sales of narcotics, assault, and attempted burglary. Mr. Lopez was found in the hallway of an abandoned apartment building on the corner of Cypress Street and Third Avenue. He had been shot three times.

Ms. Kuhl was not a suspect at the time of her surrender. Desk Sergeant Thomas Rodriguez said that Ms. Kuhl entered the precinct around 7 A.M. and calmly explained that she had shot Mr. Lopez the previous night. She took from her purse the alleged weapon which was wrapped in a bloody towel.

There is no known motive yet for the murder.

Chapter 2

EVE AND CHARLIE STRETCHED OUT on a blanket on the roof of her apartment building and looked up into the soul of a warm Bronx night. She rested her head on his shoulder. He smoked a Kent and blew tight gray rings into the air which she grabbed at with a finger trying to catch and hold.

When she needed to tell him something she tugged at his shirt and spoke in sign. There was beautiful passion in those long slender fingers. She would talk and talk, and sometimes he would grab her hand and affectionately bite it to get her to slow down.

She wished she were wearing lipstick when she kissed him. She hoped he'd noticed and liked her new perfume. She was seventeen and he was twenty-one. They existed within the simple prose of the human heart. The urgencies of now, the tides of tenderness. Every moment a meaning unto itself.

After all she had suffered and lost, after all she had survived, she'd never expected on God's earth that such happiness could be hers.

From his shirt pocket Charlie took a tissue wrapped present no bigger than the tip of his thumb.

———[1] For you, Eve Leone, he said in sign.

She reached for the present all surprised and excited and he pulled his hand away to tease her. She reached again and he eluded her once more and the two hands moved like butterflies in the darkness, one chasing the other.

He finally relinquished when she put on a look of coy exasperation. He felt a stirring warmth as he watched her pull away the tiny sheets of tissue paper to reveal a necklace. It was a necklace from which hung letters in silver: I-L-Y[2].

---

1   When a character speaks in sign a dash (———) will be used in place of parentheses (" ").
2   "I-L-Y" is "I love you" spoken in sign.

PART ONE

GOD WAS NOT LISTENING

CHAPTER 3

CLARISSA LEONE WATCHED another dinner she'd cooked for her husband dry away. She put the radio on low and sat listening to the big bands playing live out at the Glen Island Casino.

She poured a half glass of wine. She drank in silent disgust, the turbulence of her life running through her. A woman awash in hopelessness, caring for a sick and deaf daughter and a husband who—

She heard workboots outside scuffing on the cement floor, the shuffle of keys. Their apartment was in the basement of a five-story walkup, just off of Tremont in West Farms. The janitor's apartment, wedged between the incinerator room and the boiler room. Four brick walls, a steel door, an alcove that pretended to be her daughter's room, a sheet across the opening for privacy, and two street-level windows of wired glass that faced the alley.

Romain came into the apartment carrying a small garbage bag all rolled up. Clarissa noticed there was dirt on the bag, and when he bent down to kiss her she could hear things jingling inside that bag.

On the far wall were a gray industrial sink, an ice box, and a stove, which only had two burners that worked. Romain set the bag down on the Formica table where his wife sat. She eased her wineglass away from the bag as he stoppered up the sink.

He opened the bag and began to remove his plunder. A gold engraved cigarette lighter, a cameo brooch, two silver goblets that he put in the sink, a little coin money he also put in the sink, a rabbit's foot that he tossed on the table by Clarissa. "For Mary," he said.

She looked at the rabbit's foot without expression, nodded, and knew the first chance she got, she would throw that goddamn thing into the incinerator.

Romain ran the water and began to wash the goblets. "The dead delivered today."

• • •

They lay in the dark in their Castro. Romain leaned over to his wife. She could smell the wine on his breath. "I want another one," he said.

There was no point in faking sleep, no point in pretending. He would find her wherever she hid. "I want one that isn't sick, and isn't deaf. I want a boy, or at least a girl that I'm not..."

Her voice came out flat, in the barest manifesto of defiance. "No."

• • •

Something woke Mary. Had she picked up on the unnatural vibrations around her, was it the shadows moving in violent fragments beyond the sheeted doorway that always led to her mother coming into the alcove crying, curling up on the bed beside her baby. Sometimes there was blood trickling from her mother's nose or mouth.

In the feral silence that followed, a mother reaches out and takes her three-year-old's hand and even without understanding, the child understands the fear, feels her mother's fear, absorbs her mother's fear.

"Please God," begged Clarissa, "don't let me get pregnant."

CHAPTER 4

BUT GOD WAS NOT LISTENING. Just a week shy of her twenty-ninth birthday in the year of our Lord 1950, Clarissa found out she was pregnant. She did not tell Romain.

Clarissa worked in a small warehouse just off Gun Hill Road in Williamsbridge. She was a cutter in a non-union shop that made terry cloth robes. Eight hours a day she cut patterns from long thick strips of terry cloth. Young as she was she already began to suffer from arthritis.

She'd bring Mary with her to work. A few of the other mothers had to do the same. A playpen of sorts was set up in the corner where the women could watch over this small brood. The air was always filled with particles of terry cloth, and against the huge warehouse windows, the light looked like the inside of one of those glass balls you shook and it got all snowy.

During lunch break the girls celebrated Clarissa's birthday with coffee and cake. While the boss wasn't looking one of the women took a flask from her purse and winked at the others. She spiked the coffees and they all told a few stories they wouldn't have otherwise.

In the washroom later Clarissa confessed to a Jewish woman who always brought two small boys that she was pregnant. There was a rumor the Jewish woman had had an abortion.

• • •

Clarissa would often go over to St. Philip's on the Grand Concourse because for years they had celebrated the Mass in Italian and it gave her joy. Mary had also been christened there.

She sat alone in a pew with her Christ and her demons, grasping for some ultimate truth, or at least a deliberate direction.

She wanted to undo her life. She did not want to bring another child into the world in which she lived. How could she apply everything she had been taught to such a painfully desperate situation? How could she find the courage, or at least the will to defy everything she had been taught, knowing what it meant to her soul?

A woman along the far vestibule was lighting a candle and praying. Clarissa hoped the woman got what she prayed for.

At the bottom of each church window was a stained glass panel from a moment in the Bible. The one of Genesis caught her eye, with daylight burning through a naked Adam and Eve, stooped in sin, and hiding from their God.

She was just a simple uneducated woman who believed everything that happened had been her fault. She believed, on some deeply misunderstood level, she was to blame for a deaf child, and for the abuse she suffered at the hands of her husband.

And as much as Clarissa did not want to believe what she had been taught, as much as she wanted to break away from the beliefs that would keep her from giving up this child she could not undo the mystery around her heart that life was a sacred province and the suffering she endured daily would be rewarded later by an all-loving God.

AMERICAN FLAG PILLOW

CHAPTER 5

CLARISSA RODE THE BUS every day to work with one child at her side and the telling roundness of one within. She endured the slush of winter and the cold warehouse hours cutting terry cloth with an aching back and swelling legs.

She would often stare at her reflection in the bus window. Faces floated there in the dark of her memory. The girl she'd left behind, the one she might have been.

She looked down at Mary, alone in her silent world of child thoughts. Mary liked to touch her mother's stomach. It hadn't been easy using homemade signs to explain the coming of a baby sister or brother, but when Mary did understand, she drew a picture with crayons of a baby inside a bubble that was her mother's belly.

Mary wanted the picture taped to the wall beside her bed and every night before she went to sleep Mary would kiss the picture good night.

• • •

Romain was a building janitor, but he also worked at St. Raymond's Cemetery doing lawn maintenance and digging graves. He worked with his cousin Dominic who had gotten him the job.

The little plunder he brought home came from rifling caskets before the dead were shoveled away. In the spring of '51, William Thomas, a police sergeant in Brooklyn, was killed in a car crash on the Whitestone Bridge. His wife put in the casket their wedding picture, photos of their children's first holy communions, and a .38 she had given him for his previous birthday. She'd had the gun engraved:

> —*To my straight shooting husband*
> *Love, Kiki*

Romain held up the wedding photo before he tossed it aside. "Not a bad-looking piece of ass."

Dominic pointed at the gun. "I'll flip you for who keeps the piece."

• • •

The baby was born prematurely. Seven months. Mary was born prematurely and she'd ended up deaf. Clarissa was frightened.

She delivered the baby at home, in their basement apartment on a sweltering day in July, lying there on a Castro Convertible with her legs up. Dominic's wife, Gail, brought along a midwife. Clarissa recognized the woman as a cashier from the religious bookshop over at St. Lucy's.

What Clarissa remembered most about delivering the baby was staring at those street-level eyelet windows that looked down on her while she prayed the baby would be born healthy and whole.

While she struggled through labor, Romain and Dominic got a sixer of Schlitz and sat on a bench in the playground behind the house. They drank and smoked and watched a dog pack of boys play salugi and chase each other over the playground fence in a wave of Indian shouts that echoed along the apartment walls. Watching them made Romain all the more anxious.

They were well into a third sixer when Gail came out. She bummed a cigarette and took a can of beer from her husband. She wiped the cool wet can along her forehead.

"It's a girl," she said. Then she looked at those empty beer cans stacked up. "I see you boys have had a tough afternoon."

CHAPTER 6

ROMAIN SAT AS GENTLY as he could on the edge of the Castro where his wife lay in exhausted sweat. Beside her the baby slept. She was small, so small. She had dark skin and a full head of black, black hair. Her two tiny hands were balled up into fists.

"Ready for the world," whispered Romain.

Mary cuddled in beside her father. She waited for him to notice her, but he did not. Romain was caught up in one thought, don't let this one be fuckin' deaf too.

Mary tapped her father on the shoulder. She pointed at the baby, gave a big smile and began to dance around trying to tell him how happy she was to have a little sister.

But Clarissa also saw what Romain did not. The child was trying to do everything not to be left out.

• • •

Gail ran a cool cloth across Clarissa's forehead. "Any idea about a name?"

Dominic, who was sitting at the Formica table nursing a beer and lighting a cigarette, said, "How about Susan?" He winked at Romain. "As in Susan Hayward."

His wife gave him a burning stare. "Don't smoke in here with the baby. What are you stupid?"

The cigarette dropped into a dead can of beer.

As Romain began to say, "We got time—" Clarissa, in a spent voice, answered, "Eve…I'm going to call her Eve."

Romain looked at his wife. This was the first he'd heard of it.

Clarissa kept on. "I just like the name for her."

"I like Susan better," said Dominic, hoping it rubbed his old lady just a little bit wrong.

"When did you come up with this?" said Gail. "You never said a word to me."

Clarissa shrugged. "I don't know." She motioned for Mary to come close and give her baby sister a kiss.

But Clarissa had lied. She did know when she'd thought of the name. It was that day in St. Philip's Church when she was trying to get up the courage to have an abortion.

CHAPTER 7

EVE WAS SO SMALL they carried her around on a pillow. It was about the size and shape of a pillowcase and each side was an American flag.

Gail made the pillow for Clarissa when she was pregnant. Gail was a seamstress and it seemed the company she worked for had gotten an overstock of material on these American-flag beach umbrellas that had been commissioned for the 4th of July. That's how the notion was born, it was supposed to be a little cheer-me-up for Clarissa.

So here was this tiny baby, with her rich olive skin and her huge dark eyes and those two tiny fists which never quite seemed to let go, swaddled in the downy softness of the flag.

Gail thought it adorable and funny at the same time and nagged Dominic into going right out and buying a Polaroid and flashbulbs.

• • •

The overwhelming early days of having a baby, the mingled joy of sleepless nights and helplessness, the pride over the neighbors' need to look and coo and congratulate, the precious delicacy of life that brought out such feelings of love, did not cut the edge of what lay at the heart of their urgency.

They would whisper in the child's ear, call to her, shout to her, rattle unseen noisy toys, but still one could not be sure.

Every slight movement registered hope, every non-movement was its stinging reversion. A child of days—weeks—even Mary was not diagnosed as deaf until she was about seven months old.

Clarissa lay on the Castro looking down at Eve nestled in that pillow flag, with Mary there beside her softly rubbing baby sister's cheek and making noises that might otherwise have been words.

Clarissa prayed, no, prayed was not the right word, pleaded that goodness not be withheld from them. It was not without some shame she made that plea.

Though for her the answer could not come soon enough, as she saw Romain grow more touchy and depressed with each day, and she knew all too well he had no good way of harnessing all the scorn and anger that was becoming humanely visible in his every thought, word and deed.

• • •

Romain and Dominic were at the trotters, throwing away what little money they had on longshots and losers. For both men it was even worth losing to get in a couple of hours' rapt elation away from the bitches and gripes, from shoveling grave sites and incinerator trash and from everything else that smacked of too much fuckin' reality.

At the racetrack bar, working the forms, Dominic nudged his cousin. "You want another Jew's booze?"

Romain, preoccupied, only nodded. Dominic yelled to the barkeep and fingered up two, "J and B."

An ass went by that demanded Dominic's attention. "No latex holding that fuckin' thing in place."

Dominic glanced at his cousin. Romain wasn't looking at the form, he hadn't given the ass a glimpse. He was strictly sipping his scotch and staring at nothing. Dominic fanned his hand in Romain's face to get his attention.

Romain's eyes drifted over to his cousin. "You still got that .38 we copped from the casket over in Section 11?"

"Yeah."

"You got shells for it?"

"Yeah...whatch you want it for?"

The call for the next race went out. Romain finished his drink. He motioned for his cousin to hop to.

CHAPTER 8

THE APARTMENT WAS DARK when Romain returned but for a crease of light slipping through the partly ajar bathroom door. The sound of the shower running was somewhat soothing, at that moment, in its own odd way. The apartment, if you could call it that, smelled of stale cigarettes and babies. Clarissa had not heard him enter.

He moved with a nervous solemnity toward the small crib, which had been placed next to a bureau on the opposing wall, the one farthest from the alley windows. The room was darkest by the crib. He could hear water moving through the exposed pipes that ran the length of the ceiling. Romain tried to take the gun from his coat pocket but it clumsily caught up on some torn cloth. An omen, a warning?

His thoughts were stark, more so compared to the simple sleeping beauty of a baby. The tiny chest lifting, the face achingly serene. The way we all are, he imagined, before the world has had its say. The thought betrayed him. A wave of anger came on like the rush of too much caffeine.

He cocked the hammer, he aimed the gun. He fired.

The room exploded. His shadow burned through a flash of light and onto the brick wall for a bare heartbeat. Clarissa screamed out.

She scrambled from the shower as he stood there. The bathroom door swung open. Naked, dripping wet, she saw him turn toward her. The light framed the gun. It framed the smoke floating across the crib, a sickening acrid yellow. Somewhere from a window above the alley came a voice shouting, "What was that?"

Romain pointed the gun at the crib. "She's deaf."

Clarissa, trembling, lost, dripping as she came forward, arms clenched around her chest, looked from her husband to the baby lying there asleep, to the gun in his hand.

"She's fuckin' deaf," he said again. There was a righteous fury to the way he pointed the weapon, as if necessary to make his case.

From the alley came an echo of more voices. People calling back and forth to each other…"Did you hear a shot?"…"It sounded like a shot"…"Was that a scream?" All of them could hear, thought Romain, all of them but my own.

Then, out loud, "They could all hear it. All of them up there. And she's still—"

Romain's actions were so unspeakable, so freakish, it frightened Clarissa in a way she could never have imagined.

He put the gun down on the bureau. His eyes were red from the liquor and the fact that he was about to cry. "It's all your fault," he said. "Yours."

She was shivering. A puddle of water collected on the concrete at her feet.

He sat on the edge of the Castro like someone shunned from all that the world had to offer. "Say something," he said. "Say one goddamn thing at least."

She felt so starkly alone at that moment, caught in a tangle of unspeakable emotions. Her crossed hands went up around her throat as if to help along what she was about to say, or to stop herself from saying it. "They're our daughters."

CHAPTER 9

IT WOULD NEVER BE THE SAME AGAIN. On some primal level her relationship with Romain had been effectually altered, if not devastated.

She would be forever in a semi-crouch. While she cooked she would steal glances over her shoulder. She would let herself be made love to, though she would never be touched.

But she also knew she was going nowhere. She was that basement apartment, the warehouse where she worked, and whatever she could fit between.

Her personal needs, she buried them. The sense of shame, the sense of failure, she'd let it all just wail away inside her soul. She would bear the cross but not let on, not let on.

When they were out, Romain would walk ahead or behind Clarissa and the children, so it would seem like they were not together. At the Festival of Assunta, Romain was nothing short of hostile as Clarissa tried to explain to the girls in homemade sign a float with the Virgin Mother moving up the Grand Concourse.

As she struggled to decipher the code of finger pointing and head shaking for ices that the girls wanted from a street vendor, while a crowd stared and waited, Romain had had enough and coldly ordered the ices and that was that.

Clarissa was sitting on the stoop one night with the neighbor women, listening to Julius La Rosa on a radio one of them had placed in the apartment window so they could enjoy the procession of summer outdoors.

The music was all innocence and the invocation of memory. Strings that sang with anticipation, moonlight, romance. Mary sat beside her mother. Eve rested her head on the pillow they'd used to carry her around on as a baby. It was so especially hers, something she went nowhere with, without a struggle. Eve was not docile like her older sister.

The music…it was a world that would never be within her children's reach and the thought of it hurt Clarissa so. Her children, that is how she had come to view them. How she spoke of them. Inarguably she realized she had drawn a line in the sand.

How do I bring the world to my babies? How do I affect their lives so they do not end up like me?

At Orchard Beach with Gail, Clarissa got up the nerve to ask, "Are you afraid of Dominic?"

Gail was smoking a Chesterfield. She stubbed it out in the sand. The beach was crowded and loud. All those people made Gail feel smaller and even less important than she was.

She bent her head and covered her eyes from the sun as she looked at Clarissa. The question led to dreaded answers they would never speak of again.

AT CHRIST'S FEET

CHAPTER 10

EVE'S FIRST MEMORIES were of twinkling Christmas lights across the ceiling of their basement apartment. She would lie on the Castro with Mary staring up into the beauty of those magic shadows. And the tree, with all its tinsel and crepe paper ornaments, the few presents wrapped with such ornate delicacy it almost hurt not to reach out and touch them.

There were the smells of espresso and cookies baking and the brick behind the bed so warm from the building boiler, churning out heat just on the other side of the wall.

She and her sister would spend incalculable time watching this great illusion of human magic till they dozed off into the quiet of each other's arms.

Eve also remembered the beatings. She remembered them first when waking to feel her sister's trembling hand take hers and watching the sheet across the alcove entrance moving, trembling as her sister's body trembled, and knowing eventually, whether a short time passed or longer, that her mother would appear and curl into the bed with her babies. She would be crying often and often there would be blood.

Sometimes, the worst times, the sheet would be pulled aside and her father appeared. His mouth would be moving frantically and his face would take on shapes that seemed to burn in a way that made her mother tremble and her sister tremble. And even then Eve understood, he did not love her like her mother loved her and Mary.

Once when her father reached out to grab her mother, Eve swiped at his hand. She did not remember doing it, she did not know she even did do it. There was just some place in her, some ancient place that had not yet been found and defeated, that still belonged to the soul of the body that carried it.

• • •

And there was that day in church, the one that formed and informed the rest of her life, when just after Christmas Mass, as the parishioners were making their way out of St. Philip's and her mother stood talking with a friend at the edge of a pew, Eve managed to slip loose of her sister's grasp and unseen make her way between the pant legs and the dresses and the children no bigger than herself, till she reached the altar rail.

There was some primeval awe Eve felt standing at the altar with its statues and light that came through long windows and made the reds and golds and purples swim with shining color.

But it was the crucifix on the back wall, the imposing hugeness of the suffering face, and the blood. She did not understand what it was or why it was but it surely was her mother's face she saw there on the nights when she hid in the alcove. The lidded eyes, the wounds, the way the body bent with pain.

Chapter 11

FRAN KUHL DID NOT OFTEN go to church. The reality of all that had died for her during the full flower of Naziism. But she was at St. Philip's that Sunday playing Good Samaritan for a neighbor who was too infirm to make Christmas Mass on his own.

While helping the old man toward the aisle Fran noticed this tiny dark-skinned waif of a thing open the rail gate just as assured as she could be and start up toward the altar. Fran watched with fascinated eyes as an altar boy who was snuffing out the candles called to the little girl, but she kept right on a path of her own.

When Eve reached the crucifix she looked up and up and up. A woman, Fran assumed it was the girl's mother, had started quickly after her, apologizing to the altar boy as she went saying, "She can't hear…She's deaf."

Fran saw Eve, still one with her thoughts, reach up and begin to tap the feet of that crucified body tenderly and she kept tapping, as if to say what? I'm sorry you are in such pain. It will be better. It will be all right. That simple act of such childlike sincerity filled Fran with a pain that cut right to the heart of memories which floated up into her throat.

Fran reached the center aisle just as Clarissa and Eve were coming down through the altar gate. There was another little girl there waiting. Clarissa motioned for her to come along also.

Fran shepherded the old man into the line of people, and once alongside Clarissa and the girls, she said, "Adventurous," meaning, of course, Eve.

Clarissa looked exasperated, if not out-and-out embarrassed. "Once they can run at full speed in two directions at once, you're finished."

Fran smiled at the two girls. The older one had a quiet, almost forlorn look, but the stare on the face of the younger one gave Fran pause. Maybe it was some incommunicable struggling need remembered, or the obscure ripples of life surfacing that caused it. Children can do that. They can bring up the lost in our beings.

Then, for whatever reason, though Fran was sure from what she'd seen neither mother nor children knew the language, Fran took a moment, released herself from the old man and signed to the girls.

"That's actual sign language, right?" said Clarissa.

"I was telling the girls," and Fran again repeated in sign, as she said, "Merry Christmas."

The children had an indefinable expression watching, something akin to intense curiosity and playful confusion.

"I saw a peddler once," said Clarissa, "by the Bruckner Boulevard subway station using some kind of sign language."

"And Merry Christmas to you too," Fran said to Clarissa, taking again the old man's arms and starting down the church steps.

Clarissa watched the woman walk off. She was so nicely dressed, and the way she appointed herself with her hair pulled back and those glasses. She had the look of a teacher, or at least someone successful.

• • •

Fran was helping the old man into a late model Ford when Clarissa called out to her.

Fran turned to see two struggling children being dragged through the slushy cold toward her.

"I know this is Christmas and you're probably in a hurry, but, could I have just a word with you?"

CHAPTER 12

IT TURNED OUT FRAN KUHL owned a candy store just east of Crotona Park near the corner of Longfellow and 173rd Street. There were two apartments in the building above the store. Fran lived in one of those apartments. She also owned the building.

Fran had Christmas dinner with relatives and friends of the old man. His family was from Birkenwender and part of a clique who had left Germany before the war, or escaped later, to avoid the sterilization laws. For them Christmas in America was more than just an expression of sentiment.

Christmas night Fran spent alone with a bottle of wine and the radio tuned to a station that featured holiday carols. At the desk mirror Fran thought she looked much older than most women of thirty-two. Even taking off her glasses and undoing the bun didn't help. No wonder, she thought.

She glanced at Max's picture there on the desk. In his basketball uniform, standing outside the gym of the Vocational School for the Deaf at Griswald, the ball tucked under one arm, the other leaning against the open gym door. All pomp and splendor for the camera. Eighteen and looking boldly at the world. She tenderly adjusted the frame. Max—he would be eighteen forever.

The holiday, the wine, the music, the snow sticking to the window as it fell, they fleshed out and tinted memories for Fran, and she would always end up going through boxes of prints and proof sheets taken in Germany when she'd dreamed of being a photographer.

But even as she relived those black-and-white instants of her youth she couldn't get the image of that little girl at the altar out of her mind. Even as her mother, what was her name, Clarissa, asked to come by and seek advice about her deaf daughters, the image of that child brought up everything Fran had ever felt about love…and anger.

A STOLEN CAR AND A CASKET

CHAPTER 13

CLARISSA AND ROMAIN WENT to a New Year's Eve party Gail and Dominic were throwing. The night ended at a bar down their block. It was a murky little place with a few tables. Each table had a candle on it and Romain kept walking around with his drink saying, "Those candles make you feel like genuflecting right here, don't they?" And that's what he'd do. He'd get down on his knees by a nice pair of legs and say, "Father, forgive me, for I have sinned. I need to confess I have impure thoughts." Then he'd lean down like he was trying to look up Gail's dress and he'd get his head swatted and amidst the laughter he'd say, "Oh yes, Father. I have some bad fuckin' thoughts."

Clarissa had had a few Camparis herself. Just enough to cut the edge off her fear. And when she was sitting with a couple of the girls, she started to tell them about this woman at the church who could speak in sign language. "For the deaf," Clarissa emphasized, "and the woman wasn't even deaf herself." And how the woman offered to give her advice concerning Mary and Eve.

Clarissa made sure Romain could hear what she was saying, using this as the safest way she could think of to get the subject out in the open. But she made sure she punctuated every notion with, "Of course, I have to talk it over with Romain first."

• • •

They were on the elevated riding home, sitting side by side. Out the subway window a nightworld of buildings and lights trundled past that screeching iron carriage.

"My father was right," Romain said very, very quietly. "You're all fuckin' cunts."

Clarissa did not look at him. Instead she chose to stare straight ahead at his reflection in the window across from their seat.

"You think I don't know the shit you were trying to pull back there. Try to get all the bitches behind you." He curled up his mouth, mocking her. "'I got to talk to Romain, of course.' Total chicken shit."

"I want to be able to talk to my children."

"*Your* fuckin' children is right. Otherwise they'd be able to hear."

Clarissa closed her eyes. She'd come this far, how much would it cost to go just a little bit further?

"The lady at the church told me about a school called St. Joseph's—"

"They stay with you at work. They learn what you learn."

"That's just filled with possibilities, isn't it?"

"They'll learn to make a living."

She huffed at the very thought of it. She opened her eyes. Romain's face took on that look she knew too well. She felt suddenly trapped. Complete desolation set in. She knew she shouldn't say any more, but she cleared her throat enough to get the words out. "They need to be able to talk to each other. They need to know the world. We go to church, they don't even know who God is, what God is. I can't tell my children I love them."

The train began its descent into the tunnel. The sound of metal on metal knifed at the ears. Romain took to staring at a drunk curled up on a seat by the door.

"Look at that piece of shit there. They ought to drag his ass out and toss him under the wheels of the fuckin' train."

When they reached their station and Romain was sure no one could see him, he hocked on the sleeping drunk as the car doors jerked shut.

• • •

Romain carried his sleeping children from the apartment of the old lady who had been watching them. While Clarissa got the girls tucked into bed Romain went down the corridor and unlocked the incinerator room door.

He turned on the light. He pulled over a tied-up stack of newspapers, stood on it, stretched up and unscrewed the bulb. The incinerator room went dark. He stood down. He kicked the stack of newspapers back where they'd come from and flung the bulb against the back wall.

Clarissa had only just gotten her shoes off when Romain walked back into the apartment. "Come with me. I want to show you something."

"What?"

"Come on," he said.

She listened for a hint of anything in his voice that might warn her.

"Come on."

She nervously reached for her shoes.

"Forget the shoes. You won't believe this. Come on."

He led her out into the hall.

CHAPTER 14

ROMAIN WAS ALWAYS CAREFUL not to fight with his wife in public. He had one face for the world and the about-face for his family. The tenants in the building found him affable, a hard worker, charming. "He's too bright to be a porter," they'd tell Clarissa. And she would nod.

Romain would carry the tenants' groceries up flights of stairs. Any little thing in their apartments that went wrong he'd fix with a wink and a nod. "Don't tell the landlord how good I'm treating you," and they'd slip a little something into his shirt pocket.

When he found those cheapo nudie magazines or a calendar some tenant snuck into their trash so no one would know what they were reading Romain would stash them away. "Hey, Mr. So-and-So, you're an optometrist, right? What do you think about this for an eye chart?" Or, "Hey, Mr. So-and-So, you teach geography, right? What country, exactly, do you think we're looking at here?"

He repaired people's cars, their kids' bikes and toys, always getting a little something forced into his pocket for the favor. What they did not know was that Romain would sneak into the carriage room where the kids kept their bikes and wagons, and he'd slit a tire here or wreck a wheel there. "Mrs. So and So...a flat? Looks like a tear...I got a patch kit'll fix that. Your boy's sure growing...could be another Mantle."

He'd do a little moonlighting in the garage too, and the next morning he'd show up just when Mr. Schmuck was bent over all stupid looking at his car engine. "What's the problem...Sure, I'll have a look. We'll get you to work on time...Thanks, Mr. So-and-So, but you don't have to—"

He and Dominic would meet over at a tavern on White Plains Road where they made book with the barkeep. "Look what that dumb kike slipped me for fixing his car after I niggered him."

When they reached the incinerator room Romain grabbed his wife by the arm and shoved her through the doorway and into the darkness.

She stumbled. "What are you—?"

He let her loose and before she got her footing he had walked out of the incinerator room and pulled the door shut.

She rushed forward blindly, feeling the space before her. "Romain?"

She heard the bolt-latch slip into place. "Romain?!"

"Take a few hours, hon, to get sober. And watch out for the rats."

She started pulling frantically at the doorknob, but it was useless. She slapped at the steel door, but it was useless.

Her chest began to immediately constrict. Beads of sweat started to string across her neck. A wave of nausea gripped her. She was deathly afraid of rats. And she was claustrophobic. Romain knew. For Christ's sake, she couldn't even bear to have the bathroom door closed all the way.

She pressed her head hard against the steel door. Harder and harder. She wanted to scream but she could not bear the humiliation of anyone knowing that she'd been locked in the incinerator room by her husband like some pathetic—

There was a skittling of claws across some empty bottles in a trash bin. Her breath came in numb threads. It felt as if matter itself were crumbling all around her.

She slipped down to the floor. Pulled her legs in close. Locked her arms around her legs. She made herself into as small a ball as she could.

The darkness she'd been shoved into felt as if it were leaking its way into her body. Like some filmy black substance filling every vein, flooding her lungs. She was becoming something frozen and dead, while alive.

• • •

The subject was not brought up again after that night. Clarissa did show enough nerve to travel all those blocks to the address Fran had given her.

She watched the candy store from across the street and up at the corner of Longfellow. It was a gray day with a flaw of beautiful sky. It was a mystery to her why she had come this far.

She saw Fran at the back of a double-parked truck signing off on an order of soft drinks. When Fran turned to go back inside she seemed to stop for a moment as if something up the street caught her eye. Clarissa could have stood there and let herself be seen, but instead, quickly turned and got around the corner.

Whatever the future would have become, whatever would have lain ahead, for better or worse, all that changed with Mary's death.

CHAPTER 15

ROMAIN GOT WORD of the accident when he was over at St. Raymond's working. Mary had been rushed to Calvery Hospital. He and Dominic arrived in the faded light of afternoon. Gail was sitting in the corner chair with Eve on her lap. A nurse was just leaving the room. Clarissa was at Mary's side.

Romain came over and put an arm around his wife's shoulder. Mary was drifting in and out of a coma. In those few moments of clarity, Clarissa saw how frightened and confused the child was. She wanted to be able to tell her… "Mommy's here"…"It will be all right"…"Mommy will take care of you"… "Don't be afraid, Mommy loves you"…but all she could do was listen to the vague but panic-stricken sounds her firstborn made.

Romain walked over to Gail, leaned down and whispered, "What happened?"

Gail lifted up her head to whisper back, "She was jumping on the couch and fell. She hit her head on the concrete floor."

• • •

It was near midnight when Mary died. Romain was sitting in the chair with Eve asleep across his lap. He knew as soon as he saw the way Clarissa's upper body began to shake.

It's over. She's better off, he thought.

There was a faint wail of traffic in the street.

• • •

To pay for the casket and funeral, Romain and Dominic drove to Flushing and hunted out a car they could score. They sold it to a fat Russian Jew called "The Cossack" who ran a chop shop over by the wrecking yards in Whitestone.

• • •

Eve more than remembered the wake. Her sister in the tiny white casket. Being lifted by her mother to kiss Mary one last time. The closing of the cold, white, casket lid. The sleeping face forever put away.

Her father had to pull Eve from the casket. She kicked and fell to the ground.

She made her father drag her out of the funeral parlor. She tried to slap at his hand.

Mary had, alive and dead, her sister's undivided allegiance against their father.

The pilgrimage to the cemetery, the headstones in the autumn sun, her mother sobbing into a white lace handkerchief, her father's empty stare. These images became an indelible part of Eve's history.

Mary gone, Mary gone.

THE SCARLET LETTER

CHAPTER 16

GAIL STAYED AT THE APARTMENT with Clarissa for a few days. Romain bought a used television thinking it might give his wife something to take her mind off her sorrow. Even Gail was surprised at how compassionately Romain was acting.

Romain had to go out one night on an errand for the landlord. At least that's what he told the girls. Truth was, he walked over to a club on Westchester Avenue that was a hangout for hookers.

He picked up a reedy thing. Young, probably alcoholic. She had a room in the tiny hotel that was above the club. After they fucked, Romain wept, telling her about his daughter's death. He was gentle, the hooker thought, in a way most men never are.

He laid up with her for about an hour, pitching out his soul, confiding his disappointments, working through the inconvenience of any guilt he felt.

• • •

For Clarissa, after Mary died, a certain fear died.

There was a six-stool counter in the candy store Fran owned. She was sitting there alone at closing time, having coffee and doing the day's receipts. The fountain man was finishing up. When the front door opened and Fran turned, there in the dusty light were Clarissa and Eve.

Clarissa came forward uncomfortably reintroducing herself. It had been nine months since they'd met at the church, but seeing the little girl again, everything registered.

Fran invited Clarissa to sit. Eve was wide-eyed walking an aisle of greeting cards, and then one with boxed and packaged toys.

"How have you been?" Fran asked.

"How have I been," repeated Clarissa. And in a moment of complete honesty while she fidgeted with the buttons on her coat said, "My daughter, Mary, died last month and…and…" her voice faded plaintively, "I never got to tell her how much I loved her."

Fran watched this woman's mouth purse up to keep from crying. Eve was spinning a stool chair. Wiping down the counter, the fountain man heard everything.

"Dr. Frank," said Fran, "will you close up for me please?" He nodded silently.

Fran took Clarissa's arm. "We're going upstairs to my apartment to talk."

There was a door at the rear of the store that opened on the hallway stairwell leading up to Fran's apartment. Eve's shadow followed the women up the tiled stairs. "You called that man, Dr. Frank?"

"He was a doctor in Germany before the war. But things were done to him."

• • •

Clarissa sat in the dining room while Fran made coffee. She looked the apartment over. The furniture was well-made and had the feel of old Europe. The rugs were dense and their designs a dream with the end of daylight falling upon them. There were aromas in the house different from those Clarissa was accustomed to. And the photographs. Everywhere photographs. On the breakfront, the mantel, even the sitting room desk where the phone was kept.

Clarissa was doing her best to keep Eve from grabbing and handling everything in sight, when Fran came back into the room with a serving tray.

"You can let Eve roam."

Clarissa noticed that on the tray there was not only coffee, but a bottle of sherry and two glasses.

"You have a lovely home," said Clarissa. "The kind of home I once imagined having."

Fran did not remark on this, but only held up the sherry bottle and a glass.

"I shouldn't," said Clarissa.

"Don't let me drink alone." This Fran said as if she were asking for a much needed favor, and Clarissa smiled.

Chapter 17

THE WOMEN DRANK AND TALKED. Fran watched Eve slide along the buffet looking at the framed photographs as if they held some grand mystery.

"My...husband thinks my daughter is better off being with me instead of going to school. I work in a factory cutting terry cloth robes. She'd have a trade, you see."

Eve had moved on to the sitting desk and was staring with helplessly huge eyes at a cloth doll with long cotton fingers of yellow hair.

Standing, Fran asked Clarissa, "What do you want?"

Clarissa took a moment of hard thought at the challenge of actually separating her will from Romain's.

"Eve can only tell me what she wants by pointing. And she doesn't understand why I can't always do for her when she asks. She doesn't even know she has a name. When it comes time for school—"

Clarissa hesitated. Fran walked over to the desk. As she reached for the doll her eyes fell upon Max's picture. There was a glinty bit of light on the silver frame.

When Clarissa saw Fran hand Eve the doll, she said, "Oh no—"

"Please," said Fran. "My old friend here doesn't get the kind of attention she was used to."

As Fran returned to the dining room table and sat, Clarissa asked, "How did you learn this sign language? Why? I mean, you can hear."

Fran poured more sherry. She was on her third glass before Clarissa had even finished her first.

"My parents were educators. They started a school for the deaf." Fran pointed to a photograph on the buffet of a tiny building with a steepled roof and gables. "I lived at the school. I was the only completely hearing child, so I had to learn if I wanted anyone to play with." Fran glanced at Eve. She was making sounds to the doll. "I learned what it was like to be the outsider."

"Were you trained as a teacher? When I saw you in church, I thought you were a teacher."

Fran felt for her bun. She was quietly mortified at the thought. "I'll have to try harder next time not to go out looking so—"

"I didn't mean to suggest—"

"It's alright, I'm only poking a little fun at myself. I don't really feel I begin to look quite right till I've had at least four or five glasses of...whatever."

Fran waved her hand from spot to spot in the apartment. "I wanted to be a photographer. That's why all these pictures. But with the war and coming here. This business was an uncle's. My father's brother. Some of our family money went into it. *This* is all that's left now."

Eve came over to show her mother the doll. She pointed at the doll's hair and then at Fran as if to remark how much they were alike.

"What would you do if you were me?"

From the little Clarissa had said, and the vaster amount she'd avoided, Fran had a sense that whatever she answered could become the cornerstone of a conflict. It gave her pause.

Fran glanced at the sitting desk while she surmised. She took another drink of sherry and thought of Max lying there, trying to string together words with his hand against a backdrop of bloody snow. All within the profile of his captor's cold breath.

Fran closed her eyes. She needed another drink to restore her spirits. And more than that.

"It's all my fault," said Clarissa.

"I don't understand."

"There was no deafness in Romain's family. It must have been mine…but…I was an orphan you see. I lived in a home for Catholic girls in Castle Hill till I was sixteen. Maybe it's just God's will."

As Clarissa reached for her wine, Fran said, more as a cold afterthought, "The old heresies strike again."

CHAPTER 18

"WHAT?"

Fran sat there for a moment with her rooted thoughts. Repelled by the bare slavishness to a notion that those born deaf or blind, those infirm or unimaginably ill had their origins in God's will. And if it was God's will, it must be a righteous act. And if it's a righteous act, the raw calamity of our existence must be our fault. And if it *is* our fault, whose fault is that?

Whose fault? Whose crime of long ago disobedience was the basis for this unspeakable agony? Who was the weakest one? Who deserves the most blame? Who should pay the most for this subversive philosophy?

Fran looked at Eve. She was at the table playing with the doll, serving it an imaginary cup of coffee, or maybe a glass of sherry.

The more you believe God is at the heart of it, the more you deserve what you get.

"You asked," said Fran, "what I would do if I were you. I'd find someone to

teach you and your daughter how to sign, so at least by the time she was ready
for school—"

"What does a thing like that cost? How much?"

Fran felt Max's picture there over her shoulder. The stolen possibility she
could never quite overcome. Fran thought of the countless night lost hours
since. Of moving through the half-life of the world. Being in this place, but not
truly of this place. Not since they'd cut the heart of it, out of her.

She kept looking at the child and looking at the child and seeing her that
moment in church with the brocaded light of winter streaming through the
stained glass windows and Eve tapping the bloody feet of that crucifix.

Fran got up and walked to her desk. From it she took paper and a box of
colored pencils. She sat at the dining room table and using a red pencil wrote a
capital **A** on the paper.

She turned the paper around for Clarissa to see. *"The Scarlet Letter,"* she
said.

Fran saw Clarissa did not understand the reference.

"It was a book," said Fran, "about a Puritan woman who had to wear an **A**
on her chest for everyone to see because she'd had a child out of wedlock. My
mother used to tell all her students," and Fran pointed at the **A** on the paper, "this
was the true scarlet letter. Because it represented education…and knowledge.

"And these can be troublesome allies. Because as you begin to realize there
are choices, that the world is more than what you knew, you may get a taste for
the new.

"The people around you, closest to you, may want, demand, that you stay
the way you were. Because if you change, you become a threat to their way of life.
And in not doing as you are told you may risk a lot worse than being told."

Fran sat back and took her wineglass. Clarissa began to process what Fran
had said and as she did a marked feeling emerged that took on the shape and
form of her husband.

Fran watched this dark and rather comely woman, uneducated, reluctant,
modest in every way, come to her decision.

Fran then held up her right hand, closed the fingers down in a soft, flat
fist and placed the thumb upward against the fingers. "This is the letter **A**," she
said.

It took a hesitant moment for Clarissa to realize.

Clarissa copied Fran's hand with her own. Eve was looking back and forth
between the two women. Fran took Eve's hand, shaped it to mimic her own. She
pointed to the picture of the letter A and back to her hand.

Hand—picture. Picture—hand.
The war had begun.

DUSK AT THE GLEN
ISLAND CASINO

CHAPTER 19

AS THE MONTHS MOVED ON, the alcove wall became a mosaic with pictures in colored pencil of each letter of the alphabet and below each picture was taped a cutout of the corresponding hand sign. Clarissa thought the J and Z would be the hardest because they demanded the movement of fingers, but for Eve it turned out they were the easiest and most fun of all.

The world began to clarify through this beautiful silent witchcraft. Time being measured in tiny increments of knowledge. Eve grew to understand the signs for rudimentary words. Hungry…bed…happy…scared…daughter…mother…together.

The world of the basement and the bus ride to the warehouse took on amazing proportions and expanded to the candy store with its comic books and bags of toy knights and princesses and swiveling stools and Dr. Frank serving her jelly donuts and egg creams at the counter, and friends who came to see Fran and talked with fingers like she did. Passageways of the new and inviting, soundless voices.

• • •

After breakfast one Saturday morning, Romain ordered Clarissa to put a nice dress on Eve as he was taking her with him for a couple of hours.

It was the first time he'd ever suggested such a thing, and knowing Romain as she did it gave Clarissa pause. "Where you taking her?"

"Listen to the fuckin' way you say that. You of all people."

"I'll get her dressed."

Romain came and stood in the alcove entrance while Clarissa slipped her daughter into a simple blue frock. He looked over the alcove walls. He looked at his daughter who was looking up at him. He winked at her and smiled and it was the first time he'd ever winked at her and she beamed.

"You think you're putting something over on me, don't you?" Romain said.

Clarissa glanced up at him. "I'm trying to get our daughter educated so she doesn't have to end up—"

"Try not to kill her in the process."

The words cut right into the heart of her. Clarissa closed her eyes. Got her daughter's shoes on. She tried not to cry before Eve was out the door. She didn't want Eve to see her like that as she was leaving.

Romain pointed to the letter A and made the sign with his hand. It was the first time he had ever signed to Eve about anything. It was a day of firsts.

"Why did you ever marry me?"

Romain took his daughter by the hand. "My dick thought it was a good idea at the time."

• • •

Romain picked up Dominic and they drove out to Flushing to see the Cossack.

"I'm a little nervous," said Dominic.

"Take a fuckin' breath and think money."

Eve stood in the doorway of the Cossack's trailer and looked out over the high walls of wrecked cars, their metal grim and glittering in the light. It was like some enormous castle to play in.

When it was explained to the Cossack he thought it a nice smart touch bringing the child. Who would suspect a couple of dagos with a kid were carrying? When the Cossack found out Eve was deaf he gave her a lollipop and patted the top of her head affectionately.

• • •

Eve sat between her uncle and father while they drove back to the Bronx. Dominic held three cigar canisters bound together with rubber bands. Eve watched as he unscrewed the lid on one. Inside was what looked to be sugar.

"I never seen it before…not this close anyway."

Eve reached out to grab for the canister but Romain pulled her hand away. "Close that up."

They were rattling along down Third toward the Harlem River. Eve saw a flock of pigeons race over the top of a bus and into a muggy sky. The day was all exciting and new.

"What's the name of that coon joint we're looking for?"

The Food Palace was a coffee shop down in Mott Haven. During the 'fifties, there had been a large migration of Puerto Ricans into the city. Mott Haven and Hunt's Point, both largely black neighborhoods, had been hit particularly hard.

Eve walked into the coffee shop holding her father's and uncle's hands. They got more than a few stares as they took seats in a booth.

"Coon owned and operated," whispered Dominic. "Check the food for poison."

The waitress came by to take their order. She purred over Eve, "What's a lovely little thing like you gonna have today?"

"She's deaf," said Romain.

The waitress apologized. She looked visibly hurt. It made Romain angry to have a child who had to be apologized for. Especially to a nigger. Eve had never been this close to a black person. When she could, she touched the waitress's arm. The color was so dark and creamy, like her own.

Romain tugged at his daughter's frock. Motioned no, to not be doing that. When he got her attention, he motioned her to look at the wall. There were photos from an ice cream company of delicious looking sundaes. He made the sign for hungry and pointed from Eve to the sundaes.

He'd gotten that sign too from the alcove wall in his own quiet time. All excited, Eve nodded. For the first time she was happy to be with her father anywhere.

• • •

They were to meet a man named Sam Bones. Dominic knew him on sight. He wore his hair slicked back and straightened, and when he walked past the table, Romain saw the nigger was wearing a sport shirt and slacks that he sure as shit couldn't afford.

Dominic got up a few minutes later and followed Sam, who had already gone out into the alley. Romain was to keep watch from there.

The two men made their trade tucked up in an alley doorway. Above them was a rusting fire escape where laundry hung five stories high. They could hear Spanish drifting down through that vacuum of air between buildings.

While Sam Bones did his check and Dominic kept watch, Sam kept talking about how the fuckin' PRs were moving in and how they kept chickens in their apartments and cooked on the fuckin' floor. He'd seen it, it was true.

"Can you believe the nigger?" Dominic said to Romain. "Like I should weep over his fuckin' predicament."

Eve watched as Dominic passed her father some money while they were stopped at a light.

"They smell of Spic-and-Span," said Romain, "you notice that?" They got an odor. They must bathe in the shit or something."

Eve was happy and tired and she leaned against her father, and as the car took off, she began to drowse and the last she saw of the city was reflected across the eye of the windshield where it twined and merged with the buildings themselves and then was gone.

CHAPTER 20

FISHING BOATS FAR OUT on the water, within the reaching cry of gulls, white and swooping overhead, the day beautiful all the way to Hart Island. But one boat with a white sail, alone from the others. Different, different. Bent into the wind, its sail like a delicate handkerchief.

Eve was at the edge of the City Island Pier, looking through those huge silver binoculars on a pivot stand that it takes two hands to move, where you pay a penny and get a minute's worth of view time.

Eve would pull her eyes away from the binoculars and look out over the water. The boat was no bigger now than a tiny thumb-size toy. Then back to the binoculars. The thrilling world of perspective, more magic than magic.

"It makes me nervous," said Clarissa. "I don't know where Romain and Dominic take her. It's been going on for two months. A Saturday one time, another they show up at the warehouse and take her for a few hours. He's got extra money now too."

Clarissa and Fran leaned against the pier rail flanking Eve. They ate deep fried shrimp from paper cups.

"It's not my place, I know," said Fran, "but did you ask Romain?"

"You only ask Romain once. If I go to Gail, she'll probably tell Dominic. And Dominic. Well…Romain likes to say, when one of them has to take a piss, the other reaches for his fly."

It was a moment humorous and telling. Eve now turned. She pointed to the boats. She wanted to know.

Fran cupped her hands together like the hull of a boat and bobbed them forward. Clarissa copied her, Eve did the same.

"I'm frightened," said Clarissa. "I know Romain too well."

Clarissa went and sat on a bench. Eve signed to Fran, —— Boat, happy. Fran nodded and signed back.

"You taught her more already than I ever could," said Clarissa. "I wish I were smarter. Maybe if she'd had a different mother."

Fran cut her off with, "It's the lie." She saw Clarissa did not understand. "The lie you were taught from the beginning. From the moment you came into this world. If anything is wrong with the baby, it's the mother's fault. If they don't say it, they think it, feel it, believe it." Fran wanted to get into the very religion of the idea, but she didn't. "The Nazis perfected the notion of blame, but they had plenty of help." Fran reached into her purse and took out a flask. "Scotch," she said.

She sipped, then offered it to Clarissa who shook her head no. Fishermen passed and stared at the flask, the women. Clarissa felt embarrassed, Fran paid them no mind.

"As far as me teaching Eve more than you ever could. What she has, you can't teach. And that came from your body."

• • •

There was no need for Clarissa to be back home and cook dinner. Romain had told her he was going out for the night. Fran had gotten it into her head they would buy sandwiches and beer and drive over to the Glen Island Casino. It was live band night and they could sit outside on the lawn, listen to the music and watch the couples dance.

They'd spread a blanket on the grass near the old cannon by the Sound. They watched as a pink dusk fell across the horizon, its color soft as the petals of a flower. They watched the couples arrive in their cars. Young with life. The air smelled of roman and the casino was luminous along a line of French doors that reflected out onto the water, which rippled like the silk in a painting.

Fran went to the trunk of her car and took from it a camera. She was more than a little drunk. "I want a picture of you two."

She posed mother and daughter by the cannon with the light of the casino behind them. A world so bright, so filled with mood. Eve's eyes winced when the flash went off.

In the days to come when Eve saw that picture it spoke with such feeling and memory, a dream would be awakened inside her.

• • •

CHAPTER 21

FRAN HAD DRUNK TOO MUCH to drive. As they made their way down Shore Road back toward the Bronx, Eve slept in Fran's lap.

Windows open, the warm breeze upon them. Through soothing miles of darkness they rode silently until Fran said, "You don't know how much I envy you."

There was a little scotch left in the flask which Fran finished. Fran had let her hair down, her glasses were off. Her head was back against the seat.

Clarissa thought Fran's profile aristocratic. All sharp lines and straight. And the face gave off an intensity, even when relaxed, even when high.

"I never told you about Max. The boy in all those pictures."

"You don't speak much about yourself, but it's alright."

She told Clarissa about the boy she'd met at fifteen. She had seen him at a basketball game. He was running upcourt, his hair all blond and fine. Max was so lean and aware, and Fran had felt a surge of girlish romance that was never to leave her.

She'd met him weeks later in a shop talking with a schoolmate. The way he expressed himself with his hands. They were an art form in themselves and seemed connected by some alchemical process to the passion in his eyes.

Then the sterilization laws had been introduced. This came as a hard punctuation to all that Fran had said before it.

"Do you know about those?"

Clarissa did not.

"Anyone who was deaf, or if there was deafness in the family, had to be sterilized. Jew, Catholic, gypsy. A good Nazi or not. It didn't matter. Deafness in the family, you had to be sterilized. If you were pregnant by a deaf person, you had to be sterilized."

Fran paused for a moment. Her mouth was very dry. And there was no more scotch. "If you did not agree, if you did not go voluntarily they came to get you. If you tried to run they sent people after you. If you fought back, you could pay with your life.

"Max fought back. We ran away in winter. It was very cold. So cold it hurt. But not cold enough to stop them from coming.

"We were not far from the border." She could still see that last piece of minutes. Bits of photographic memory burned into her consciousness with horror. The police official pulling the gun. The warning. The shots. Max's body trembling in the snow.

"He was eighteen in that picture on my desk. The one by the phone. It was the last picture I took of him. He will be eighteen forever...and I will be forever without him."

She had tried to tell Clarissa all this as dispassionately as possible. As if it might save her undue pain. But that very attempt could not belie the truth.

Fran closed her eyes. She did not hear Clarissa say, "I'm so sorry."

CHAPTER 22

THEY ARRIVED LATE AT THE APARTMENT. Clarissa double-parked and the women got out of the car and passed a sleepy Eve from one to the other.

Clarissa noticed Romain and Dominic by a newish GMC pickup angled in a driveway. The doors were open and she could make out their silhouettes by the interior light. A couple of the local men in T-shirts were walking around the truck and admiring it. She could hear her husband's voice. He was coming on with that tony attitude of his around others, all chum and charm.

Romain saw the women and approached alone. He was pretty sure who that skank with his wife was. The first words out of his mouth, "Where you been?"

Clarissa, trying to be polite, said, "Romain, this is Fran."

He put on a roughneck smile. "So you're Fran. Well."

She put out her hand to shake. "It's nice meeting you, Mr. Leone."

"Jesus Christ, Mr. Leone? That's the way a judge addresses you. Call me Romain."

He stood there basking in his own little play of humor. Clarissa kissed Fran good night.

Fran watched them walk back down the street, through the dim light from apartment windows, Romain a few steps ahead. He was better looking than she'd imagined. Softer featured really. It didn't surprise.

• • •

"Whose truck?"

"Mine. You're drunk."

"How can we afford that?"

"You stink of booze. You and that Fran both."

Romain yelled to Dominic he'd be back in a little bit.

"I'm asking you. How can we afford it?"

They started down the steps and through the basement door. "I don't think I like you and the kid hanging with some skank who brings you home drunk."

They were moving along that silent brick hallway beneath the street.

"Fran has done more for Eve than either of us."

Romain stopped and turned. On warm nights the smell of ash from the incinerator room was particularly pungent. "I don't like being told shit like that."

"Where'd you get the money for the truck?"

"I don't answer to you."

"This girl is going to school in the fall. Fran is gonna see to—"

"Fran!"

"Fran is gonna see to it she gets into St. Joseph's School for the Deaf."

"Keep your fuckin' voice down," Romain told her in no uncertain terms.

"You don't want trouble do you?" said Clarissa.

Romain got that look on his face, the look right before he turned violent. She saw his eyes flash for an instant toward the incinerator room door.

"Eve doesn't go to school, people are gonna show up from the city asking questions. You keep her out after that, maybe people start looking into our lives. Maybe they bring the police into it. You ready for people looking into our lives? Are you, Romain?"

"You fuckin' threatening me?"

• • •

Romain sat on the edge of the Castro in the dark. He watched his wife through a strip of light step out of the shower. As much as he wanted to slap her face, he felt this raw and dusky sexual desire come over him as she dried the long strip of thigh that led up to her ass. And the slight sway of her breasts with their almost black nipples against the harsh bathroom white. The small beads of wet on her vaginal hair shone like small bits of glass.

It was more than sexual desire he felt. There was this ambiguous thunder in his body that seemed to carry the force of the world with it.

Her fighting back, her antagonism, the look on her face, to fuck that, to make all that accept your cum, just the thought of it filled his whole sense of identity.

THE MYSTERY IN A
PAWNSHOP WINDOW

CHAPTER 23

DR. FRANK HAD NEVER CALLED Clarissa so when he did she knew something was wrong.

He was sitting at the bottom of the stairwell when Clarissa and Eve entered the building. He looked more like a tired boy than someone who had been a doctor. He pointed up to Fran's apartment.

"She's drunk. And in pain. She needs…someone."

As Clarissa started up the stairs, Dr. Frank said, "She doesn't know I called you."

* * *

The apartment was silent. From the foyer Clarissa could see the dining room. On the table was a near empty bottle of scotch and another of sherry lying on its side.

Clarissa was about to call out when she heard a low dullish groan from the back of the apartment.

There was a long hall that led to the bedrooms. At the end of that hall was the bathroom. Fran was lying on the tile, curled up. She was naked but for a bathrobe.

As Clarissa rushed down the hallway she motioned for Eve to stay, but Eve would not listen. Fran opened her eyes at the sound of Clarissa's voice.

She looked out through eyes glazed and sunken. She tried to get the bathroom door closed before Clarissa could reach her. In a voice both ashamed and angry, she said, "Go away. Go. I don't want anyone to see me."

Clarissa reached her too soon and in that space of moments, while she pushed her way into the bathroom and Fran sat and struggled to at least get her bathrobe pulled in tight around her, Clarissa saw the scar across Fran's stomach. This lip-colored, hideously long mound that looked more suited to a gutting than surgery.

For a moment Clarissa froze. She just stood there, unsure, hands pressed against her thighs. She also saw there was blood in the toilet.

Eve had come slowly, quietly along the hallway wall, toward the bathroom.

"What are you doing here?"

"We just stopped by to—"

"Dr. Frank, right? Shit. I'm ashamed to have anyone see me like this."

"What can I do for you? How can I help?"

Fran tried to stand. Clarissa wanted to help but she did not know how or where to place her hands. Once she got to her feet, Fran leaned back against the bathroom wall. She was woozy and got one arm on the door.

Fran was sure Clarissa had seen the scar. "Pretty, isn't it? A sign of the times."

Clarissa helped Fran to the bedroom. She sat up with her back against the pillows. Fran's skin was a sickly, bloodless color. Gray from all that sweating pain.

"This is what you could look forward to if you got pregnant by a deaf person."

Eve stood alongside her mother, who sat on the edge of the bed. Clarissa had a moment of awful understanding.

"The night in the car you told me about you and Max running away. Is that why?"

Fran moved according to how the pain inside her moved. "I was six months along. If I could have only run faster. Or maybe, if I'd had a gun."

Clarissa had never heard a woman speak like this before. And within that washed-out stare, the eyes still carried the flame of hatred.

"They took out my uterus. And they were not too careful about how they did it. Racial hygiene…the little things men think of in their spare time."

Fran reached out toward Eve. She tried to ease the pain off her face so as not to frighten the child. "Clarissa, would you get me something to drink. Not sherry either."

When they were alone Fran noticed, as Eve had, there was blood on the inside of Fran's robe.

Fran signed to Eve——I have pain. Here and here.

Fran pointed to her stomach and chest. Eve reached out and touched Fran's leg.

It brought back that day in the church, a moment within a moment, and Fran said, as if Eve could hear, "You talked to me that day, you know. From far, far away. You talked to me."

Fran touched her heart and pointed to Eve. She knew the child didn't understand. They would have this talk again, when she was older. Maybe, hopefully.

Clarissa came back with a drink. She went to the bathroom and flushed the toilet. She wet a facecloth with cold water. While Fran drank, Clarissa soothed Fran's neck and forehead with the cloth.

"Sometimes the pain is unbearable. Sometimes that's why I drink. Sometimes I just start bleeding. I never wanted you to know this. It isn't fair. And to be honest, I am ashamed. I am ashamed of my body this way."

"I wish…" Clarissa stuttered, grew silent. "God will do something good for you. You'll see. He will."

Fran put her head back. She gave a cynical laugh. "He? I didn't know God had a dick. It wouldn't surprise me, though. I hope there isn't any deafness in the family."

Clarissa kept easing the face cloth lightly across Fran's skin. Fran had closed her eyes but Clarissa saw tears begin to trickle through the tightly closed eyelids.

Clarissa pulled Fran to her. She got Fran's head down on her shoulder. Fran's crying turned to sobs. The sound was like something you'd expect spilling out of a broken vessel. It went on for exhausting minutes.

Fran, in an aching whisper said, "I would have been a good wife and mother."

CHAPTER 24

FRAN HANDED EVE A COPY of the photograph she had taken at the Glen Island Casino. Eve curled up on the big chair in Fran's living room. She sat there in the quiet looking.

There she was with her mother. One leaning against the barrel of the cannon, the other sitting on it. Holding hands. Their world lit by that long aisle of French doors, beyond where young couples danced and the surface of the water sparkled with their reflection.

The joy of emotion Eve felt that night, the mystery and excitement. It was all there. All just as new. A moment of simple memory, the abyss between then and now, had been connected.

Eve touched the photo as if this might explain the tactile reality it left her with. What she'd felt, what she'd experienced, what she did not really understand, but what had made itself known—this was another way of speaking.

• • •

Eve taped the photo to the alcove wall next to the snapshot of herself as a newborn lying on that pillow flag, her face amelt with sleep.

In the dark she cuddled up to that very pillow, and using a flashlight her mother had given her, stared at the two photos. Engrossed in every little detail. Imaginings within imaginings.

It was a special moment of selfhood. Maybe Fran would let me take a picture, she thought. Before Eve turned off the flashlight and went to sleep she signed her name on the alcove wall using shadow fingers.

• • •

St. Joseph's School for the Deaf was just east of the Hutchinson River Parkway, the school literally backing up to St. Raymond's Cemetery on Lafayette.

St. Joseph's was not a private Catholic institute, but a state-funded school, and to get in, a child had to be recommended by the Committee on the Handicapped; this was after a special examination determining the child's degree of deafness.

Fran, through her contacts in the deaf community, made the introductions for Eve, handled all the preliminary paperwork and even set up the exam.

As Eve was nearly one hundred percent deaf, she was accepted into St. Joseph's. Of course, that degree of deafness also meant her ability ever to speak would be incredibly limited. She would though, probably be able to lip-read.

Both women were there that first day holding Eve's hand, leading her along a hallway of swirling activity where teachers and parents moved all businesslike and smiling through introductions.

The wordless moment came when both women watched Eve walk hand in hand with a little boy, following the teacher, and at a classroom doorway, cut with light, Eve turned and waved goodbye.

Simple as that. No crying, no dramatics.

• • •

"I'll drive you to work," said Fran.

"I can take the bus."

"No buses today. Let's get to share this a little while longer."

As Fran went to put the key in the ignition Clarissa reached out and took her hand.

"I don't know what would have happened to Eve without you. I know you don't believe, but God answered one prayer for me. And you were it."

Fran's voice got husky as she went to speak, so she retreated back into silence. She found herself looking at the school where she could see that assemblage of little ones in the glinty light of the windows, all desk-straight and brimming with nervous energy.

Fran took Clarissa's hand in her own. She opened the hand tenderly, and on the tiny theatre of the palm, Fran signed——Woman, sister, friend. Thank you.

CHAPTER 25

EVE'S LIFE BECAME THE THREAD of many lives. She began to see and know and understand others like herself. Whereas she used to watch the neighbor children skip rope or play hide-and-seek as she sat alone, she was now part of the others.

She went to school, she learned, she had fun. And the petty grievances of childhood, the harsh insults, the harbored resentments and jealousies, these too she became aware of. She was to learn that non-hearing children enjoyed the same cruelties hearing children enjoyed.

She was neither the best student, nor the worst. There was nothing about Eve her teachers would have said was extraordinary. But she did have one passionate curiosity. She wanted a camera so she could take pictures. And not a toy camera either.

• • •

Of all people to fulfill that dream, last on the list would be Romain. But he did.

There was a pawnshop in Throggs Neck, not far from St. Raymond's Cemetery where Romain fenced anything of value he had taken from a casket: wedding rings, jeweled broaches, studded tie clasps or cufflinks.

Constantin, the pawnshop owner, was a spiritless little shit of a Greek and whenever he handled any of Romain's contraband this superstitious crawl came over him, especially if it were engraved. A name, a personal inscription—it wasn't until he got those filed off did the feeling leave him. When that was done it was as if the person's soul were now as dead as the body and erased from his existence.

Constantin didn't like meeting Romain at his shop for these transactions so they'd get together at night at the Whitestone Drive-In, which was just blocks from his shop and the cemetery. They'd park beside each other. Romain usually brought Eve. Just another father and daughter out and bumping into a friend.

Eve would be left alone in the truck. She loved coming to the drive-in, being up late, eating ice cream and watching the screen with faces and actions almost as big as the sky itself. She could not understand the words, but it did not take away from the pleasure and excitement. And when the titles of the film would flash across the screen in huge blazing letters, Eve sometimes now understood a word here or a word there.

• • •

After they had finished their business Romain asked, "Did you bring it?"

Constantin reached into the back seat of his Packard and handed Romain a box inside a Daitch Shopwell bag. When Romain got back to the truck he handed the bag to Eve. He signed in his rudimentary way——For you.

Surprised, she opened the bag. The box inside was beat up and held together with tape, but she knew what it was right away from the picture on the box.

A camera. A simple, used tan Kodak box camera. With breathless excitement she took it in her hands.

Years later Eve would learn that these cameras were part of a public relations campaign sponsored by Kodak for their fiftieth anniversary in 1930. Cameras were given to children who turned twelve that year. One of the teachers at St. Joseph's School for the Deaf had written to Kodak requesting cameras for their students turning twelve.

The trail from St. Joseph's School to where Romain saw it in the pawnshop window was anyone's guess. A forgotten mystery along with all the other forgotten mysteries, hocked in moments of desperation and need. The pawnshop ticket had no name, and was yellow with years. The camera had been little used. That would change.

CHAPTER 26

IT WAS FRAN WHO TAUGHT EVE how to use the camera. Clarissa watched. Eve now signed too fast for her mother. She knew too many words. Moments like this were left to Fran.

It made Clarissa proud, yet it also frightened her. Will I be as unable as before to talk to my baby, because she will have outgrown me?

Clarissa felt a turn of jealousy wishing Fran's hands were her own. But she knew better. She silently prayed and asked God for help to forgive this unChristian of all spells.

"I know why Romain gave her the camera," said Clarissa.

Fran looked past Eve. She reached for her glass of sherry on the dining room table. "Is it as bad as the way your voice sounds?"

Eve wanted to take pictures, so they went up to the roof where the light was better. The sky was bleached with clouds, the breeze turned the hung laundry on farther rooftops into a motif of beautifully waving flags.

"He's selling some kind of narcotics. He and Dominic bring Eve along so no one will suspect." An inconceivable disgust showed on Clarissa's face, but that soon bled into the danger of this knowledge.

Eve was snapping pictures of her own feet, of the sky. She even leaned over the ledge of the roof to get a shot of the street below and had to be pulled back and away by her mother.

"How did you find all this out?"

"Gail had been drinking a little too much wine. She opened up to me when we were alone. She knew she shouldn't have. She said to be careful. Careful." Clarissa despaired.

Fran wondered if Gail had opened up on the chance Clarissa would do something and save her a dangerous responsibility.

Eve wanted to get a picture of her mother, but Clarissa was nervously walking the roof and she shooed Eve away. Fran followed behind them both.

"Did you ever think of leaving him?"

Clarissa looked out across the rooftops. The world paused on that thought. "If I tried, I don't know what would happen. And I have to think of Eve."

Clarissa kept walking the roof toward a crude makeshift hutch that had once been used for keeping birds. Eve traipsed alongside the women trying to catch their faces in the camera.

"And anyway," said Clarissa, "where would I go?"

"You could both come here and stay with me."

Clarissa looked back at Fran. It was more kindness than she had ever been offered.

"You don't know Romain."

"But I do."

Eve shook her mother, signed for her to smile. Clarissa tried. Eve clumsily got the picture.

Clarissa looked again at Fran, thought back to the mad truth of what Fran had been through at the hands of a different kind of Romain. "Yes," she said, "I'm sure you do."

"I don't know how to say this, or if I should say this. But, what if you warned him that you'd go to the police if he didn't—"

"No." Clarissa leaned, or what might be more accurately described as slumped, against the bird hutch's weathered slats. "No, no, no."

"What if you just went anonymously to the police?"

Clarissa stood there with all the uneven fragments of what she felt. What she wanted to do, and not do, while Eve took her picture.

Suddenly Clarissa said, "Oh, my," then just as suddenly she started around the hutch bending down as she went. "Oh, my," she said again.

Fran followed, Eve too.

On the far side of the hutch, near the ledge, a wounded dove lay on its side desperately trying to right itself. Clarissa bent and fragilely, carefully, folded her hands around the crumpled and trembling body.

The wings made a papery attempt to flee. Clarissa sat on the ledge with the bird in her hand trying to find out what was wrong. Fran sat beside her. "Oh, my," Clarissa said again.

• • •

Fran was alone at her dining room table browsing the just developed photos Eve had taken on the roof days before. The first were childish fun. The urgency of the new and desired shown through. The next few caught the women walking along the roof and talking. Their faces, even in those herky-jerky photos, showed the strain of the conversation about going to the police.

That had come to nothing, but Fran knew Clarissa was now wrestling with some fateful choices. Fran had considered going to the police on her own, without even telling Clarissa, but she was unsure what kind of repercussions it would have against her friend.

Then Fran came upon one picture that gave her pause. The two women were sitting on the ledge tightly together with that broken dove in their hands. The wind blew their hair, the sky was a cooling fire. It was a moment filled with unerring simplicity and truth. With a tenderness that was nearly tactile. Fran could only stare in amazement and ask herself—Was this a perfect accident, or the eye of intuition?

MOMMY AND DADDY TAKE MY HAND, TAKE ME OUT TO FREEDOMLAND

CHAPTER 27

THE EISENHOWER ERA and the immigrant kingdom known as the Bronx gave way to the changing color of cultures, the coming of Kennedy and the drug nicknamed Horse.

Eve was like a pilgrim at the dawn of a nascent decade. At the shore of a continent breeding new dilemmas.

Romain continued to use her as a front, a shill, a visual decoy, as he and Dominic delivered heroin for the Cossack to the new slums of America.

They were wops trying for the petty bourgeoisie. Neapolitan trash on the prowl for an infinite number of things. Street guys trying to box fate, not understanding they were out of their weight class in thought, word and deed.

• • •

Romain did not do as he threatened and take Eve from school. Instead, he worked his drops accordingly. He bought his daughter's affection with rolls of film. And at this, he was effective. Little by little he even began to learn the rudimentary signs, which touched Eve and tempered her view of who he was. She became as much his, as anyone's.

Time became a silent struggle between mothers and a father. The cold efficiency versus the efforts of joy and love. The callous and calculated versus the cherished afterwards.

It was not a child's world Eve grew up in. Yet, it was the world of children everywhere, and for all time, who live at the epicenter of conflicts.

Everywhere Eve went, that box camera went with her. From the Food Palace and drops for Sam Bones to Fran's candy store, which became her second home. From a shoeshine stand where a lame Puerto Rican boy spit-polished for dimes while his father and Dominic made the swap, to trips with her mother to the zoo and an ice cream parlor just off of Fordham Road. From a beauty shop in Mott Haven where black housewives got their hair straightened and bleached while heroin was being scored in a storeroom, to St. Philip's for Sunday mass.

The eye of the child, but leaner and more prosaic than most other children. Maybe that's because Eve didn't spend as much time with other children her own age.

Even at school, during recess, she played...yes, she had fun...yes, but the camera came first. She took her schoolmates' pictures, her teachers' pictures. The camera was her special friend, her closest companion.

It was also her way of being in and of the world. It bridged all forms of silence and separation. And more than that. It was her memory.

Even at night, when she slept on her American flag pillow and dreamed, the camera was right there beside her.

• • •

When Freedomland opened in 1960, it was the largest entertainment center in the world. The theme park was shaped like the United States, and you could go from riding a tugboat in Little Old New York to watching the San Francisco earthquake. In Satellite City, one could experience a simulated flying saucer trip with two hundred others over the Western Hemisphere. There were runaway stage coaches, a Civil War battle, a Casa Loca house that defied gravity, an ore bucket ride going in two directions at once over the park, a fur trappers' ride with falling bridges and a Skeleton City, and the Chicago fire being put out every twenty minutes. It was American entertainment as only Americans can conceive it.

It was also a pleading must on Eve's list of musts, so one Saturday Romain surprised her. The two of them "Followed the Fun Road" to the site over by the Hutchinson River.

Romain played daddy in the broiling sun while Eve did the rides and got so many photographs both their pockets were filled with rolls of film.

But it was all just preconceived show from the mind of a lower-middle-class junk dealer. A set piece of hours dragging from one bullshit ride to another until Romain bumped into this Italian guy he recognized with his wife and three kids. Eve seemed to remember him from someplace before with her father, 'cause she thought the man was cute like Frankie Avalon.

While they were inching their way along in the line for their turn with Danny and the Dragon's tour of famous children's stories, the guy did a disappearing act, and a few minutes after so did Romain.

Over by the Chicago fire, Dominic was waiting. He and the Italian did a spot check of the crowd and made for the bathroom. It was there they did the trade, with Romain keeping watch outside.

Romain thought it was all the perfect stick-it-to-you joke. "Freedomland," he told Dominic over the phone that night, "is fuckin' right."

CHAPTER 28

ONE OF THE DEALERS THE COSSACK worked with was found murdered in back of a gas station over in Astoria. He'd had a safehouse there for cutting the heroin.

Romain had an idea, so he and Dominic went to the Cossack and told him for a cut they might be able to come up with a place in the Bronx.

The Cossack sat on his broken-down trailer office couch, considering. "What kind of place?"

"A private garage. Behind a candy store, faces an alley. Quiet."

"White neighborhood?"

"White neighborhood."

"Who owns the place?"

"The woman who taught my kid to sign."

"Is that the German drunk you told me about?"

"Yeah."

"Alright…but not if she's a Jew."

• • •

Romain stopped by the candy store near closing time. It was a totally unexpected visit. He sure had never been by before.

Fran was alone when Romain walked in. He had on a clean sport shirt open at the collar, and almost natty slacks. He was freshly shaved and his skin hinted of cologne. He was carrying a bag, and the way he was carrying it suggested a bottle of either liquor or wine.

"Clarissa and Eve aren't here," said Fran.

"Yeah, I know," said Romain. He smiled, but it didn't offset the dusky loveless stare to the eyes. "I brought this for you."

In the bag was a bottle of J&B scotch. "Maybe," he said, "we could sit and talk. Maybe have a drink."

• • •

While she poured them drinks, Romain walked the living room looking over Fran's furniture and photos. He made small talk from the other room. How great it was she'd helped Eve, the change in her life…

When Fran came into the room with their drinks Romain had his hands in his pockets and was jingling his loose change. A rattler come to visit, she thought, and handed him his scotch.

"Now, what is it you really want, Romain?"

He sipped at his highball. He saw she'd floated a couple of extra jiggers in her glass, and when she drank he told himself, this bitch is hardcore.

"Clarissa tells me you own the whole building."

"That's right."

"Rent out the apartment downstairs."

"That's right."

"And the store makes money."

"It does enough."

"Very nice."

The way he was looking the place over you'd have suspected it was getting sized up to be burglarized.

"You still haven't told me what you really want."

"I saw you had a garage down in back and I was wondering if I could rent some storage space."

She looked at his scotch glass. "You must have known that before you got here. But you've never been here before."

She's a fuckin' question mill. "Yeah, well," he said, "I drove over once to see if Clarissa and Eve were around, but the store lights were out and I didn't want to bother anybody so I didn't stop."

"Right," said Fran.

She sat in a chair. She did not offer for him to sit.

"I'd pay you whatever you think is fair."

She crossed her legs. She was wearing those ugly pants cunts wear so you can't tell what kind of ass they got. Typical dyke material. He wondered if she was a dyke.

"I use one garage space for my car. The other is for my own storage."

"I don't need a lot of space. Maybe a dozen boxes' worth. It's a bitch over at the apartment. The landlord only gives me so much space in the storeroom. And with Eve getting older, you accumulate more with a kid. You'd be helping her and Clarissa—"

Fran put her scotch down on the end table, took off her glasses. "You're not gonna use me like you use your daughter. And you're not gonna use your daughter to try and fuckin' use me."

He stood there like someone who'd just been slapped. "What is that supposed to mean?"

His face had lost all its charm. She took her drink and stood. She brushed past him on the way to the kitchen. "You heard me. That's enough. Now get out of here."

"I don't know where you get off talking to me like that."

"And by the way, I have a few policeman friends. Do you understand? Men who have deaf children and might not appreciate your 'fatherly' actions."

She knew more than he'd suspected. "You fuckin' cunt licker," he said.

She flung the remains of her scotch into the sink. She came around and stood in the kitchen doorway. "You..." Furious now, she said again, "You... you are the very definition of a breed. A...a corpse of memorialized traits and actions. A nihilist with a guinea smile. And I'll bet you don't even know what a nihilist is."

He slammed his glass down on the dining room table. "If you were a man and talked to me like that—"

"You'd do nothing." She started to run off in German. Then, "You're just another sawdust Caesar. Another petty Mussolini."

"You Hun vampire. You cunt dyke Dracula."

All the old hates, pure and simple, had her. She grabbed the scotch bottle. It was open. She tossed it at Romain. "Get out," she said.

He tried to grab it, catch it. The liquor spilled all over his shirt and his almost natty slacks. The bottle slid through his hands and landed on the floor splashing his socks and shoes.

He turned on her like something cured in poison. Cursing her out in dialect, he grabbed her by the blouse.

"I'm not your wife," said Fran, "so see what happens if you touch me."

For all he wanted to lay her out right there on the floor, to hit her so fuckin' hard she'd shit right through her pants, but he let her go. "Dyke." He spit on the carpet. He grabbed his cock. "Dyke."

He kicked the scotch bottle. It spun out and across the kitchen linoleum.

"I could make you give me that garage space. I could go right home now, pack up Clarissa and the kid and be out of here. I'll fuckin' go west. I'll dump the old lady in the desert. How 'bout that? Then where would you be...dyke."

Whether he would really do it or not, no matter how much the thought of it completely attacked her sense of existence, no matter...She would not let on.

She tore away her blouse while she kicked off her shoes. Romain had no idea what he was watching. She undid her pants and flung them at him. He caught them as they hit his face.

She was standing before him in her bra and panties. Defiant. The light from the kitchen offset the scar, the horrible scar. It looked like she had tried to smother a hand grenade.

"I'll get on the phone and call the police and say you tried to rape me... How's that?"

Realizing, he dropped her pants on the floor. He stepped back. "Holy shit," he said.

CHAPTER 29

ROMAIN WAS GODDAMN SHAKEN by that incident. Driving under the El his hand crabbed beneath the front seat searching out a pint of scotch he kept for emergencies. At a stoplight he bent his head down getting in swig after swig.

That skank. She'd gotten a handful of him and he didn't know how to deal with it, where to place it, how to get loose of it. Even after the booze had a little run at his system he felt like she was still clinging to his flesh. And that scar across her stomach. It was like going to a horror movie and seeing some kind of she-beast.

He stared at himself in the rearview mirror to make sure he was still there and in one piece. He realized he had been shamed and defeated and that was a humiliation somebody would have to suffer for. The express thundered by overhead and he could feel its blind power all the way down into the concrete.

• • •

"Forget the German bitch's garage..." he told the Cossack over the phone. "...I found out a cop just moved in across the alley to an apartment that faces the garage. And he's already like a local plague nosing into everybody's business."

• • •

Fran sat on the foyer floor trembling with the truth of many things. Despicable as Romain was, that moment he saw her stomach and his hatred turned to shock, to disgust, it hurt had her. It hurt her as a woman, even as it empowered her, even as it gave her dignity over his indignity.

You either defeat reality, or you are defeated by reality. For Fran, there was no reality in between.

• • •

Fran never once told Clarissa about what happened that night. And that night Romain looked for the most trivial excuse to lock his wife in the incinerator room. To leave her in the darkness in her petticoat, with the eyes of a trapped animal.

She tried to find her sanity begging for God's protection, but what she found was quite something else. She found it while rats skittled over trash that stunk, and the concrete floor was as cold as death's own accomplishment and the moonlight hinted at the wire-mesh glass of a tiny window which shone like a woman's eyes high above Clarissa.

She found it like an assassin finds its probable victim, like a powerless flower finds a scar of cracked asphalt to rise through.

The scorned irregular heartbeat howling inside her steadied, and the claustrophobic madness slipped back and away with the thought on how she might destroy her husband.

• • •

Clarissa made it almost like a game. She and Eve sat at the Formica table in their tiny apartment looking through all the snapshots Eve had taken. There were already shoeboxes full.

The ones of the Food Palace, the shoeshine stand, the beauty shop, the Cossack's, anyplace Eve went on those repeated excursions with her father and Dominic, Clarissa put in a separate pile.

When Clarissa heard Romain's keys working the lock she quickly, and without Eve realizing, slipped those telling snapshots back into a shoebox and then just quietly went along as they had been. Clarissa felt a sense of guilt over what she was doing and how, but she didn't let it shade her decision. The wine she was drinking helped give her a boost of courage.

Even so, Clarissa went all sickly inside when Eve held up a picture of Romain at the Cossack's teasing, a chained and vicious-looking shepherd with a long shank of meat bone.

Eve signed——Mean looking.

Romain took the picture, turned to his wife. "What did she say?"

"Mean looking." Clarissa took the picture from her husband as she slid the box with those other snapshots off to one side.

Romain signed——Yes. Then he pretended to shiver. He ruffled his daughter's hair on the way to the refrigerator.

Clarissa looked the picture over while Romain opened a beer. The moment caught with that dog, fighting against the chain for a greasy scrap. Stretching out and up on its hind legs so far it would have fallen but for the chain. And at the door of the trailer, Dominic and the Cossack watched, even slightly enjoying the animal's miserable predicament.

"I'm going to Jersey with Dominic," Romain said, on the way to the bathroom.

He drank his beer while shaving. He kept the bathroom door open so he could half watch International Showtime. He liked Don Ameche, he liked the way he carried himself. While Romain showered, Clarissa closed up that shoebox.

Dominic had a girlfriend in Jersey. Her family owned a bar in an Italian section of Woodridge. It made Gail crazy, her husband sleeping around like that. She used to say she wanted to slit her wrists from the shame. Clarissa only hoped Romain found some slut he was crazy about and choked to death on her.

THE JEROME BEACH
AND SWIM CLUB

CHAPTER 30

THE IDEA WAS SIMPLE ENOUGH. Tell the police about Romain, at least what she suspected, then show them the snapshots. Maybe something would come of it, maybe they would go after him. Maybe—

The only problem, when that wine courage wore off Clarissa couldn't manage the same kind of willing fearlessness. She sat at her workstation in the warehouse cutting terry cloth and second-guessing herself. She rode at the front of the first subway car as it drove through the darkness, deciding and deciding and deciding.

She watched as platforms of strangers flared out of the black only to be swallowed again in a rush of seconds. If she and Eve could just disappear that quickly without running away. Without leaving the school, and Fran.

• • •

Fran had gone to Bergen Avenue to see a movie while she waited for Clarissa. *West Side Story* was playing at the National. The romance and tragedy had left her crying as the passion-ridden tale spilled into the cup of her own memories.

Because she sometimes did cry at movies, Fran preferred to always go alone. She hated anyone seeing her in that state of vulnerability. The only people who had were Clarissa and Eve the night they found her bleeding and in pain on the bathroom floor.

It was still early so she went to a bar and had a drink. She sat in the cool afternoon darkness by herself.

Occasionally the few men in the bar eyed her through the shadows. But she sat there like an aloof regent, stirring the ice in her scotch glass and watching the street through a small window.

The movie's music still played in her head, and it brought up all her womanish wishes. The ones she still clung to in the quiet dwindlings of night. She realized as she sat there and watched the impersonal and disjunctive comings and goings along the sidewalk how alike she and Clarissa were. How much they were victims, prisoners of their lives, and their pasts.

Fran was to meet Clarissa at the escalator station up to the El at 149th Street. From there they went shopping in the Hub. It was a street-busy afternoon. Walking a people crowded sunlight from shop to shop, Fran noticed Clarissa seemed unusually preoccupied, closer to anxious, actually. It wasn't until they stopped at a luncheonette and were having coffee Clarissa confessed to Fran what she had been plotting.

"I lay up at night thinking about it, with him right there beside me asleep, and even though I'm sure it's only in my head," Clarissa whispered now, "I feel like he suspects. Even when he just looks at me. I feel guilty and about to be caught."

Fran put down her coffee cup as her back arched tensely.

"Do you think it's something I should do?"

Fran took off her glasses and rubbed her eyes. Why didn't luncheonettes serve liquor?

"Do you think it would work?"

Fran flashed back to the night she and Max were standing in a doorway alcove with the snow bitter and blue cold around them deciding and deciding and deciding, if they could get away.

"Do you mean," asked Fran, "can you get him arrested and sent to jail?"

"And out of my life."

"I don't know."

"If it didn't work and he found out it was me—" Clarissa closed her eyes at the thought.

For Fran, it was exactly like a moment a lifetime and a continent away from another moment that took her to the black edge of life.

Weighed down by dread, doubting, Clarissa said, "I have no one else to rely on. No family, no friends. No real friends, but you. Tell me I should and maybe I can do it."

• • •

Against a backdrop of naked stone-faced buildings Clarissa approached the precinct house—the 48th. Her heart pounded with horrors of what might, could and would go wrong if she went through the station house doors.

She had the pictures in her purse climbing the steps as beat cops passed, smiling at her, and she tried to smile back but couldn't make her facial muscles respond.

It was suddenly avalanching down on her, misgiving after misgiving. A man in handcuffs was led out of a squad car. A solid-looking bastard flanked by two detectives. She stood aside. Let them have the door. She didn't have to, but it gave her time. Too much time.

• • •

Fran was working the candy store register and watching the clock. Her mind was timing out the day, where Clarissa should be by now. When the pay phone by the counter rang, Fran was certain it was her.

"How did it go?"

A deathly long stretch of silence followed.

"I didn't have the courage." Clarissa's voice was seized with despair. "Fran, I know this is wrong of me to ask. I know—"

Chapter 31

THE BLEEDING HAD STARTED, the pain a poisoned shade of agonizing. Was it the stress of a decision or old wounds raging back, reminding her about suffering and retribution, of what it really meant to have been a woman in her place and time?

In the dark on the floor of the kitchen huddled up in a robe, drinking to blind painlessness, stripped of her youth and one of women's most cherished possessions, at that witching hour when the world can turn suddenly dangerous, she stared into the dark and saw the true face of existence—when you surrender your life, when your life is no longer your own, and then for that purpose, you finally come to own your own life.

• • •

Fran went to the warehouse where Clarissa cut cloth. During a lunch break they talked in the hall. The air was a gauzy haze from specks of terry cloth. Fran smoked. Through the enormous wire mesh windows the sun burned down on Fran's back. She thought of those cathedral windows in St. Philip's the morning she first saw Eve.

"You get me the pictures, I'll do the rest."

"Are you sure?"

"Are you?"

Clarissa took Fran's hand as she turned to go. "Forgive me."

"For what?"

"For not being strong enough."

"Together, we'll be enough."

• • •

There was a bowling alley and billiard hall on Third and Brock where the El ran close enough to the apartments along the street that you could spit from one to the other. Fran was to meet a detective there. He was married to a friend of a Swiss woman she knew.

They sat in a black leather booth back of the alleys where they served cocktails. Fran was still in pain, still leaking a little blood. The place smelled of cigarettes and cool foul air, which only made her nausea worse. She and the detective had to talk around the stinging licks of hit pool balls and the hollow echo as bowling pins were struck.

As he looked over the photos and asked questions, Fran explained. The detective had been born in Heidelberg. They spoke German, so if they were overheard, the odds were small anyone would understand.

"Italians," he said. "They're colossal morons. Overindulged street cleaners, really. Hitler should never have allied himself with them."

Fran's stomach muscles went taut, anxious. She leaned back in her seat.

When the detective looked up he realized how he'd said, what he'd said. "I didn't mean it like it sounded."

Fran wasn't so sure. "Of course not."

They sat looking at each other amidst the dull noise of talk, and the trivial pursuit of pocket shots and spares.

"Where's his wife in all this?"

"She's afraid. She gave me the pictures."

"I need to take them with—"

Shaking her head no, Fran reached out almost automatically. "If you have the pictures and he finds out—"

"They can possibly help identify people."

"No."

"They're potential evidence."

"No. I will not allow his wife to be violated. You have enough now, to know."

CHAPTER 32

WHATEVER THEY THOUGHT would happen…didn't. The summer went by with a constant edge in the air. They all felt it, Eve probably most of all.

For her, there was a tension in her surroundings that could almost be measured. Hers being a world of silence, she was attuned to the spoken word of gesture and expression which seemed to convey untold volumes. The mundane and routine became time capsules of spare impact. That even if she did not know what they meant or why, she felt as if they carried the weight and purpose of destiny.

It was also that summer, when she was ten, Eve began to have a sense of herself as separate and apart from the physical world, and of being deaf in a hearing world. Triggers of identity were beginning to be touched off.

There were times, especially when she'd meet someone, a classmate or a friend on the street, and they'd sign to each other with the same kind of overlapping enthusiasm as kids do when they speak that she began to notice the faces on strangers—the queer looks of puzzlement, the averted stare, the momentary sadness suppressed by a quick smile. All that also began to convey untold volumes of her place in the world.

• • •

The barber had just put some talc on a sterilized towel and was patting Romain around the ears and neck when Dominic came hustling into the shop.

"I got to talk to you…outside."

"I'll be a few minutes."

Romain leaned back and closed his eyes to enjoy the pampering but his cousin told him, "Chop, chop, man…now means now."

They stood out front of the barbershop on Morris Avenue, away from the old men playing cribbage at a makeshift table.

"Gail's mother had a heart attack," said Dominic.

"When?"

"Early this morning."

"Christ almighty."

"I got to drive Gail to Trenton in an hour."

"What? We got a drop this afternoon."

"That's why I hustled over here. I can't do it. I got to take her to Trenton."

"Don't tell me."

"There's no way around it. It's her mother."

Romain stuffed his hands in his pockets. The loose change started jingling nervously. "Today of all fuckin', fuckin', fuckin' days she has to have a heart attack…and not drop dead."

"And Gail wants Clarissa to go with her. They already talked."

"Nice. And she'll want to take Eve. This whole day is turning into a disaster."

"Call that fat kike and just tell him."

"What are you talkin' about? You going dipshit?" Romain paced, gave Dominic three or four nasty looks. "You want to end up like those spastic old guineas sitting around in their shorts, with their socks pulled up over their ears? Look."

The old men gossiped and worked their cards, oblivious to the world around them.

"Call the kike," said Dominic, more as a pleadish request than anything else.

• • •

When Romain walked into the apartment he saw Clarissa's overnight bag on the bed. It was very nearly packed. She came out of the bathroom with her makeup kit. "Did you hear?"

"Gail's mother," said Romain. "Yeah."

Eve was in the alcove laying a few things out on the bed to be packed along with her mother's.

"She's staying with me."

Clarissa put the makeup kit down. "I want her to come with me. Gail wants her to come."

Romain went to the alcove, caught his daughter's eye with a wave. He signed——You, me, swim.

Eve looked at her mother. She was standing in back of Romain. She shook her head no. Romain sensed, or saw. He went over to their crummy dresser. "She's coming with me," he said.

He got out his trunks, Eve's bathing suit. He held up the suit and passing the alcove again he signed——You, me, swim. He pointed to his watch, the need to get moving.

As he started for the bathroom to get a clean towel Clarissa grabbed at the bathing suit. Eve watched the ugly tug-of-war begin. It was rage against determination over a stretch of blue and red fabric. The way the mouths assaulted each other, the grimacing bends of the body, and Romain trying to kick at his wife to loosen her grip; it was painful to watch. Eve jumped between them signing, signing. She grabbed at the bathing suit and kept signing.

"What the hell's she saying?"

Eve signed to her mother now, trying to calm her.

Clarissa slowly let go of the bathing suit. "She said, she'll stay."

CHAPTER 33

THE MORNING SKY WAS A FRAGILE BLUE. As the day wore on it grew muggy, oppressive. The sun was heating up those metal subway cars something awful as Romain and Eve rode the El down to the Jerome pool.

Romain stood over his daughter. She looked ahead and away. She was aware of feelings the nature of which she couldn't quite understand. Maybe it was a sense of being momentarily lost, of being sick and not sick at the same time. Romain nudged his daughter's foot with his own.

She glanced up at him. He tried to be conciliatory and slipped a dollar into her hand. He signed——Food, drink, yours.

All he got back was the look. The one he recognized. It was Clarissa staring up at him, all matter of fact. But the eyes, they were his eyes. Diamond dark and they could hold their fuckin' glint. No questions asked.

He tried to think of a way to get around that look. Then he told himself, the hell with it.

• • •

The Jerome Beach and Swim Club took up a whole block between 168th and 169th Street. It was flanked by Jerome to the west and Gerard to the east. There was a concrete wall about two stories high around the place. Half the club was a pool and concrete deck. The other half, separated by a waist-high wire fence was a beach with sand. Eve didn't exactly think of it as sand, but more like some torturous gravel.

Romain went to the men's locker room, Eve the women's. He carried the heroin in two metal cigar holders. He folded his towel and then slipped the cigar holders into the folds.

The place was wall-to-wall people. From the concrete tiers right down to the diving board were pale shapes letting their flesh get lobstered. The smell of suntan lotion was overpowering. Romain never imagined so many kinds of ugly-looking bodies. Broads you wouldn't fuck with a pig's dick. Worse than the beach by ten times.

Romain managed to hustle a chair from a foursome of yappy housewives playing mahjongg. He found himself a place to wait. Eve bumped into classmates by the diving board. She came back to where her father was sitting to get her camera. She pointed to the beach side of the club.

"Sure," he nodded.

To get to the beach side from the pool, you had to walk through a passageway of iron piping that sprayed down a mist of water, then step into a trough to wet your feet. This was so you wouldn't be bringing sand from the beach to the pool. Eve passed her camera over the fence to her classmates, happy to have any reason to be away from her father.

He watched her scoot between tables and into the passageway. He suddenly felt just like a father out with his kid for a Saturday. A pang of remorse, and guilt, clenched up a little fist's worth of stomach over how he'd used Eve. It was a motherfucker for all of about five seconds, then his contact showed.

• • •

Nick Caparelli dealt on and off. He also sold insurance out of Fort Lee. Mostly to vets, a lot of vets, especially the Korean War crowd, were closet mainliners. So to pay for that new split-level in Tenafly and the kids' education at Bergen Catholic, Nick did some moonlighting in the junk trade.

Romain knew Nick. Caparelli cruised the pool, took a cigarette from a pack in his shirt pocket, and when he passed Romain, stopped innocently for a light.

"Where's Dominic?" he whispered.

"In Trenton. His mother-in-law had a heart attack."

"Who's gonna cover?"

"We're it."

Caparelli was straight out of the Frankie Avalon School of Looks. Perfect prison rape material. His face didn't handle worry any too well. "You sure this is right?"

"Locker 211. Give me fifteen minutes."

• • •

Nick was down by Romain's locker when he approached out of the shadows. The room was humid and the air had the clinging odor of chlorine. There were only a few men in the aisles changing, and every time a locker slammed shut a metallic echo carried along the concrete walls.

Nick was nervous. "You didn't leave it in your locker?"

Romain tapped the towel under his arm. "Carrying it." He opened a locker, set the towel inside. "You want to give it the Maxwell House test?"

Nick scanned the locker room. There was only a balding Slav with a small boiler of flesh hanging over his swimming trunks sitting on a bench at the far end of the aisle. He was massaging his feet lifelessly.

It took all of two intense minutes. Nick floured the tip of his pinky with a dab of white powder. Worked it across his tongue. He was slipping an envelope into the locker when the Slav came up bowlegged and charging right toward them.

CHAPTER 34

IT WAS A BUST, FLAT OUT. With that Slav pulling a badge and a gun from Christ knows where. Caparelli looked like he'd been caught naked in front of a mirror fondling himself.

Was that another cop they heard rushing down the dank hallway? The Slav was calling to someone, and someone was calling back.

Romain had that street guinea sense of survival and he bolted. Screamed to Nick and the sound of his own name jolted Caparelli back into reality and he was on Romain's hip as they made a dash for the exit.

You could hear the shouts above the showers. It was a cop running right toward them. He was blocking the light to the exit, but before he could get his feet planted and his gun out Romain shoved Nick right at him and they crashed against the concrete wall in a heap of arms and legs and Romain skidded clear into the light.

. . .

Eve was getting shots of her classmates. They stood on the sand and mugged for the camera. She had them framed up with the El in the background when she saw through the lens people were beginning to stand and stare past her. A woman ran through the frame trying to keep her sunglasses from falling off. Before the expressions on her classmates' faces did an abrupt shift Eve's finger clicked the shutter almost autonomically as she turned to follow the action.

She saw a man being chased through the crowd knocking people over. Another man was chasing him. A third was taking the steps of that concrete tier at a hard angle to cut them off.

It all hung there in a Spartan moment of time as bodies scattered or were struck down that she realized the man being chased through the blasted sunlight was her father.

A blind panic hit her like that wall of air when the express crushes by. A feeling of danger, of being trapped overtook her. The fretwork of internal connections torn apart, Eve rushed toward the passageway, through the passageway, tripping at the edge of the trough.

Her father had been tackled by the Slav at the far end of the pool. It was too wet there to take a hard turn in his sleek black shoes. The two men were driven into the concrete. Their bodies hit with a jarring violence.

Eve tried to grab the man who had her father's arms vised backwards. She was knocked over as two other men swarmed Romain. The camera came out of her hands and was lost.

She was swept up into someone's arms, squirming, hitting, kicking, as her father was hauled to his feet in handcuffs. The men had no idea Eve was deaf so the more they yelled and the louder they yelled meant nothing.

. . .

Romain and Nick were in the back of the Ford handcuffed and being watched over by one of the detectives. Eve was up front squeezed in between two others. She was visibly trembling and trying to read lips enough to understand what the men kept saying to her.

"She's deaf, you stupid bastards," said Romain.

The Slav came around in his seat and pointed. "Watch your mouth. You don't want to dig the hole any deeper."

"What hole you talking about? What did we do?"

"Even having your daughter around something like that and a retarded kid no less." The driver shook his head in disgust.

"What is *this?* Hunh?"

The Slav held up the three cigar holders. "Heroin…which we got out of your locker."

Romain put his head back. He watched the lattice of sunlight as it shuttered along through the elevated's tracks reflecting off the window. Just keep it nice and straight, with a touch of arrogance. Never even hint in your voice you know you fucked up. Not like Frankie Avalon here who looks like he's about ready to drop a little stool on the seat.

"You guys screwed up big time, you know that," said Romain.

"Yeah," said the Slav. "That kind of talk is right out of Rikers Island."

"You did, man, 'cause that wasn't my locker."

The Slav eyed Romain trying to see how full of shit he really was.

Romain cocked his head toward Frankie Avalon. "I just met this guy and we got to talking. The locker was sitting there open. Stuff in there. We figure maybe some guy forgot to lock her up. Maybe somebody busted into the thing. So we checked for identification. I go to the pool sometimes, maybe I know the guy. If not, we take the stuff up to lost and found." He looked at Caparelli. "Isn't that right?"

"Yeah," said Nick.

"This kind of crap is so bad I can smell it," said the driver. Then he sniffed at the air as he pushed that Ford through a yellow light. "Crap," he said again.

"Check my daughter's pockets. I gave her the key to my locker so I wouldn't lose it. I lose things."

The Slav glanced at the driver. Romain saw the way their looks "talked" to each other.

"Yeah, you guys fucked up big time."

JAILGIRL

CHAPTER 35

THEY WAITED TILL THEY WERE at the precinct house to get the key. If there
was a key. When it was handed to him the Slav muttered, "Fuck."

Eve didn't understand why they were taking her father and the other man
down one corridor and leading her to a cubbyhole office where she was to sit
alone and wait.

She was scared, she was hungry, she had to go to the bathroom. She wanted,
needed her mother; she needed, wanted Fran.

"See the kid's alright. Get her a Coke or something."

The man who'd been driving gave the Slav an imploring look. "Not me. I
don't know how to talk to a retarded kid."

"She's not retarded. She's deaf."

"Same fuckin' thing."

The Slav kept staring at that locker key in disgust. "Write it down. 'Are you
thirsty? Do you have to take a leak?'"

• • •

The ride back from Trenton was pure hell. Clarissa had gotten hold of Fran before
they left. After explaining, she begged Fran to drive right over to the station
house. She was petrified they'd end up putting Eve in a temporary detention
center like Spofford.

No matter how much Fran assured, promised, swore she would not let that
happen, that she was leaving as soon as they hung up, on this one issue, Clarissa
was uncontrollable.

A storm had come in off the coast. Route 1 was slick and heavy with traffic.
The wipers on Dominic's car barely worked against the streaking lines of rain.

"How many times did I ask you to get the wipers fixed? How many?"

"Say it again, Gail, and I'll drive us right off the goddamn road."

"Both of you shut up! Do you hear? Now shut up!"

Things got immediately quiet, leaving only the scratchy sound of the wiper
blades. Dominic went back into dead man's space, sweating it out, hoping there
wasn't some warrant with his name on it. The only stroke of luck, so to speak,
was him not being at the pool.

Clarissa was in the back, off alone, imagining Eve in some grimy closet of
a room, lonely, scared. Clarissa bit at her nails to ease the tension. She figured

this was all her fault. She could fill a book with her feelings on the subject. But Spofford, or anything like it…

"How much farther?" she asked.

She felt Gail's hand on her own.

"You don't know," she told Gail, "what happens in a place like Spofford. You don't know."

• • •

On the desk in the room where Eve sat alone waiting and waiting was a photograph of a father, mother and son. That triangle of faces, she couldn't take her eyes off it. It warmed with its familial affection. With what she imagined was the true color of love.

Eve stood. There was not one photograph. She approached the desk with trepidation. Not one of her and her parents together. She took the photo in her hands. Not one that in any way approximated that moment. Not one. You can't hide what she saw and felt there from a photograph.

It made her sad. That kind of moment had been something she'd wanted, hungered for, but knew, even then, would never be. A photograph had showed her that, taught her that.

Eve suddenly realized, the thought snapping into her head: Her camera. She'd lost it.

She felt hopeless, helpless. She did not understand what was going on, and no one could or would explain.

The room had a tiny window. It opened to a flue of space between buildings. She leaned out to look. The night was fearful dark and spotted with rain.

She wanted to be strong and not cry, she wanted to be home and safe, she wanted this frightening to stop, she wanted—

The office door opened, and there in the harsh and canted light of the hallway, was Fran.

The child ran to her crying. Fran knelt down. At no time in Fran's life had she ever been held with such blind unrestrained need, such overwhelmed trembling that looked to find the safe harbor in, and of, you.

CHAPTER 36

EVE FELL ASLEEP ON FRAN'S BED almost immediately with her mother stroking her hair. Fran had decided they all should stay at her place, at least for the night.

Fran was in the kitchen making tea for Clarissa, she herself was drinking sherry. Clarissa came into the kitchen very quietly, she was an exhausted wreck.

Fran handed her the tea. "This will calm you."

"What have I done?" said Clarissa.

"You?"

"This, tonight, what she went through, is all my fault."

"And how is it your fault?"

"I should have never let him use the child, even if it meant her getting to go to school. I should have left Romain or—"

She put the cup down without even drinking. "Look what I ended up putting her through. There are so many things I could have done."

"Drink the tea. It will help you sleep. You need sleep."

Clarissa reached for the bottle of sherry instead. "I think I need this."

Frank took a glass from the cabinet. Clarissa poured and drank, then poured again. "If you hadn't gotten there as quickly as you did…I was just petrified they'd take her to one of those detention centers."

"That's over now. She's here, she's safe."

Clarissa went to say something, then hesitated. She filled her glass and walked into the living room where it was dark. Fran followed her.

"Don't put on the light, please."

"Okay."

Fran remained in the doorway, a slight distance from her friend.

"I was put in one," said Clarissa. "A detention center."

"Yes?"

Clarissa could not look at Fran. Instead she used the darkness to allow herself to look away.

"When I was at the Catholic school for girls, a family came and took me in. I ran away after a year. I was fourteen. I took some money when I ran. I ended up in a detention center."

Clarissa drank more sherry. The room was so quiet, but for the rain. The nightmare of brutal years. Shut away, but not out of sight or mind. The body in a perpetual state of humiliation and hurt. Like having a sickness that never ends and somewhere along the way you become what they made of you. You're weak in ways you don't even know you're weak. And you're fighting back sometimes without even realizing it. And there are scars where there are no scars.

Clarissa wanted to tell Fran all this, but it was not in her upbringing or character to describe what she had suffered. All she could manage was, "I can't say the things that happened, even to you. And you, more than anyone, would understand."

Fran came over and put a hand on her friend's shoulder.

"I'm sure that's how I ended up with someone like Romain."

Clarissa went to drink more sherry, but her glass was empty. Fran took Clarissa's glass and gave her her own.

"I thought about that all the way back from Trenton. I had never allowed myself to really think about it before. He's just like…those others."

"That's over now."

"Is it?" Clarissa walked toward the kitchen. She leaned against the door frame. The light was harsh on her eyes. "Romain won't end up going to jail. No. The devil is looking out for him."

Fran came up behind her. Clarissa turned. The women just stood there understanding, sharing that possibility.

"If anything ever happens to me—"

"Nothing's going to happen," said Fran.

"Promise me you'll never let Romain keep Eve."

"He's her father, and I'm just—"

"Promise me."

"Nothing's going to happen."

"Promise me."

"Clarissa."

"Promise."

Clarissa looked so unbearably tired.

"You have my word."

Clarissa handed Fran the glass. "I need sleep now."

• • •

Clarissa slept in the room with Eve. Fran could see the one shadow they made as she closed the bedroom door. Fran sat in the living room, drinking in the dark.

They were alike, she and Clarissa. The woman's body as state of mind. As the place where others had exorcised their demons. Where others had evened the score for their own misfortune or abuse. Woman as cutting board, woman as serving tray, woman as toilet seat.

On the table beside her chair was the detective's card. She used her lighter to see the number.

As the phone rang she lit a cigarette. "Detective Berghich, please…Fran Kuhl…The woman who picked up the Leone girl from his office."

Fran waited. The rain against the windows offered a slight, obscure covering of sound. The smoke from her cigarette felt of loneliness as it drifted across the empty room.

"Hello, Detective. Yes, fine. Asleep now." A pause. "I called because there is something you need to know. It's something I told another detective. No, not at your precinct." Another pause. "It's about some pictures."

CHAPTER 37

IN THE MORNING CLARISSA AND FRAN sat down with Eve and explained, as best they could, why her father had been arrested and what it meant. They had to use words they knew little about. Words like narcotics, heroin.

The little that Eve understood of what she heard was that her father had done something bad, and he might well go to jail for it. Eve did not want to believe the worst. It was shameful and ugly, but neither woman lied to save her from the truth.

Later that day Eve's classmates showed up at the candy store with her camera. The two from the pool had now become an entourage of four. Fran watched from the register as Eve was hounded with questions. What did your father do? Is he in jail? Did they arrest you? Did they put you in a cell?

There is no form of inoculation against the disease of infectious curiosity. When her classmates left Eve stood in the candy store doorway watching them go, the camera dangling from her hand. She seemed so slender and hurt.

The camera turned out to be broken. And at school, Eve got an education in the unwelcome comment, the backstabbing dig, the sly joke that works as well as a slap across the face.

She became, for a time, marked. Her new nickname was the sign for JAIL and the sign for GIRL.

More than once Eve came home scraped up from a fight.

• • •

Romain and Caparelli held to their stories. On the q.t., the Cossack hired an attorney who had a track record in these cases to defend Romain. "One of the Cossack's brethren, and straight off the money boat," was how Romain described him to Dominic.

He was not only the Cossack's insurance policy on Romain's loyalty, but the attorney was also to be the Cossack's eyes and ears on what the prosecutors might have against him.

The attorney was confident Romain could beat the indictment until investigators uncovered a stack of snapshots in a shoebox they found under Eve's bed.

Sam Bones, the Cossack, the shoeshine man whose street name was Little Boy, Dominic. It was a fuckin' who's who of who was in Romain's life.

Bones had a record, Little Boy had a record, the Cossack had a record. It opened them all up to possible investigation, and worst of all, there was a photo of Romain with Caparelli and his kids taken at Freedomland right before the 4th of July weekend, which completely blew the sworn affidavits they'd never met.

The whole con of using his kid as cover, all sweetness and light with a camera, while he played daddy—talk about a rich screwjob. Talk about paving the roadway the cops got to drive right up your asshole. Smile for the camera, you dago fool.

It took the jury less than an hour to convict. Snow was falling outside the windows of the Bronx County Courthouse when the judge read the sentence. Romain sat there like a man with endless time on his hands.

Romain was hoping for probation or maybe a few months at Rikers. What he and Caparelli got was two years at the State Correctional Facility in Ossining.

The prosecutors offered Romain a reduced sentence if he testified against the others, but Romain was too old-world street for that. Besides, he was hoping to buy himself a few favors down the road.

Clarissa was silently thankful he did not take the prosecutors' offer.

• • •

The little time Romain had to say goodbye he used trying to convince his daughter all this had been a mistake. That he'd done nothing wrong and had never used her.

Having to judge between parents as to the truth—it was not her mother who had been chased like a wild beast, it was not her mother who had been on trial, it was not her mother going to prison, it was not her mother's fault they called her Jailgirl.

"Tell her," Romain said to Clarissa. "Tell her what I'm saying is true."

Clarissa held onto the collar of her dark red coat. "I won't lie to her that way."

Romain did not press his wife. There was no profit in it at the moment. He tried to kiss his daughter goodbye. But she just stood there bundled up in her sweater, stone deaf to his attempt at affection.

Romain was taken in a facility bus to Ossining along with other prisoners. The heat in the van was for shit; the men shivered.

He watched the skyline as it disappeared in the gray distance, and with it went his freedom. There was no slang right enough to describe that instant you realize everything about you belongs to somebody else. He was now gonna get a taste of what it must have been like to be his wife all those years.

• • •

Big black letters on the side of the bus said STATE CORRECTIONAL FACILITY. The metal grilling on the windows was also a dead giveaway.

Romain watched the everydayers in cars staring at the bus as they headed north on the parkway. Incomplete features going from window to window. Wondering, probably, if they could get the whole fuckin' story in one glimpse before being tucked in for the night.

Beyond all that Romain was mind-busy. Busy, busy. He kept going over one fact. It had become a fixation since after his arrest, but he'd never mentioned it. Never let on what he thought or felt. Figured he'd sneak up on them about it later, when he had an edge.

It was those goddamn snapshots.

THE M2

CHAPTER 38

EXISTENCE TOOK ITS DIFFERENT TURNS. The rent was brought to Clarissa each month in cash, courtesy of the Cossack, for Romain's silence.

Clarissa took it, and used this as an opportunity to save as much money as she could from her job for the time when she was emotionally ready to file for divorce and have to support Eve on her own.

Not only did she need to overcome her fear of what Romain might do for walking out on him, but divorce was contrary to the deepest beliefs of her religion.

In confession she once worked up to the very question, explaining to the priest what her life had been like all those years. In spite of the suffering, he gently scolded her over the very notion of divorce, offering as an alternative the pathways of prayer, patience and perseverance.

"It doesn't matter what some idiot excuse for a human being says," Fran told Clarissa, waving her scotch glass as she spoke. "Two years of not being locked in an incinerator room will be worth more than any goddamn 'sacred vow.'"

• • •

Eve had never been much of a student in her oral speech classes. Being so profoundly deaf, speech for her had only distant possibilities and she showed worse than little interest. She was part of a small number of students that almost defiantly resisted any attempt at trying.

As for lip-reading, Eve was taught you could pick up thirty to thirty-five percent of what people say. And that, under optimum conditions.

If the speaker had a jitterbug head or unbearably thin lips, if they were like those Santa Clauses at Christmas time with a frosty moustache drooping over their lips, you could forget it. But Eve being so visually oriented, she more than held her own.

A school for the deaf, in some regards, is vastly different than other schools. Children in a place like St. Joseph's find their likeness in the other children. The comradeship of similar difficulties. It is their world within the very different world around them.

It is not only where they are taught, but where their teachers serve as guides ushering them together out into the streets so they can practice taking buses, getting library cards, buying sodas, become prepared for the complications of having to make their way in a hearing world. Yet for Eve, even in this environment, she now stood apart. Her father was in prison.

The teachers at St. Joseph's put a stop to Eve being called Jailgirl, though the name still did have an underground following among the students. The long-range effect of this factioned drama forced Eve to a deeper form of personal resolve. A willfulness, is how Fran described it, not to be hurt by others' need to be hurtful.

But who knowingly wants to force themselves to be different in order to be stronger? Eve had already gotten too good a taste of the struggle. At no time did she feel it more so than when she looked at those last pictures taken with the Kodak at the pool the day of her father's arrest.

A picture is worth a thousand words. And that black-and-white of her classmates with their innocent smiles and their beefcake poses as they signed the word——Tough, unaware of people behind them running, their faces etched with strain. And now in the grainy background Eve could see more clearly an anxious woman calling out to someone.

The shot went right to the basic state of all she felt. She was her classmates, deaf, innocent, and unaware at a moment of chaos.

Everywhere she had gone with her father had been *that* day. He had used her, he had used her deafness. She hated him, but she hated more the fact that she could not hear.

She sat there at the candy store counter watching other children, adults, Dr. Frank, even Fran making change at the register, as they all talked and listened. She felt each of them would have known what she didn't.

She went back to looking at the photos so as not to see anything else. Her shoes scuffed at the chrome footrest as if her body were somehow trying to get her somewhere. And while she was caught up in a maze of broodings, something else happened. The exquisite parallel, is how Eve would much later describe it. Where the mind begins to make creative connections out of separate moments.

The snapshot did not just tell one story, but other stories. You knew the boys were deaf because they signed, but if you didn't know sign you didn't know what they were saying. That would be as much a mystery as what was going on around and behind them.

In the picture Eve could feel a tension. The gulf between her smiling classmates and the strained and frightened faces around them was as wide as the gulf between the hearing world and the deaf world.

Planes of existence began to open up. A photograph could catch a gap in the world. Could show you what was missing. Could make you wonder. Eve felt this tingling sensation rush from her feet right into her head and she couldn't sign fast enough to try and explain to Fran right there at the register what she had experienced.

CHAPTER 39

FRAN BOUGHT THE M2 at a camera shop on Mt. Eden that she'd haunted from time to time. The owner had survived the Holocaust, and had the brand on his arm to prove it. He and Fran had spent their share of quiet time talking through the angers and grief of a shared past.

The M2 was used, but it was still a Leica. The quality of the lenses, the flatness of the film plane—

"The camera of the modern times," said the shop owner, and Fran nodded.

"Remember their poster ads?" he said. "There was one in black and white, with a girl on a bench, looking back over her shoulder." He sighed in that way memory has of moving us. "Beautiful eyes. White, white teeth. I had such a crush on her. I kept that poster for years." Then his face went quietly dark. "I read an article that she died in Dachau. She had been a very fine model, but—"

• • •

Fran outfitted the camera body with a light meter and a 50mm Summicron. She fired up the shutter on all speeds checking for hesitation. She made sure there was no condensation or fungus inside the lens. She went out into the street testing to see if the rangefinder images were correctly aligned.

Fran felt this rush of joy just handling the camera. She and Clarissa intended to give it to Eve. Feelings deep in the shadows of the self, long dormant, filled Fran with a kind of youthful light, as if in some small way, through this, she herself would be starting over again.

• • •

It was on the dining room table when Eve got there after school. A wonder of black and chromium beauty.

Fran and Clarissa were having coffee, acting as if the camera didn't exist, or was nothing more exciting than a pot of plastic flowers.

——What is that, Eve asked.

——What is what, her mother answered.

——That.

——Just a camera.

Eve reached for the card that leaned against the lens looking in bewilderment from one woman to the other. The card read: **Because we love you—Mommy and Fran.**

The women watched as Eve lifted up the camera in a state of completely overwhelmed awe. In Eve's hand it was a thing of sturdy grace and sleek solidity. An alchemy of dials and levers and numbers.

——It's beautiful, but I don't understand what all these numbers mean or what they're for. Is it hard to take pictures?

Fran told her, "It's like learning to sign and lip-read all in one."

• • •

It proved to be at least that hard. Heady exaltation was bled down by mistake after mistake. Threading the film, alright. Getting the camera focused, alright. But when it came to reading the light meter on the top of the camera and adjusting the aperture opening for the ASA of the film, never mind the depth of field you wanted, never mind if the frame was part burnished shade and part iron hot daylight.

What had been simply point-and-shoot now demanded the rhythm of practiced learning, of overcoming the strife of confusion. It was that moment again when she'd learned her first letter in sign, and stood with her mother at a bus stand on the Post Road and realized the words on shop windows and signs at crosswalks, on the sides of cabs and the front of newspapers and magazines were a language just beyond her reach. Something she could touch with her fingers, but could not taste with her mind.

And it didn't get better, and it wasn't just about the camera. There was the complex world of school, of Romain demanding his daughter come to see him in prison, and the unsettling knowledge that her life would always be a pantomime fraught with wishes she couldn't hear.

In a moment of frustration she flung the camera and it caromed off the Castro and onto the floor.

"What did you do?" said Clarissa. "What in the world. Go pick that up. And you better not have damaged it."

Eve shook her head no. She turned to walk out but her mother grabbed her by the arm. Clarissa began to pull Eve toward the camera but Eve had gotten stronger. One hard yank and she was loose.

Clarissa demanded Eve pick up the camera, her arm stabbing at the spot where it lay while Eve backed toward the door, her chin pitched defiantly.

"Don't walk out of this house without picking that camera up. I'm warning you. Don't!"

Eve closed her eyes like she wasn't going to see what her mother had said. Clarissa repeated everything in sign, and Eve answered back as angrily and defiantly as she could——Fuck, no.

Clarissa's neck bent disbelievingly as she watched Eve keep on defiantly. It was a ghastly rush of sign from out of nowhere and absolutely heartless——It was your fault Daddy used me. Your fault. You let him. You never stopped him. You didn't care. You let him because, you were afraid.

And with that Eve was out the door and running up the basement hallway.

CHAPTER 40

FED BY ANGUISH Eve wandered that metropolis of blocks, the only world she'd ever known, really.

Bits of sadness began to stand out in the swell of human traffic. An old woman on a bus bench with discolored legs and badly torn stockings. A boy about her age crying in a tenement doorway and on the hall stairs behind him a shadowy human outline. The downcast face of a woman in a luncheonette window as life streamed across the glass.

She felt herself in these images, but she didn't know how. And the silence inside her, the one she'd lived with since birth, became so profoundly deep, someone could disappear into it and never find their way back.

She became frightened, walking nowhere, just blocks and blocks of nowhere, then instinctively she changed course.

• • •

When Eve got to the candy store Clarissa had already called Fran on the pay phone by the register. Eve must have seen something in Fran's eyes because the first thing she signed when they were alone upstairs was——Please, don't hit me.

Eve's hands were trembling when they spoke. She stood leaning into the high back of a fabric chair and broke down crying.

——I don't want to be deaf, Eve's hands railed.——I hate being deaf. I hate it. If I hadn't been deaf my father would never have been able to use me.

Fran crossed the room but Eve backed away shaking her head, wiping at the tears and signing, lost in the cutting painfuls of who and what she was.

——We're told the wind makes a sound. The rain. When people cry has a sound, when they laugh. People's voices are all supposed to be different. What does music sound like? They tell us everywhere is sound. And I can never hear it. Never. Never.

——What did I do wrong? Why did this happen to me? I don't want to be deaf. *I don't want to be deaf.* I don't want to be deaf. I've done nothing to deserve being deaf.

Eve finally allowed herself to be held. She surrendered enough to let Fran daub at the tears with a handkerchief. Eve's breath sucked in through a diminishing roll of sobs. The two women's foreheads touched. Fran smelled of candy store and toilet water.

When Eve calmed enough, Fran spoke and signed, "I could tell you I'm sorry you were born deaf. The world could tell you they're sorry you were born deaf. But you are deaf, and you will always be deaf."

Eve began to cry again, but this time Fran shook her hard. "You cannot escape what the world has made you, because it is part of who you are now. Life is not the special province of kindness. You've seen *that* when your mother has been locked in an incinerator room. You've seen that when I was on the bathroom floor in pain and bleeding. And the scar that caused it."

These were stark comparisons to be sure, and the images, to Eve, felt like heartshaking blows. She sniffled, then signed——But if I hadn't been deaf, he wouldn't have been able to use me.

"He would have found another way to use you, and he'll try again, if he gets the chance."

——But she didn't stop him?

With that Fran removed her glasses. Her aquiline features bore down as she explained about the shoebox of snapshots and how much fear Clarissa had to overcome to see that one act through.

Fran walked over to the desk. From it she took a folder. Max's boyish face caught her eye.

She walked to the dining room and motioned for Eve to join her. She opened the folder. Eve noticed dozens of cut-out magazine articles. Some appeared recent, some were stained by time. Fran laid them out on the table. All had photographs.

"Look at them, the photographs."

Eve went from one to the next. Most were black-and-white, a few were color. There were avant-garde shots, and studies of the human body, there were shots taken on the streets of places Eve had no idea existed.

Fran next pointed to the names by each photograph. "They were all taken by women."

Fran went to the breakfront and brought the framed snapshot Eve had taken on the roof of Fran and Clarissa holding the wounded bird in their hands. She set it on the table with the articles.

"You can do this. You can learn. You have the eyes."

She drew Eve's attention to one of the photographs. It was of the Statue of Liberty in the pristine light of winter, with snowdrifts so high around the base it seemed as if that woman was a presence standing in the clouds.

"What is that?" Fran said.

——The Statue of Liberty.

"Is it a man?"

——It's a girl.

"And she could be a 'fuckin' deaf girl', right?"

Eve's eyes flinched.

"You like using the word 'fuck', so she could be a fuckin' deaf girl, right?"

Eve nodded. Fran took Eve's snapshot and now placed it side by side with the photograph of the statue.

"She could be you."

Eve took in the two images and all kinds of ideas that went along with them.

"I'll tell you something else, Eve. There is no sound in our dreams. So in that reality, there is no difference between the hearing and the deaf."

• • •

When Eve got back to the apartment, Clarissa was sitting at the Formica table. She was smoking, which she rarely did, and drinking a glass of wine. Dinner was waiting, the light through the windows was fading, but softly so. It framed her mother's sadness all the more emphatically. The moment was a photograph she wanted to remember.

The camera was still on the floor where it had been hours ago. Eve walked over and picked it up. She looked the camera over, as Fran had taught, to see if there was visible damage. She set it on the table.

——I'm sorry for saying what I did.

Her mother's face creased where it had been so painfully tight.

Clarissa took Eve by the hand. There are no reasonable omissions, she thought, not now.

"I knew he used you. But it was the only way I could think of…to…to insure you would not, not…" she squeezed her daughter's hand, "…end up like me. Me…You don't want to end up like. Uneducated, beaten down."

It hurt too much to see her mother so. With eyes brim full and defenseless naked.

——Don't talk like that.

"I did my best…all I could bear to do. Terror is a miserable destination. Be strong, not like me." Clarissa signed for impact——You were born deaf. If that's anyone's fault, blame me. Not yourself. Not ever yourself. Never.

The light had gone from the windows and left a fleeting and imperceptible dusk. That short time between worlds which only hinted at the distances we all had to cross. Clarissa tried to hide whatever other torments she was feeling. Eve kissed her and hugged her in a way to let her mother know she was truly sorry. Eve then asked——What do we do when he comes back?

THE CONFIRMATION NAME

CHAPTER 41

THOUGH ST. JOSEPH'S was not a Catholic or parochial school, it did celebrate St. Joseph's birthday on March 19th and everyone got to dress up in purple and gold. The week was also filled with special activities, and one of Eve's favorites was when they were taken down into the boiler room where there were the remains of a tunnel and laundry cart tracks that had once led to dormitories across the street.

As most of the students were Catholic, the school also performed the sacraments of the First Holy Communion and Confirmation.

Confirmation was a ritual Catholics of the time went through when they were about twelve or thirteen. It was also a sort of conferral of grace, where you came into full communion with the Church. A spiritual strengthening for a life ahead of goodness and service. With the laying on of hands you were a Soldier for Christ, so to speak.

To Clarissa the ritual was important and meaningful. Not only did it signal the coming of womanhood for a girl, it represented another anchor of goodness to hold you firm in spite of the world.

To Fran, any Catholic ritual was just a pageant of silliness, a magic show to mire the gullible in confusion and collection plates.

Of course Eve wanted Fran to be at her Confirmation.

"I'll go anywhere you want," Fran told her. Then she smiled mischievously, "Except confession."

Later, Eve wanted to know,——Why do you think it's all so silly?

They were shopping in Alexander's at the time. It seemed an out-of-place moment to have the conversation, with all those women around them, shoving each other for position over bins of clothes, scrapping for what was on sale.

"Since I don't believe in God, I don't believe in going to church or dressing up for a ghost."

Fran was always so matter of fact, and in this she was no different. And her ability to be flawlessly direct was something Eve wanted to emulate.

——I thought everyone believed in God.

"No," said Fran.

——Can you go to heaven if you don't believe in God?

"When you don't believe in God," Fran answered, "you don't need heaven. Because the only hell is here on earth."

Eve looked to understand. Fran looked back at her unconditionally. For

Eve there was no accepting or rejecting what Fran said. The answer seemed too unreal to be imagined.

"I talk to you like a thoughtful woman," Fran told her, "so that is what you will become."

They continued on down Fordham Road. It was a conversation and a day Eve would never forget. Because a little farther on, near the Valentine Theatre, people were gathering up outside a shop.

Faces crowded the windows as Eve and Fran reached there. The expressions had an eerie kind of shock to them. The shop sold televisions. They were all on, and loud.

Eve watched a man with a thin moustache in a white shirt and loose tie. She read his lips as best she could: President...shot...Dallas.

CHAPTER 42

EVE WATCHED THIS PLACE called America struck by a violent tragedy, reel with sadness and shock. She saw this place called the Bronx live out a shared sorrow that went from street to street, building to building, home to home, without regard for color, race or creed.

Though she could not describe it, there was a feeling everywhere she went: people had discovered that a dark iniquity lay hidden among them. That somewhere in the keep of apartments and parks and roadways, in the slums and schools and shops, there lurked a beast that beset us and had destroyed a part of what had been our best.

Eve now also sensed that others—classmates, neighbors in the building, children at the candy store, even strangers—felt as she did the moment at the Jerome pool when her father was arrested for a crime. The word Fran used to describe these feelings was...violation.

It was during that winter Eve learned to understand her camera and its relationship to light. From pictures of a street, cold and snowy with loneliness, to a Christmas tree in the candy store window, luminous and warm with twinkling lights and season's greetings in a dozen different languages.

It was that winter Eve found the first spots of blood on her underpants and felt the growing mood of boys. She investigated cigarettes, alcohol and a little thing called "pot."

It was that winter she rebelled against going to the state correctional facility no matter what her father threatened.

She watched the Bronx, and by extension the country, move on from the brutality of an assassination to the adoration of the Beatles. Her mind and body were a journal of change.

• • •

That spring, Eve was confirmed at St. Joseph's.

There is a culminatory point during Confirmation when each child announces what is to be their Confirmation name. This name is of their choosing and supposed to be that of a saint who will be their symbolic mentor and inspiration. But Eve broke with tradition.

When it was her turn, and since Eve did not speak, it was left to the bishop. As the child's forehead was anointed with oil and balm he said, "Eve... Franconina...Leone."

He spoke in that low and somber priestly fashion, so that at first, Fran didn't realize it was her name Eve had chosen. She glanced quickly at Clarissa, who smiled.

Fran took off her glasses and closed her eyes for a few moments to compose herself. She felt as if she were suspended on an airy thread. She was that dizzy with happiness, that touched by emotion.

Eve stood in the white dress, designed and sewn by her mother, and started back down the aisle to her seat. All legs and eyes, her skin olive beautiful against the white cloth.

This was a moment Fran would take to her death, a moment of unquenchable affection and humbling pride. As Eve walked past she glanced toward her mother and Fran, and in a secretive and rebellious way, she winked.

"You knew all the time," Fran whispered to Clarissa.

Clarissa leaned toward Fran nodding, "It was the unanimous choice."

A KISS ON THE CHEEK

CHAPTER 43

ROMAIN'S LEFT CHEEK was black and swollen. He had a gash along the eyebrow. As he sat down at the long table Clarissa asked, "What happened?"

"Ahhh…some Rican tried to fuck with my respect."

Coming to the prison always made Clarissa uncomfortable. She looked edgy and tired. Romain glanced at the guards.

"Three more months," he said.

"Three more," she answered flatly.

"Did you bring cigarettes and aftershave?"

"Yes."

She had learned they used the aftershave to make some prison booze cooked up in the kitchen, which was where Romain worked.

"The trip up okay?"

"It was a nice day for a bus ride."

"How is Eve?"

"She's doing well."

Clarissa was still a good-looking woman, he thought. And her body hadn't gone south. He'd like to bag her, but beyond that—"

"Dominic been around?"

"Never."

"I'm not surprised. The rent still come regular?"

"Yes."

For the whole twenty months Romain had kept wondering: the thing of it with Clarissa was like some pathetic refuge, but from what he didn't know. It was like some part of him had been born prematurely dead. He would lay in his cell at night thinking, why not just blow her off. Do the "fuck you, sayonara."

But somewhere at the edge of his life there was a piece of him that couldn't let go. That fed on a lineup of all the brain awfuls he could think of. Conflicts that put a revolver loaded with angers right to his head.

"Did you ever, ever love me?" asked Clarissa.

It was a goddamn queer question and coming right out of nowhere. He looked around, searching out the guards in case she'd been overheard.

"I don't know what love is," he said. "And I'm sure as shit, you don't either."

She nodded, as if acquiescing to the fact he was right. Then she wished she could have taken the nod back.

"We may be moving to Philly when I get out."

He saw the unguarded expression on her face. This was gonna be more than an issue.

"I may have something going with the cousin of a guy in my block."

Clarissa wanted to get up right then and there and start running.

"Eve still taking pictures all the time?"

"What?"

"Eve…" Romain mimed like he was taking a picture of Clarissa, "…all the time?"

"Yes. All the time."

Then, Romain kind of half whispered, "Those fuckin' snapshots the cops found. Bad day for me, hunh?"

• • •

On the bus ride back from the Men's Correctional Facility, Clarissa was caught up in a crossfire of emotional conflicts. She could still hear herself asking Romain, "Did you ever, ever love me?" That she could, at this late date in their excuse of a life, even ask such a humiliating question made her doubt her own sanity.

Before picking up Eve at Fran's, she stopped at St. Philip's Church. She sat in a pew alone and looked at the stained glass window, the one of Genesis, with daylight burning through a naked Adam and Eve, hiding their shame from God. She'd sat in that same pew years before, grasping for some ultimate truth, or at least a deliberate direction, deciding whether or not to abort Eve.

Divorce. It shamed her to even have to consider it. Divorce was against every credo of Christian life, against everything she'd been taught about the way we are supposed to live. Then in the silence of that church, she began to wonder was she using that credo against divorce as an excuse because she was afraid of leaving Romain?

The very notion of that possibility panicked her because it eroded the foundations of support she'd used to survive all those years.

And if they were gone, then what was there? That great church began to close in on her. She got up and ran. She ran back to her apartment, alone.

• • •

In a panic Clarissa began to pack her and Eve's things. Get out now while he was in prison. Run.

But where? Leave the city, the state. Start over. Those two words—start over—they landed on her like a ton of concrete. She did not want to leave Fran. Fran was all she and Eve really had.

And if she did run while Romain was in prison, wouldn't that only incite him to find her? Wouldn't that make him sure she had been the one who turned over the photographs? And wouldn't Fran know where she was? Couldn't Romain follow her sometime or physically try and force her to tell? What if he and Dominic went to the police and created some kind of lie against her? Romain and Dominic were good at creating lies.

A sense of uncertainty came over Clarissa. She sat on the bed beside the open suitcases and considered her predicament. She could move to Fran's. She wanted Eve away from Romain, she wanted Eve to stay at St. Joseph's. But if she moved to Fran's, of all people, wouldn't that only enrage Romain, as much as he hated Fran? Wouldn't she be bringing the threat of him right into Fran's house?

Maybe it was best to do nothing till she was sure. Where does the fear stop, so the real choices get to take over? Where do the real choices stop, because the fear has taken over? Are all these reasons for not going just excuses to cover my fear?

Maybe Romain would just tire of her. Maybe he would get out of jail and just want to be done with her. What does he want me for anyway?, she asked herself. Then, out of the confusion, the ghost of a notion. Maybe he was too weak to leave.

If that was the answer, as much as it made her sick to feel it, a sense of power came over her. Power…and fear.

She sat on the bed beside the suitcases for a long, long time. An hour, maybe more. Looking at nothing, thinking. She then began to unpack her things.

She could not run. She did not want to run. She just wanted to not be afraid. She wanted to be away from Romain and not afraid. She just did not know how to be unafraid.

CHAPTER 44

FRAN AND CLARISSA WERE SUNNING themselves up on the roof. They'd brought beach chairs and stretched back. The sun drew out the smell of tar. Clarissa made sandwiches. Fran contributed a six-pack of Rheingold.

They'd been up there long enough to get a little pink. There were traces of sweat on their eyebrows and necks.

"Somebody once told me," said Fran, "I drink like a man."

Clarissa opened her eyes. Fran was sitting up and reaching for another beer.

"Who was it?"

"I don't know. Some man."

Fran set the beer can on the beach chair arm. Hooked up the opener and popped. Twisted the can. Hooked the opener again and popped. She was a model of swift and seasoned efficiency.

"Do you ever think," asked Clarissa, "you might find someone you could be comfortable with, and marry?"

Fran took a drink of beer. Clarissa shaded the sun from her eyes and waited. Fran tossed the opener back into the bag with the other beers.

"No," she said. "What about you? I mean after Romain."

"After Romain. Will that even be possible?"

"There will be a time after Romain."

Clarissa sat up. The long nights and days in question between that kind of happiness. She folded one hand over another and looked at the wedding band that now just took up space on her finger. It might as well belong to someone else.

Clarissa took the beer from Fran. "I'd like to be well loved once before I die."

She drank.

"Sometimes," said Fran, "when I think about Max, I try to imagine what our life would be like now if he were alive. What our children would be like."

Clarissa ran the cold and sweating can along her throat while she listened.

"I make up imaginary stories lying in bed. Like scenes from a movie. Sometimes I go to movies just so I can have new places to pretend about. What if we lived on that street, or in that town, that country? What would our life be like? Who would our friends be?"

Clarissa handed the beer back to Fran. After a little bit, she confessed, "I see kind looking men. Men with their wives and children. On the street, in church. Holding hands. What if…you know?"

Fran nodded. She took another drink of beer, then offhandedly said, "I let men pick me up now and then."

A look of embarrassed shock came over Clarissa. It made Fran almost smile.

"Not here. I go to Manhattan or Brooklyn." The veins along Fran's temple flashed, her eyes drew in. "But I make sure they're very drunk, and the hotels we go to are very, very dark."

Fran laid back then. "I think it was one of them who told me I drink like a man."

Nothing more was said for a while. They remained as they were, engaged in this little moment. The simple honesty of it took on a quiet force.

"I never had anyone to talk to about things like this," said Fran.

"Me neither," said Clarissa.

With that Fran closed her eyes. And with that Clarissa leaned over and kissed Fran lightly on the cheek.

THE BUNGALOW BAR
ICE CREAM TRUCK

CHAPTER 45

DURING RECESS, JUST DAYS BEFORE school let out for the summer, the Bungalow Bar ice cream truck pulled up to St. Joseph's playground. The speech teacher corralled her class so they could practice their oral and lip-reading skills by ordering ice cream. Some of the students, like Eve, could only sign and needed an interpreter.

It wasn't as if Eve, who had intentionally slipped to the back of the line, was experiencing something for the first time and yet—

So much effort had to go into even as simple an act as ordering ice cream. It *was* like learning to use her camera.

That scene of fleeting nervousness and urgency, of students chatting among themselves in sign around the truck, their hands moving like the wings of birds and the ice cream man with his lined and wrinkled face watching from a place of weary patience.

Eve had seen that moment how many times at the different parks and projects and summer recreation centers, but never, like how she saw it now.

She slipped back from the line without anyone noticing and slid the camera off her shoulder.

She managed one picture after another without a student catching on. Moving back she noticed just out of frame a woman bagged down with groceries staring disconcertedly over her shoulder at the scene. Eve got that too. It was all happening in momentary intervals. Stepping back again the school's chain link fence slipped into view and Eve felt this little rush of imagination.

• • •

When Fran lined up the photographs, she knew. It was right there. Each shot seemed to be an attempt at a series of corrections and alterations. The mind of seeing, at work.

There was an earthy poetry to the shots. A clear-eyed treatise of an everyday scene contraposed with those deaf children signing.

And that last photograph through the fence, with the chain links just out of focus enough to highlight and separate the action beyond. It had a dynamism and tension that had to be felt before it could be photographed.

It almost baited the notion, who was taking the picture? Was it someone imprisoned by separation? A moment of curious spying? The innocent onlooker?

• • •

The *Bronx Home News* was notorious for publishing shots taken by Bronxites about their neighborhoods. Unfortunately the *Home News* was out of business since '48.

The *Bronx Press-Review* published the same kind of shots, but much more rarely.

Fran went to the *Press-Review's* offices in Parkchester, found the right editor in charge and made her case with the photographs.

For sheer delirium of pride, nothing could match that moment when the vice-principal tacked to St. Joseph's *Bulletin Board of Achievement* the cut-out section of the newspaper with Eve's photograph.

There it was—Ladies and Gentlemen—with the caption: Eve Leone gets a snapshot of her classmates at St. Joseph's School for the Deaf. Students practice their speech technique for a treat of ice cream.

Eve sat in class those first days after, just tickled silly as her insides double somersaulted every time she passed that picture on the bulletin board. But as far as the whole school went, Jailgirl and her camera played it completely cool.

THE SUNDAY MISSAL

CHAPTER 46

ROMAIN WAS RELEASED two weeks early. He didn't tell Clarissa, but had Dominic come and pick him up. The weather that day sure as shit wasn't like when they'd hauled his ass up to Ossining. Dominic brought a six-pack and some Jew's booze. On the ride back Dominic filled in the last two years. To Romain it was nervous talk, like Dominic was trying to keep from saying something.

They stopped at a Howard Johnson's to eat. Romain figured he should feel more out of sorts, being off the street two years. Truth was, only the hairdos and the clothes had changed. Everything else was a dead ringer for how it used to be.

While they were sitting at the counter Romain flat out asked, "You gonna tell me what the fuck is wrong?"

Dominic was hunched over his sandwich. He tried to act like Romain was mistaken, but Romain was not mistaken.

In the car Dominic copped to it. "The Cossack's got a connection in vice at the 43rd. He picked up a rumor, okay."

Romain said nothing. He just sat there waiting for Dominic to get on with it.

"The cops had been tipped about the snapshots."

Romain's eyebrows bunched up.

"I heard about a year ago," said Dominic. "I didn't want to tell you while you were inside. Didn't want you doing anything crazy."

Down in the deepest part of the self, where those intuitions pool like water at the bottom of a sewer, Romain had known. "It was Clarissa or the dyke."

"Clarissa or the dyke," repeated Dominic.

• • •

Romain didn't come home for days. He got street loose in Woodridge, sleeping in a room above the bar that Dominic's girlfriend ran for her family.

Romain went back to West Farms late one night. He passed a guy walking a dog who lived in the building and was greeted with the kind of gutless half-stare he expected when the con returns.

Romain knocked on the apartment door hard, and strictly on purpose. Nothing. He still had his keys. The place was dead quiet and dark. No Clarissa, no Eve. Just plenty of photographs. Framed, taped to the walls. They were fuckin' everywhere. You'd think the apartment was a shrine. A friggin' Lourdes to his daughter.

He thought of the snapshots that had done him in and he wanted to cyclone the place. But he kept it in check.

There was food in the fridge. He went out and bought beer. He ate at the Formica table with only the television on, he'd even shut off the sound. His mind kept diseasing on one thing—it was Clarissa or the dyke.

Afterwards, he went up to the roof. He set his beer on the ledge and smoked. He breathed deep that free fuckin' air and watched the light spill on miles' worth of windows and street traffic. He could see the elevated, its cars all bright and wildly flickering as the train shuttled between buildings. It was like looking into the heart of an endless foundry that was constantly on shift.

All that energy and go. There were thousands of scenes being played out right at that moment, by people who didn't have to be on the watch, weren't forced to look over their shoulder. Who didn't have a record, and weren't flat-ass broke.

And who did he have to thank for that?

Chapter 47

It was Sunday afternoon when Eve and Clarissa got back to the apartment. They'd stayed at Fran's and gone straight from there to church. The television being on, the Castro open, they knew the inevitable had happened.

Romain stepped out of the bathroom. He had been combing his hair. Neither woman knew what to do. Clarissa managed a feeble, "We thought you were coming home in—"

"They let me out early. Dominic picked me up. I thought I'd…well, surprise you. And I see you are surprised."

Romain looked his daughter over. She'd grown, taken on more of her mother. Only Eve was taller. And those eyes. Nothing beats a taste of that stare to tell you what shit is like.

Romain roughly signed——Taller.

Eve walked right past him.

• • •

There was nothing. Just dead space and bare emotions. They were shadows moving past shadows no matter what time of day it was. Dinner got to be the worst of all. The Formica table felt no bigger than a playing card. The whole meal passed in silence.

Everything for Eve and her mother was about self-preservation; for Romain it was about biding his time. Whenever Eve got the chance, she signed to her mother, even when Romain was in the apartment——Divorce the shit before he does something else.

• • •

Weeks of nervy half-sentences and men coming to the apartment meeting with Romain. Faces Clarissa didn't recognize except for Dominic. Most spoke Italian, but a couple were Spanish. Romain's Spanish had gotten pretty good in prison. The men treated Clarissa with suspicious politeness.

When Eve was around her father would tell them, "My daughter's deaf. But watch what you say, 'cause she's a pretty goddamn good lip-reader."

• • •

Clarissa never went anywhere without her Sunday missal. She'd kept it in the bottom drawer of her dresser along with a few nightgowns and a pouch of potpourri.

She carried the missal with her 'cause that's where she hid her bankbook with all the money she'd saved while Romain was in prison. It was tucked into a flap in the back cover. Since he'd gotten out, she hid the missal in her purse.

Romain and Clarissa were alone in the apartment late one Friday. Romain was shaving. As Clarissa passed the bathroom he called out, "Say a prayer for me, hon."

She stopped, uncertain of what she'd heard.

He turned to her. "Yeah. Head over to church and deposit a little prayer for me."

She felt this sudden twine of muscles in her throat, the words caught. "I don't understand."

"Like you been doin' every Friday since I was in jail. Take your missal. Go to church. And deposit a few prayers." He went back to shaving, smiled at her through the steamy mirror. "I always knew my wife was deeply religious, but you give new meaning to 'In God We Trust.'"

CHAPTER 48

WITHOUT THINKING OR WAITING she put the purse down on the arm of the Castro. Romain watched her fumble through her possessions for the missal, flipping pages to the back flap, looking for the bankbook.

It was right there, right where she always kept it.

He cocked his head, and moved that razor coolly across his jawline. "I found it the first night I was back," he said.

She couldn't turn the page to her last deposit fast enough. The money, it was still there. She looked up.

"If I wanted the money, I could make you hand it over."

She held the bankbook and the missal to her chest. "What is it you want?"

There was no necessity for an answer.

"What do you want?"

She'd almost screamed it, but he kept on shaving as if he were deaf.

"Answer me."

This time she did scream it.

"I'll tell you when I'm ready," he said.

• • •

He'd found a new way to torture Clarissa. Just put the thought out there in the universe. Leave it hanging in the air like a sign, while he worked some angle for making money. Let her feed on it every waking hour——I will tell you when I'm ready.

He imagined even when she was taking a piss it was on her mind. What's the bastard gonna do? For two years he'd had to live with "the how" of those snapshots. So why not let her get a good dose of just how *uncertain*, uncertain can be.

Sometimes he'd even show her the barest trace of affection. He'd come up on her really slow and kiss her on the neck. He could feel the strain just creep up her body every time.

He never hit her once, never locked her in the incinerator room. He was gonna rub her face in it his way. Let her quietly fear till he was ready to deliver.

As for his own life, he couldn't get that on track. He didn't need a roomful of theories to explain it either. The ex-con was poison. The Cossack slipped him some short money, but couldn't face the risk of having him back.

• • •

The three women sat at Fran's dining room table facing a moment of truth.

Eve kept at her mother——Leave him.

The apartment below Fran's, the one she rented out, was being vacated in a few months. The plan had always been for Clarissa and Eve to move in there.

Out of sheer hesitation, Clarissa said, "I don't know if we could afford it."

Eve cut in with——I'll get a job.

"You're not leaving school," her mother told her.

"The hell with the rent," said Fran. "We'll figure something out. Just decide."

This was no time for reflection, no time to turn things over in her mind. This was about finding that place inside where you can begin the fight to not be afraid. She'd been waiting years to find a way to get out from under. If she didn't, it was gonna be death by the silent treatment until one night she went to sleep and woke up to find herself in some newly-constructed hell.

Clarissa stood, while Eve kept at her. She just stood and Fran knew. Fran grabbed Eve's hands to quiet her.

"I won't spend my life rehashing tragedies." Clarissa looked at Eve. "And I won't spend yours."

That was how Clarissa said it.

"Leave us," Clarissa told Eve. "For a few minutes."

The two women walked downstairs alone. Stopped at the bottom of the stairwell by the door. The tiled hallway was still cool, though outside the night was turning muggy.

"I'll go over and tell him. Pack some things. Come back."

"You want me to drive you? Sit in the car and wait?"

Clarissa shook her head no. She tried not to look too afraid.

"You sure?"

"I have to learn to not be afraid. So, I have to start acting not afraid."

"If you go over there alone, he could—"

"Hit me? Lock me in the incinerator room?"

"Yes."

Under the shadow of these possibilities, Clarissa said, "If he does, this time, I will break the window to the street and scream till someone hears me or till morning, and when I get out, I will still pack up and leave him."

"Why be alone with him at all...ever again?"

"You know as well as I do, if he wants to confront me alone, if he wants to get ugly, the only way I can stop that from happening is if I find another incinerator room somewhere." She paused. Her look wandered a bit before it settled back in on her thoughts. "I have to know, I have to have him know...I'm not afraid."

"At least let me drive you there."

"No."

"I'll drive you and then just leave."

"It's only ten blocks and I need the walk. Because...the walk is when I'll get the weakest. When I'll be the most scared. And I'll have all those chances to just turn around. Like that day when I went to the police station with the photographs and I couldn't bring myself to go inside. That walk killed me."

Clarissa's lips were very dry. She felt this great widening void she was about to face. "I need that walk. You see, I want my daughter to respect me. I want you to respect me."

"Oh, Clarissa."

Fran reached out and held Clarissa.

Clarissa started to go. But she wanted to say something more before she left. Clarissa took Fran's hand and like that moment in the car on Eve's first day of school signed across her palm——Woman, sister, friend.

"Yes," said Fran. "Always."

TIME AND MUD

CHAPTER 49

ROMAIN WAS SITTING on the edge of the Castro. He'd pulled it open to sleep some, but now he was drinking a glass of red wine and watching International Showtime. Some daredevil act was highwiring it between two buildings above a Paris street. Romain hoped the fuckers would fall into the crowd and land on Don Ameche, give the show a little boost.

He barely turned when Clarissa came into the apartment. She stood by the door after she closed it, leaned against the wall. She was getting up the courage for what she'd come to say.

He finally turned, almost as afterthought. He looked her over. He was like a force of nature throwing off enough bad feelings that if you ran a Geiger counter over him, the crackling would jump off the charts.

"Why you standing there like some mope?"

She was now looking at the long chance to a new life. She hadn't even put her purse down, when she said, "I'm going to file for divorce."

The bastards on the highwire made the cross. Too bad. He finished off his wine, drained it to the last swallow of red. "You gonna divorce me?"

She started to enter the room. "That's right."

"Then you can kiss your daughter goodbye."

"What?"

"You're out of our life. Finished. Gone. Dead. Maybe we'll keep a couple of *snapshots* of you."

"Fran already brought me to an attorney."

"Fran brought you—"

"And he told me you won't get custody. This is one place where a mother has—"

"I'm not talking about custody. I'm talking I pack up Eve and you hit the fuckin' street."

"You can forget that idea. Eve is at Fran's and that's where she's gonna stay till—"

"Fran."

Romain stood in a slow and silent way. Fran. Good old fuckin' Fran. A cunt's friend. He went to the sink and set the glass there. Then he turned.

It was the way he turned. "Go on," she said. "Lock me in the incinerator room. But I'll scream till someone gets me out. And then I'll have you arrested."

He started across the room. She knew it was now that she couldn't give up on herself. "And I'll still file for—"

Romain spit in her face. It was more a shock than anything else. She went into her purse for a tissue. She wiped his spit from her skin. All that fear she'd lived with, she could feel it start to flatten out. And on the inside, she began to experience hidden caches of self-reliance organizing up, moving toward her defense. Her willfulness had made it so.

"Romain, that's the most affection you've shown me in years."

She went to walk past him. Be done and gone. If she could. "I'm going to pack a few things. Eve and I will be staying at Fran's until the divorce."

Romain grabbed her by the arm. "One thing, first. The snapshots. It was her who told the police, right?"

Clarissa was staring at her arm, she noticed more spit on the sleeve. "I don't know what you're talking about."

"Don't." He shook her hard. "Not with me." Again he shook her. "I'll sneak into the Nazi's place one night and put a two-by-four across her skull if I have to, to get the truth."

Clarissa did not try to pull away. It was Romain who let her go. Just like that. He motioned, almost mocking, for her to get her stuff. "But remember one thing. You walk out that door and I don't have the answer, you can tell the dyke, there's not a night she can hope to be safe for the rest of her life."

CHAPTER 50

ALL THE TOIL in that tiny apartment as a self-imposed prisoner meant nothing, nothing compared now to the wall of threat standing there staring at her.

It was a fight he wanted. Give me the answer or else. Finally she was able to stand between him and someone he meant to hurt, including herself, and there were no compromising contradictions to hold her back.

The television was on. Just like that night. A curious sensation overtook her. Exactly like that night. The moment shaped out in a black-and-white memory of her at the table with Eve and those boxes of snapshots.

"It was me, Romain."

She said it like someone coming out of a long and beaten dream.

"I was right here with Eve." She pointed at the table. "We were going through all the snapshots and you walked in. You went over and turned on the television to…to that same stupid show. Do you remember? Do you? Do you, Romain?

"You got a drink and you went to shave 'cause you were going out with Dominic to see his 'hump' in Woodridge."

As he stood there listening to all this his shoulders creeped up toward his neck.

"While you were being so smart and so cruel I was going through all those snapshots, putting the ones aside. It was me who called the police. Not Fran. It was—"

He hit her so hard, so fast with a fist across the jaw, she was out on her feet.

Her legs jellied and she dropped back onto the Castro. Landed in a sitting position like a rag doll just dumped there.

There was no blood. She woozed from side to side. The whole room felt displaced and in midair. She almost tipped over, but braced herself with a hand.

She wanted to throw up, but she wouldn't out of spite. She wanted to stand, but she wasn't sure which way was up.

He saw her begin to try. He let her. She came up head sagging left, her body fighting the pull of gravity. She used a hand as leverage. There was a nasty gleam in Romain's eyes.

As she stood up enough to get some leg under her, Romain swung. Her head had tilted back from a wave of dizziness. The second blow was silent and fast. He meant to hit her in the face but his fist caught her in the throat. The punch was delivered with all the shoulder he could muster out of forty years' worth of pure hatred. His fist stove in her windpipe.

She hit the Formica table flush. A chair toppled over. She was flat out on her back. Her body began to convulse. She was just conscious enough to know she was suffocating.

He stood over her for a moment like a prizefighter waiting to go another round when he realized.

She was grabbing for her throat. Trying to somehow piece it back together. To get at some air. Her legs thrashed and kicked, her body writhed. Her mouth kept opening and closing in horrid desperation. Romain could hear his wife gasp.

The thrashing legs, the desperate motion of the mouth. This went on, and on, and on. More frantically fighting the seconds to death. Her hips rose as if somehow they could lift the body one last time. The legs spread, the knees pulled up. The muscles jerked down one side of her body. And then her life was just taken.

CHAPTER 51

HE STARED AT HIS WIFE lying there on the concrete floor. He felt his breath come through his teeth in sharp bursts. Coward's breaths, he thought. His chest hurt. He wanted to run but he was flat against the wall holding on for dear life.

Her dress was hiked up to her panties. Her legs spread apart. She had urinated on the floor. He could not look at her face. He dared not. His eyes went to the ceiling. To the water pipes that ran the length of the apartment. There was sweat along the pipes.

One rabid desire overcame him. How do I get away with this? His insides were starving for an answer. Panicked, but still motionless. A frozen imprint against a brick wall. Like someone before the firing squad.

The incinerator! Could he just burn her into oblivion? But at this hour, what if that nosy Slav of a superintendent smelled the fire? What if he couldn't stoke up enough heat to ash the bones before Eve or Fran or some other shit got suspicious and showed? With all the times he'd locked her in the incinerator it would be the first place they'd look. No...Not the incinerator.

• • •

At the storeroom door, he dropped his keys. Hands shaking, the taste of vomit in his mouth. He looked back up the basement corridor. An overhead light filled out the darkness by the stairwell.

The storeroom was pitch black when he closed the door behind him. He fumbled his way to a filthy corner where they kept movers' tarps and heavy cloth belts. He heard clawed feet scurrying over a rooftop of boxes.

• • •

He wrapped the body in a tarp. He bound it at the chest and legs. He pulled the tarp over the head like a hood. He shoved the loose ends down inside the cloth belt.

He did all this without ever really looking at her, without really seeing. Inside though, fear told him, the face was there waiting.

He looked out the basement door. He had to carry the body to the garage without being seen. He used the darkness, moving carefully along the stone wall and down the red brick alleyway. The windows above, lit squares of danger where at any moment, any moment—

He carried the body bent over, gambling on that dozen yards to the garage door. Just let me get to the truck, he begged.

He could feel an arm against the side of his throat and down along his chest bobbing as he ran. The touch of it made him sick.

His mind was in pieces as he drove up Tremont Avenue. He glanced in every direction at once. Trembling hands with dirty fingernails bloodlessly tight on the steering wheel.

Every stoplight burned him. Every blazing storefront window heightened the shadows around what he had done. He drove through the steam coming up from a manhole cover. It was ghostly against the windshield.

His face got sticky pale. Make it go away, God. Make it all go away.

But God wasn't listening.

CHAPTER 52

HE SWUNG OVER TO PELHAM PARKWAY, crossed Eastchester Bay. The tires stuttered violently on the metal drawbridge.

He was on what was called Shore Road. There were long stretches of marshland and heavy woods along that road.

The road bent around a treed island of sorts. It made a complete circle, in fact, where you could turn out to City Island or up into Westchester.

He rode the circle. He rode it and rode it. Only once did a car pass, heading south on the far side of that island.

He hunched down in his seat as if he could be seen. Feverish waves came over him as he drove and drove, looking into a murky wilderness of undergrowth and willows for a place to park and hide.

· · ·

He used a hubcap from the truck to dig a hole in the mud. His pants grew wet at the knees.

He pushed the body into the shallow hole. He pressed down and he pressed down, but the earth fought back. The body lifted slightly and buoyed amidst muddy bubbles.

He scoured the darkness. He found a huge rock he could barely hold. He dropped the stone on the bound-up remains of his wife. The low thud went through him with horrifying directness, and seconds later, the earth began to relent. He found another huge stone and another. Carrying them, his bony fingers stretched to the breaking point. He dragged them if necessary.

The brown ooze began to tide over the gray-green tarp leaking its way between gaps and folds in the binding.

He knelt again and filled in the mud using the hubcap as a shovel. The smell of marsh water was nothing compared to the smell of vomit in his nose.

Headlights rode up out of the distance and he cowered. He shook like an infant, his whole body channelways of fear. The light was taken apart by the trees, fragmented into a thousand starburst shards and he could see all too well now what he had done.

He tried to erase what he saw from his eyes. He tried to blind it out with excuses and reasons. For a moment the old angers unsheathed. Scarcely a reflex before he told himself, tried to convince himself that she had caused all this to happen.

It was her fault, with her flawed children and her fighting and her cunt friend. She had been God's own war against him. It was her fault she was lying there like that.

He tore out willows and took the remains of dead trees and covered up the grave. Time and mud would take care of the rest.

PAPER CUPS ON A

WINDOW SILL

CHAPTER 53

As soon as Romain hit the Bronx, he called Dominic, told him to get over to the apartment. To say nothing to Gail. Make sure no one saw him—fuckin' no one. From the way Romain's voice was, Dominic knew it had to be bad so he packed up the .38 they'd copped from the cemetery.

• • •

Dominic was across from Romain's apartment smoking, just out of reach of the streetlight. His pug hat slouched low on his forehead as he leaned against the ugly brick of an alleyway wall. His nerves were snatching at him as he waited. When he spotted Romain's truck swing into the apartment garage he crossed the street quiet and fast.

A shadow rolled up on the wall by the truck and Romain nearly about caved till he realized it was Dominic.

By now Romain's eyes were deeply pocketed, his pants stuck to his legs with mud and sweat. He felt bad enough to be a thousand years old. There was not a fuckin' inch of his body that wasn't trembling.

"What happened?"

Romain couldn't hold it together. He broke down right there at the steering wheel. All that tension and edge of collapsing manhood. To Dominic it was flat-out scary.

"I fucked up...I...I killed her..."

"What? Who?"

"Clarissa, man. Right there in the apartment. I hit the fuckin' cunt till—"

At the far end of the garage a door opened then shut with an echo. Footsteps on the concrete floor. Both men slid down in the cab seat like a couple of delinquent punks. It felt like those footsteps walked right across their throats. Dominic had to force Romain's shirt up over his mouth to muffle the rattling sobs.

CHAPTER 54

EVE'S INSTINCT TOLD HER enough was enough. Fran wasn't so sure. Her feeling, "Clarissa and your father could have gotten into a serious talk. Let's wait."

Eve walked over to the desk, grabbed Fran's car keys and held them up.

• • •

When the two women got to the apartment Romain and Dominic were at the Formica table playing briscola and talking over the sound of the television. A stack of empties had collected up by the draining board.

When the women walked in things went pretty dead for a few seconds. Sound dead. Fran picked up on it. But for Eve, she was good at the nervous things faces do, especially her old man's, which she knew too well. It was that postcard fuckin' moment of Romain Leone unease.

Eve demanded——Where's Mama?

Romain shrugged. "I don't know." He looked from one woman to the other.

Eve started to walk the room for signs. Anything, that her mother had been there. The purse she'd been carrying, a change of shoes, a missing suitcase.

"What's going on, man," said Dominic.

"Clarissa was at my apartment, and a few hours ago she said she was coming over here and that she'd be right back."

Fran avoided certain facts on purpose. Eve crossed the room after finding nothing and grabbed her father's work keys from the table.

"What is this? Why you acting so—"

Before he could get a hand on Eve, she had slipped his grasp and was out of the room.

Eve went right to the incinerator room. Romain could hear her trying key after key in the lock.

The goddamn nightmare truth was starting to have at him bad. Even with all the beers he couldn't keep Clarissa's body from surfacing up through the mud of his insides. A vision honest and deadly as the hand that killed her.

Dominic got up from the table. "Clarissa might have bumped into Gail somewhere and the two of them just started yacking away." He opened another beer. "When those two start—"

Fran stopped listening and stepped out into the hall to see what Eve was doing. In those few moments, when they were alone, Dominic whispered to Romain, "You look like you're about ready to have a fuckin' heart attack."

As he stuffed the beer into Romain's hand Eve undid the incinerator room lock. She flipped on the light. It was a ghosthole of garbage. Of bundled newspapers, of cans topped with bottles. And the rancid smell of recently burned trash. It killed her to think how many times her father had locked her mother in there.

• • •

Romain could see the women signing to each other in the hall. When they walked back into the room Eve went right for the phone and held it out toward her father.

"What?" he asked.

"She wants you to call the police," said Fran.

Chapter 55

It took twenty-four hours to file a missing person's report. The authorities, though, could Jane Doe the hospitals and morgues.

Fran made calls from Clarissa's apartment. Eve sat guard on the front stoop watching every figure moving starkly alone from streetlight to streetlight. It was an unbreathable tale of waiting and each shadow wore a surge of hope before it bitterly disappointed.

Mama, please be alive.

Dominic suggested he and Romain walk the blocks from the apartment back to Fran's store, hoping to find out if maybe there had been an accident, or if maybe Clarissa had bumped into a friend. Maybe, maybe, maybe.

Fran eyed them with cold detachment from over the rim of her glasses. Dominic thought of her as a fuckin' Hun devil.

• • •

On Bronx River Road the two men ducked into a bar. They slinked down into a back booth by the johns and pool tables where they could be alone.

Dominic was leaning into Romain, railing how he better be the "grieving father" a lot better than he'd been showin' so far.

They were talking how to handle tomorrow at missing persons when Romain noticed the barkeep saying to someone he couldn't quite see, "You girlie. You can't come in here. You hear, girlie?"

Romain had no idea it was Eve until she edged in alongside the matchbox square of light from above the pool table. She stood there like a white moment in a dead black night.

She had followed her father. For unseen seconds she had witnessed the jittering leg and how he kept rubbing at his lower lip with the back of a knuckle.

An unnoticeable collection of visual trivialities. But not to her. He had been that way at the Cossack's more than once, and at the Food Palace. Then at the precinct house right after the police arrested him. Who'd forget that?

"Hey, girl. You."

Dominic looked around just as Romain slid out of his seat.

The barkeep had had enough. He was staring at his scotch-eyed patrons going, "What the hell gives here? Hey, girlie. I'm talking to you."

In a fit of misdirected emotion Romain went right at the barkeep. "That's my daughter. And she's deaf, okay. Fuckin' deaf." Romain grabbed Eve. She wrenched loose her arm.

"Hey, I'm sorry," said the barkeep, "but she's underage and——"

"Her mother just fuckin' died, okay. So ease up."

The barkeep threw his hands out apologetically, but Romain had already kicked the black leather front door open.

• • •

Eve swung about. She and her father stood facing each other while headlights flared across the face of the buildings and tided up out of the gutter.

Eve gave her father a severe expression——Why are you drinking? Why aren't you out looking for Mama?

The moment was raw and charged. Romain tried to explain himself, to defend himself, but he was having to grapple with everything at once.

Then Dominic had at him. "You know what you said in there?"

"What?"

"Inside, to that fuckhead."

Confused, Romain glanced at the bar trying to flash on—

"You said your wife just died."

Eve saw Dominic had angled his face so she couldn't lip-read something he said to Romain, who turned queerly fearful over what he heard.

Dominic stabbed his middle finger repeatedly into the side of Romain's head. "Think…think."

CHAPTER 56

"EVE IS STAYING with me tonight."

Romain was sitting at the table. Dominic was leaning against the sink smoking. "I don't know if that's such a good idea," said Romain. "I'm pretty upset. We both are. All of us are. I'd kind of like having my daughter with me tonight."

"Eve decided already," said Fran.

Romain stood. He walked over to his daughter. He tapped her on the shoulder. "It'll be all right."

She accepted her father's meager show of affection with grim reluctance.

"You know," said Dominic. "I think it's a good idea, too. Romain'll stay with Gail and me tonight. We'll leave Clarissa a note. That way when she comes back, she'll know—"

"Clarissa is not coming back," said Fran, "and both of you men goddamn know it."

• • •

Eve sat at the window looking out into a darkness she'd never imagined. She could smell her mother's perfume on her clothes. The scent always spoke to her heart of kindness, gentleness.

Fran watched Eve unknowingly signing out private thoughts, pleadings. Fran drank but it did little to still the anxiety. She stood by the photograph of her and Clarissa on the roof with that wounded dove. From hidden corners came whisperings.

"If anything ever happens, promise you won't let Romain keep Eve."

Fran's eyes closed. A sense of dread, like being back in Germany, returned.

"Promise."

Fran got Eve to lie down in her bed, at least for a while. Ear to the door, she could hear the child whimpering.

Fran walked downstairs and sat on the landing step at the bottom of the stairwell where she and Clarissa had talked earlier.

With its white tiles bordered in black and single light bulb in the high ceiling above, the entrance had an echoey quiet, something at that moment almost tomblike. She could feel Clarissa signing in her palm——Woman, sister, friend.

The words reached down into a deep of wounds and memories and needs. Fran wanted what she knew to be true, to not be. She wanted to be held and comforted, but knew that was not to be. She covered her face and cried into her hands, trying to hide the sound from the world as best she could.

But the tears ran down her arms till the blouse cloth in the crease of her elbows was soaked with anguish.

· · ·

A missing person's report was filed at the 48th Precinct station. Husbands and wives disappeared all the time, some even stayed away, for better or worse.

The police would have shown little interest but for the fact there was a child involved.

Mothers tended to run away less when there was a child involved. As for fathers, children had no such significant effect on their actions. In this case, at least a cursory effort was warranted to get at the truth.

The day was miserable and muggy. Eve and Fran sat together away from Romain and Dominic in a small office just off the main stairwell.

A fan on top of a filing cabinet circulated the stifling air. On the windowsill was a line of paper cups where cigarettes floated in cold and oily coffee. And people—an endless parade of faces and types kept passing the open door and looking in. All this made Eve feel that much sicker because it told her so powerfully where she was and why.

Eve watched her father talk with the officers, answer questions. He was not the Romain from the bar the night before. He was the Romain the outside world saw. The one who conned and exploited. The grave digger and drug dealer all dressed up for grief.

It said how far they'd truly come that Eve did not for one moment, not for one sign's worth of time, believe her father was telling the truth.

When Eve got her chance through Fran to make her case, she talked about her father's conviction on drug charges, the way he'd used and abused her mother, about his little penchant for locking her mother in the incinerator room when it served his mood, and how on the very night of her disappearance, her mother had gone back to the apartment with the intention of telling him she wanted a divorce.

Eve signed all this with a fury not lost on the officer. But the most telling statement, the most damaging statement, was when the two women acknowledged Romain and Dominic were at the apartment when they arrived, and that there had been no sign of a struggle, nor anything to show her mother had come back home.

Romain bore up under all this with a quiet, passive intensity while the officer asked questions and pecked out answers on a beaten-up typewriter. The only thing the officer could assure anyone in the room was that men would be sent out into the neighborhood to do questioning.

On the way out Dominic managed a minute alone with the officer. He got in a few nasty asides about Clarissa's character. Some drunken indiscretions, a few late-night disappearances. There was even an abortion while Romain was in Correctional.

"I didn't want to tell you all this with the kid in the room, okay? I mean she's still young. Fourteen, for Christ's sake. I don't want to badmouth her mother."

The officer thought Eve older and more mature than fourteen.

"You can ask my wife, Gail. She'll tell you. More than once Clarissa said she wanted to kiss the whole marriage off. Fuck 'em…and goodbye."

THE FOUNTAIN
AT CROTONA PARK

CHAPTER 57

POLICE WALKED THE BLOCKS from the candy store to the apartment with a photograph of Clarissa that Eve had taken. They searched the apartment and Romain's truck with two different teams. He was interrogated repeatedly over the next week.

It was not that the police were easily influenced, but the range of disappearances was just too vast, and their leads nonexistent.

The money in Clarissa's bank account was still there, but the missal and bankbook were not to be found. This led to some feeling foul play was a possibility. But if Eve's and Fran's sworn depositions that Romain and his cousin were at the apartment that night when they arrived didn't all but exclude Romain, Gail's statement to the police did.

Gail sat in her modest kitchen, having made the detectives coffee, and while they and Dominic stood above her she validated every lie her husband had told at the precinct house, including about an 'alleged abortion'.

The abortion idea itself left a foul taste in the men's minds about Clarissa's character. What Gail had done was not only out of protective fear. It was, in her mind anyway, a chance, if not to actually get Dominic back, to at least compromise his acts of infidelity. Afterward, when she had to be alone, when her screams and demands Dominic not go out failed, a deep sense of emptiness came over her that she had betrayed her friend.

• • •

Coming out of her apartment some days later, late for work, Gail saw Fran. She'd been lying in wait. Fran looked as if she were about ready to rain down destruction. Gail tried to get back into the apartment, but Fran got hold of her at the door while she fumbled for her keys.

"Do you know what you've done?" Fran shouted.

"Leave me alone."

"You've destroyed Eve."

Gail saw in the glass door of the building that people who passed on the sidewalk were staring.

"And you know what else you've done?"

"Leave me alone."

"You've killed any chance you have of ever being happy."

"Leave me—"

Fran grabbed the keys out of Gail's hand. "'Cause there's always going to be a piece of her inside you, that will never let go of what you've done.

"You failed her. And her mother. And you let those bastards use everything they always use, to get away with murder."

Fran then threw the keys out into the street.

Chapter 58

FOR EVE THE FACT HER MOTHER was gone hung like a shroud over everything. It was as if some strange secret was being played out in broad daylight. And her only defense against that certainty was a state of numbness.

As a way of helping Eve past this fixed moment, of bridging the disaster, Fran sat her down and explained what had happened in Germany all those years ago that caused the scar and the bleeding.

In the quiet of that apartment above the candy store, Fran wanted the girl to know, to see, to feel, that there were shared agonies and that these could be, must be, survived.

It was also a way of explaining what the word "abortion" meant, something that Dominic had so freely lied about concerning Clarissa, which in turn led to a discussion about sex.

As Fran began, she felt, in a way, guilty. As if she were defiling Clarissa's rights as a mother. But, she knew, a promise made is a promise kept. The mantle of mother had fallen upon her, and if they bled her white and dry, she intended to see it through.

Eve, it seemed, had some knowledge of sex, and not just the gropish heartracings of a teenager, but from secretly witnessing her parents from a crease of dark between the alcove sheet and the wall.

"That," said Fran, "might be considered sex. But little more."

• • •

Romain appeared at Fran's all neatly dressed and aftershaved to bring his daughter home. Eve was in the candy store where Fran had put her to work stocking shelves and handling the register. This was done not only to keep Eve's mind occupied, but to give her the sense of earning money and being self-sufficient.

It sickened Eve to see her father smiling his way past a woman and her small child wandering an aisle of toys. Romain tried every conciliatory approach for his daughter's affection: the innocent victim, the saddened husband, the lost father. It was the public-Romain on the private scale, but Eve refused them all.

Romain finally threatened. "I could force you," he whispered, so the woman and her little boy would not hear as they passed.

Eve set down the comic books and magazines she was about to rack. She put out her arms, wrists together, fists balled up, as if defiantly telling him, handcuff me and see what happens.

She was scared but not as scared as Romain had hoped. He warned Fran as he left, "I got to be in Philly for a few days on a business deal. When I come back, have her ready to go home."

"She is home," Fran told him.

• • •

While Romain was with some ex-cons in Philly trying to work a score, Eve and Fran snuck into the basement apartment to get her things along with Clarissa's possessions.

The super caught them with the first load. Not only didn't he care, he offered to help. Romain was nothing but a nasty spaghetti-eater as far as he was concerned, who'd already been given notice for non-payment of rent.

One chest of drawers, and a cupboard-size wardrobe closet. Meager little, but still, it reminded Fran how much decency had been taken from them.

They were about ready to leave. Eve came out of the alcove carrying her American flag pillow and a shopping bag filled with all the photos that had been taped to the walls around her bed.

"We're done," said Fran. "Let's go."

Eve stood there looking. This had been where her mother had loved and cared for her. Where she had fought through weariness so her daughter could have some part of the world.

"I know it's hard," said Fran. "But she'd want us to go."

——I'm not done yet.

Eve kneeled down and searched through the shopping bag for a particular photo of her mother. It was one taken in Crotona Park. Her mother was sitting by the fountain and looking back over her shoulder as if someone had been calling out to her. Clarissa's face was tilted slightly toward the sky and the light had caught the tenderness in her features. Or maybe it was her tenderness that had caught all that light.

The photo of Clarissa reminded Fran of the woman in the ad that the man at the camera store had been so entranced by, and how the image had stayed with him all those years.

Eve took the photograph and set it carefully upright on the Castro. Fran waited as Eve wrote a note on the back of an envelope. She placed the envelope alongside her mother's picture:

> *So you won't ever forget how beautiful Mommy was.*
> *Eve*

CHAPTER 59

ROMAIN WAS DRINK WEARY and disgusted when he got back to the apartment, suffering the late night down of blown deals. The broke, uneasy blues pressed against the back of his skull and what is the first thing he sees?

The photograph on the Castro, propped up there, hit him flat out. She was staring out at him from that picture, pointless and on purpose at the same time.

He grabbed the note. It went through him like some blend of fact and fiction, and it was all the more horrible because of it.

He tore back the alcove sheet to find stripped bare concrete walls. The dresser and closets told the same story. A scheme of permanent isolation. Well, they weren't going to get away with it.

He dropped down onto the Castro. Everything about him pulled toward that piece of floor where she'd suffocated in a fit of violence.

Could he leave it behind in his memory? Build a wall of days around it? He was glad he was being tossed from this dump. He'd halfway invited it to happen. But the note, the picture. It carried a shattering simplicity. Eve knew exactly who he was, and she'd told him so.

• • •

The way the buzzer rang and then just kept on, Fran knew. The way Fran pulled her robe in tight and crossed the living room with a troubled leanness, Eve knew.

From the first floor landing they could see his outline in the frosted glass of the front door down below. He was pressing the buzzer with a fist, then standing back. "I know you're there," he shouted, staring up at the windows. "I saw you. Do you hear?"

Romain was looking up at the window when the front door swung open. It happened so fast, catching him by surprise, his body kind of snapped back.

"I came down here," said Fran, "'cause I didn't want you to think I...*we* were afraid."

He pushed past her into the entranceway. Eve stood on the first floor landing in a T-shirt that hung to her bare knees.

"Get her dressed, we're going home." He called up to Eve, "Get dressed!"

Eve looked at Fran. Fran did not move, so Eve did not move.

Romain shouted and stumbled out some sign. "Get dressed. We're going home."

Infuriated that she did not listen he started for the stairs. Fran blocked his pathway, her arm lashed to the railing. "Try it and I'll call the police."

"You'll call the police? I could have you arrested for kidnapping."

Eve saw what her father had said. She rushed past Fran and started throwing her arms into his chest. Every time he blocked her hits then stepped back she kept pressing at him signing over and over, thrusting her index finger under a downward turned left hand and twisting her wrist.

"What's she saying?"

"Murder," repeated Fran. "She's saying you murdered her mother."

There was an enormous dark power to that single motion of a word. The finger stabbing into the throat of a half-closed hand like some love gesture gone hideous.

"I swear," he said, letting his daughter hit him, "I swear I didn't hurt her. God strike me dead if I'm lying."

"Good thing for you there isn't a God to take you up on that filthy lie."

"Shut your mouth!"

"Or what?!"

Fran grabbed Eve, told her to go upstairs. "Do as I say," she ordered.

And Eve did. She backed up the stairs signing to her father——You murdered my mother.

"Get her dressed, she's going home."

"I told you before, she is home."

Now it was just the two of them facing off in the square of that alcove as if they were wrestling for the outcome of the world.

"You can't have her," he said.

"You can't keep her," she answered.

"The law is with me on this."

"How are you going to exploit her now? Do you intend to become her pimp?"

"What's a carved up dyke like you want her for?"

"You only want her so you can and convince yourself you didn't do what we all know you did. Including Dominic and Gail. But the truth is, every day you'd look at her she'd remind you of what you've done. You'd see her mother in that face, and it would destroy you. Am I wrong?"

For a moment, Romain considered. His mind slipped down into the underworld of needs and angles. That place you don't go, to just pass through. He started nervously jingling the change in his pocket.

Then he said something that frightened Fran. "I might let her stay."

Fran's hands rose up the front of the terry cloth bathrobe Clarissa had made for her, as if she were suddenly exposed. "Go on."

"Money…I need money."

CHAPTER 60

FRAN SAT AT THE DINING ROOM TABLE, SPENT. Eve brought her a glass of scotch.

"You must have read my mind."

——Am I staying?

"Staying."

For control, Fran had made a pact with the devil, to be leveraged by a down payment.

From the landing Eve had watched and seen the argument. Romain did not have the same kind of callous bravery with Fran he'd had with her mother. He didn't have that, I'll pitch right into you stance. There were half-beats of hesitation, like someone trying to be cagey or cautious at the same time they were throwing out all that terror.

And never once did Fran give him her side, never once did she step back or away, never once. It was, he moved, she moved. He moved, she moved.

Eve asked Fran how she knew to act like this.

Fran told her——Hate. She tapped a finger to the side of her head——I get lots of practice up here.

Agitated, pensive, knowing they'd have to live with the uncertainty of Romain, Fran just let out with a stream of premeditated conscience.

"When I think how they lied about your mother sneaking out with men. And this abortion. Then getting Gail to validate the lie.

"They wanted to destroy your mother's character. And they used the things they did because it is just such accusations they can use against a woman in this world. They make her out to be a tramp.

"If you're immoral enough, you always get what you deserve. That's why Dominic and Romain used those lies. Because the world is built around those lies. By men, liars worse than Romain and Dominic. Only they're called dictators, presidents and popes.

"Governments. Laws. Religion. Attitudes. Religion is the worst because it is the basis of all that has come after. And the Church is a master of using the trick of God to twist the truth of things.

"You get it in your catechism class. Who was the weakest one the devil went for? Not Adam.

"It was the woman's fault. So with that in hand, if a man is compromised, who does he have to blame it on?

"It's the same way with deafness. It's the woman's fault a child is born deaf. Your mother was taught to feel it, to believe it. So in the end the idea is passed on to you, and it becomes then your failure. Well…it's no one's fault and no one's failure. It just is."

Fran stopped right there in mid-thought. Her hands and face perspiring. She looked at Eve, read the expression on her face, trying to handle this overwhelming volley of feeling.

"I was trying to tell you things to watch out for in this world. But I must remember too. Your mother didn't believe as I believe. For her, there was a God she could pray to for support. A caring God who, in spite of His silence, looked out for us. She believed in grace and goodness and sin."

Worn with stress but charged with a deeper revelation, Fran told Eve——I must remember you have to know her side of the story too. For when you come to judge the world.

• • •

Fran had told Romain she'd be at Crotona Park with the money and to meet her there. She had picked the park on purpose. She sat on the fountain ledge, exactly where Clarissa had been sitting in that photograph of Eve's left on the Castro. Whether Romain realized it or not, he didn't let on.

She handed him an envelope. It had a thousand dollars in it. It took fuckin' years of work and struggle to save that kind of money. And there was this guinea drug seller slick counting through the fifties. It made her feel a black madness just to watch his polished fingernails edge the bills. As he counted he gave no hint of winning a small victory. On the contrary he was brief and matter of fact.

"The apartment in that building of yours. Downstairs. The one that's empty, or is gonna be."

"Yes?"

He slipped the envelope into his sportcoat pocket. The collar was up and it rose a bit as his shoulders hitched somewhat arrogantly. "Don't rent it."

• • •

Romain used the cash for a down payment on his future. He got himself a motel room by the Harlem River Station. From his second story window he could look across the river into Zululand. Here he was, starting over, streeting-it as a single act.

Of course, it was all Zululand now, or Spic City, or Little Havana. The Bronx was not "the white" it used to be. Even the Jews were complaining how the Bronx, the old Bronx, the real Bronx, was dying, and those Christ killers secretly used to cum over niggers. So, when they start complaining you know how bad it is. Heroin—that was the only thing that remained white wherever you went.

It rained that night. Hard and with thunder. Loud enough to kill the James Brown screech in the next room, but still Romain couldn't sleep.

First it was the picture on the Castro, then the fight in the hallway, then the park with her sitting there at the fountain just like—

Then taking the money. That one cut into him the most, to actually have to put his hand out to some cunt.

He lay down. He could feel the rain through the closed curtains. He could almost see it from behind closed eyes. Small rivulets of it starting through the high reeds, puddling at the edges of the mud, seeping its way down, dampening the tarp he'd buried her in.

He got up. He'd drunk his pint dead. Killed off all the beer. He wanted to have plenty of edge tomorrow so he needed sleep. He decided to maraud his stash of white powder, just enough to catch under his pinky nail, one snort, so he could sleep.

• • •

Romain showed up at the candy store with one suitcase. Eve had begged Fran not to let him have the apartment. To be just feet away from such a constant threat—

"Don't you understand?" Fran told Eve that night in the half darkness of the locked candy store. "He could take you away any time he wants and I wouldn't have the authority to even try and get you back."

——I'd come back on my own. I'd fight him.

"And he'd have the authority to take you away again. I have no legal rights. The only things keeping you here are his greed and his weaknesses. He's here—so you're here. And maybe if we're lucky, he'll do something we know about that can get him sent back to prison and out of our lives. If we're lucky."

Fran could hear Romain coming down the steps. She signed this to Eve. Fran then told her when he had gone out.

——Maybe we should just go. Sell this place and find a candy store in some other city and start over.

"You don't understand. You're too young yet." Fran was shaking her head, her eyes crystal hard with thought. "To buy a place like this you have to be able to get a mortgage from a bank. And they give mortgages to men. Being a single woman is like the kiss of death if you want a mortgage. I couldn't have bought this place, even if I had the money to. It was left to me. And it took years after that, even though I'd been working here since I was twenty, to be able to sign for deliveries. And to get credit to buy goods, even though I owned the place, was one humiliating experience after another.

"Single women don't start from the bottom. They get to struggle and claw their way up to the goddamned bottom.

"This is my home, this is your home. This is our future, this is your future. And I'm not giving it up. I'll bleed to death right here first."

PART TWO

THE RED LIGHT DISTRICT

CHAPTER 61

PEOPLE OF COLOR. You call them neighbors, or you call them animals. They were either the next chapter in the American Dream, or an ethnic apocalypse that would end the Dream.

By the mid-Nineteen Sixties, there were more Puerto Ricans in New York than in San Juan. There were more blacks than Puerto Ricans. And like the Europeans before them, the dark-skinned races, the children of the third world, were finding their way through the cracks and fissures of poverty, eyeing the streets with sidewise caution, as they moved from neighborhood to neighborhood.

But it was not so much the changing complexion of the world that cast the longest shadow over their lives, it was the changing complexity of the world. Desertions and illegitimacy, death and divorce. Households without fathers.

Fran saw it all firsthand in the candy store. Women, the day they received their welfare checks, Mother's Day, as they called it. Hustling in to buy.

There was a war going on in the far east that was beginning to split the country, music did a radical turn, movies became more violent, and bars started to appear on first-floor windows, iron grating over doors.

The Reign of Ambiguity and Contradictions had begun. And that was the era, Eve would flower into.

• • •

Eve was not only the girl whose father had gone to prison, but was the teenager whose mother had mysteriously disappeared. In school she never used the word murder. Pain gave way to resentments and rebellion.

She approached her schoolwork with a perfunctory somnambulism. Lots of nodding, but little listening. The only thing that aroused her slightest interest was when she was asked to photograph special events at St. Joseph's, an assignment that fell to her as a result of the one published photo that made the bulletin board.

She began to make the rounds of the different cliques at school. From the young cage breakers who liked to drink at Van Cortlandt Park and Woodlawn Cemetery, then cruise the Concourse with their buzzed-up grins, or check out the boys shooting hoops over at Cardinal Hayes, to the stoners who watched the twinkling stars on the ceiling of the Paradise Theatre, secure they were in possession of a hip otherness.

But beyond all the sly young digressions, or the flash feelings she was doing things no one had ever done before, the photos Eve took when she was alone spoke of the tangible sadness, and the tactile loneliness she suffered.

They did not so much capture the state of the world as they did a state of mind. A fowl floating dead on the surface of Van Cortlandt Lake while no one on shore nearby even noticed. Painted in graphic colors on the wall of a building being demolished, the lyrics from a Beatles song—*Help...I need somebody*. And this was framed with an open door that led to rubbled sunlight.

Sometimes Eve would walk the headstones of Woodlawn looking at the ages that people died, realizing how young her mother had been to go missing from the world.

• • •

Eve and a couple of friends were hanging out at the White Castle parking lot over on Allerton Avenue and Boston Post Road trying to figure how to best burn up what was left of Saturday. Eve was sitting on the curb smoking, the collar up on her pea coat, when what does she see coming out of Gino's Restaurant across the street, but her old man, all prettied up and smiling.

Her body shifted into low, dark mode. She'd never spotted him on the street before. The only time they crossed paths now was when he used the apartment below Fran's as a crash pad. And that was strictly hallway time—I don't want to know you, I don't want you to talk to me.

She watched him without moving. As if the slightest motion on her part and something bad would happen. He was with a man and a woman who Eve had never seen before. The woman, she thought, looked like the type that wore too much perfume and had her nails done fifty times a week.

The three of them were in a tight triangle talking there in the windswept autumn afternoon, when the woman slipped her arms around Romain's waist. They were all laughing at something one of them had said.

Eve felt a wave of desolation and anger. She couldn't watch anymore. She bummed a couple of Kools and took off on her own.

All the way to Pelham Parkway, all she could feel as a thought was how the world went on since her mother's death like nothing had happened. It just, went on. There was urgency to her footsteps. As if she were trying to outrun the goddamn thought, or catch up to some answer.

CHAPTER 62

THEY WERE CLOSING UP the candy store for the night when Eve told Fran about seeing her father and that woman. What Fran felt at hearing this, for Eve's sake, she kept to herself.

Upstairs, Fran told Eve, "Get the cigarettes out of my purse."

Fran was in the kitchen pouring two glasses of beer when Eve returned. Fran handed her one of the glasses.

"I assume you like beer, since I don't know how many goddamn times I've smelled it on you."

Eve knew she'd been had, but she didn't quite know how to react to this profound piece of information.

Eve took the glass. Fran shook a cigarette loose from the pack and offered Eve one. "Nothing like a cigarette with a beer."

Eve tried to fight the slightest rumblings of a smile as she took the cigarette. Fran even lit it for her.

"I prefer to know what you're doing before, during, and after you do it. What do you think of that as a plan? And I hope for your sake you agree."

Eve put her hands up, all cocky like, as if surrendering to Fran's will. Fran wished Clarissa were there to see her daughter. Eve was taller than either woman, shaping out lovely with black hair that curled toward wild, leaning back against the counter now trying to be cool and tough in that way that only makes you all the more vulnerable.

"Come with me," Fran ordered.

• • •

Back from the hallway entrance on the first floor was a padlocked door under the stairwell. Eve had always thought it was some kind of storage closet until Fran turned on the safelight and the tiny area was cast in red.

——A darkroom?

The underside of the stairwell had been boxed in to seal out dust. There was a wet bench, a higher dry bench and an enlarger.

——You never told me.

From a drawer Fran took out a folder of photographs. She began to lay them out on the dry bench.

"I've been waiting till I felt....I've been waiting for the right time."

As Fran kept laying out photo after photo Eve noticed a homemade sign of cutout letters taped to the wall above the dry bench that said:

THE RED LIGHT DISTRICT

Eve grabbed Fran's arm, pointed to the sign. Gave her a thumbs up. —— Very cool.

Fran winked. "I was just trying to prove to myself I had a sense of humor. Come see this."

Eve squeezed in next to Fran. Spread out on the dry bench were shots of the candy store taken during Fran's first years in the Bronx.

There were normal images printed in stark black and white. Images Eve would come to learn were shadow masked, and collapsed images, manipulated photographs, solarized photographs, photograms, those shot through screens and gauze, those that were tinted.

It was not only the history of techniques laid out there over those few images, but more importantly, it was one subjective transformation after another.

"Just like you can change the tonal landscape of any picture, you can do the same with your life. The one inside you." Fran pointed her cigarette at the pictures of the candy store. "The building is the same, but look at all you can do with it."

There was a stool by the dry bench. Eve sat down with a stack of photographs going from one to the next. Each was its own gift of information and feeling, yet earlier that afternoon was still hard inside her.

—— After seeing him, Eve told Fran —— I felt like, the universe had this distant animosity against us, not just me, us, lots of us, maybe all of us, because it allows evil to go unpunished and people don't take notice. It's like, my mother never existed.

"Except for us."

—— Yes.

Moments passed that felt small and daunting at the same time. Eve put the photos back on the bench. She smoked her cigarette.

—— What was your mother like?

"My mother, well…She was very much like Clarissa. Which is why, I guess, I felt a closeness to her right from the start. They both always made the person they were with, feel more important than themselves. And there were no barriers to their honesty."

Fran stood there drinking her beer and thinking. Moments of each woman were like transliterations of the other. Mergings and blendings in ways you feel before you even know you're feeling it.

Eve stared up at her, her face cast in red.

"I was down for years. Very down. That Christmas morning, I took the old man to church and saw this dark-skinned waif of a thing at the altar."

——I wasn't drinking a beer or smoking a cigarette was I?

Fran smiled, but she was still back at that cold Christmas morning. "Then your mother catches up to me at my car. When I got home I sat on that stool with the old photographs. How do I change my life? That was what was on my mind."

Fran put down the now empty beer glass. She smoked. The lines from her nose to her cheeks had deepened sharply over those few years. "Your father, men like him, will destroy your life in ways you can't imagine. If you let them."

• • •

Eve lay in bed staring at panes of moonlight. The pilgrimage all ahead. Desires coming as if in the hands of cupbearers. But as she closed her eyes she saw him and that woman, with a cleft of shade about his grinning chin.

She'd made copies of her mother's picture at Crotona Park. Now she could create her own. An endless montage of sizes, shapes and tones.

She sneaked downstairs, that guinea temper of her father's inciting her. The apartment was dark, empty as his soul. In the bedroom was a mattress on the floor, a lamp beside it, a television sitting on a chair at the foot of the bed. Life stripped of all the astounding minutiae that makes life, like pictures of loved ones, dearest ones, departed ones.

She set a new copy of the picture of her mother at Crotona Park against his pillow. It would be waiting there like a bullet to enter the skin.

She went back to bed. Panes of moonlight waiting. There was a power in fighting back that took you right to the threshold.

COCAINE, CINDERELLA
AND CHARLIE

CHAPTER 63

FREEDOMLAND HAD BEEN A BUST, so they shut it down. On the site, actually on the parking lot site, an apartment complex named Co-Op City was to be built.

Romain had to drive out to City Island to see a contact about scoring a drug that was starting to surface called cocaine. This meant he had to pass what had been Freedomland.

From the Hutch Parkway he could see giant bulldozers and lines of trucks leaving trails of a white dust drifting skyward. He thought about the fuckin' camera he'd gotten Eve and grew subdued. But the camera wasn't the only reason.

To get to City Island, he had to take the loop out on Shore Road to swing onto City Island Boulevard. The loop with all those marshes and trees where he'd buried her.

In daylight he couldn't quite tell which break he'd pulled the truck into. He saw kids walking along the road swacking at the high weeds with sticks.

What if they found her now? Was there any way they could prove it was him? His mind flashed on her wilting with rot and all that once lovely black hair. He felt this clammy sensation move up his legs and he wished he'd snorted a little junk just to ease the ride.

His contact was a Puerto Rican. A real low end slammer just like all the rest. Fresh off the boat, with clothes and machismo to match. All ready for Freedomland.

They met by the ferry pier to Hart Island. Hart Island with its potter's field where Romain's old man was buried. This was turning into a day of fuckin' deaths.

They ate deep fried shrimp out of paper cups while he and the Rican talked. They walked till they found themselves a spot of alley protected by Dumpsters behind Thwaite's Restaurant.

Romain had never tried cocaine, but the first rush told him all he needed to know. His brain was ushering in a new era.

• • •

The first time Eve saw Mimi, the child was sitting airy above a crowd of heads at the far end of a packed school corridor. A smiling three-year-old in oversized sunglasses just floating along on somebody's shoulders.

The twelve and thirteen-year-olds at St. Joseph's were putting on a play for their parents, friends of the school, and Board of Directors. That's why the crowd. Eve was to get pictures for the school yearbook.

While everybody was wedged up in the hallway waiting for the auditorium doors to open, Eve worked her way through that traffic jam of bodies signing to excuse herself as she dragged along a chair.

When Eve saw the girl her mind had done this creative little cartwheel, and when she thought she'd worked her way far enough into the crowd, she tried to clear space for the chair, easing away backs, tapping people on shoulders, excusing herself again and again. She stood up on the chair with strangers and teachers and classmates eyeing her curiously. And trying to keep from tottering as the chair was hit, Eve managed a picture across that sea of heads and shoulders and talking hands where this tiny Spanish waif and her sunflower face were innocently grooving like some angel bird open-armed there above it all.

The auditorium doors opened and a wall of adults began to move along behind a surge of school kids, and that's when Eve saw him. The little girl was sitting on his shoulders. He couldn't have been more than twenty, wearing an army fatigue jacket and funked out pants. He was lean and had the kind of finely cut features that would have looked as good on a woman as they did on a man. He was black, or maybe Jamaican, and part white.

She followed along a bit back, using that throng of bodies as cover. She felt a thrilling current like some invisible bloodbeat go right through her.

From the way his head turned and how he spoke to those around him, only half looking, she saw he could hear. But he also signed, and he signed well. His hands were graceful and quick at speaking, while he walked through the crowd with the girl on his shoulders.

He and the girl were with an older couple. They were black and neatly dressed. And they, too, knew sign. Neither he nor the girl showed any resemblance to the couple, but the way they all related with each other there had to be some deeply close connection.

They were in the middle aisle hunting for seats close to the stage. Eve made sure she just happened to slip past them. She got a closer look out of the corner of her eye as he swung the girl down from his shoulders.

She saw his face had more edges to it. It was the kind of face she imagined would know how to handle silence. And his eyes were blue blue. He took the sunglasses from the little girl and put them on.

As he came around, Eve glanced away. She hadn't wanted to, but she did.

She wondered if it were shyness, or the fact she felt in some way marked or deficient.

Chapter 64

THE STUDENTS PERFORMED *Jack and the Beanstalk, Little Red Riding Hood* and then finally *Cinderella*. Eve was allowed the freedom to be in front of all the seats, so she could get shots of the plays. There was also a curtained doorway she could slip behind to go backstage and take pictures from there.

Eve had no idea she'd caught his eye. Maybe it was her buoyant aloofness sitting there cross-legged at the corner of the stage, totally into that camera and unconcerned about what was going on around her. Maybe it was because she seemed so exuberant and heady at the same time, and attractive in that way when you can't really point to one physical detail, but you still get this slight feeling your hold on gravity has been broken.

Eve was backstage when the scene between Cinderella and her mother's ghost took place. As Cinderella decried the cruelty of her stepsisters to that apparition, the impact of the moment on Eve caught her by surprise. The curse of loss and memories at the heart of the fairy tale went to the heart of her own tale of hurt.

And even though they were just children overacting in sign, when Cinderella stood alone after her mother's ghost left the stage, Eve was brought to a place of profound and painful loneliness.

That's what she wanted to capture—a child Cinderella, in a smock made to look shabby, signing out her emotions, surrounded by a few pitiable props and a backdrop of gray curtain.

For the audience, the highlight of the play was the slipper scene. It seemed Prince Charming, and a genuinely undersized prince at that, couldn't quite get the slipper on Cinderella's foot. Finally, in exasperation, Cinderella, at least a foot taller than her prince, smashed a fist against her own forehead.

Everyone in the audience who knew it was the sign for "stupid" broke out in laughter. Cinderella, staying in character, grabbed the slipper away from him and squeezed into it herself.

That was the picture that made the yearbook.

• • •

After the play Eve was outside St. Joseph's leaning against the hood of a car with a lineup of girlfriends. They were working through a couple of beers they kept hidden in plain sight against the curb or in one of their large purses. As they talked and drank and made sure they weren't caught by any of the parents or teachers mingling on the schoolyard where tables with food and refreshments had been set up, one of them would outlandishly chime in with the stupid sign and they'd all crack up again over what had happened in the play.

But even as they laughed and drank and hung out, Eve was still seeing and feeling that moment from the disquieting shadows offstage, as the ghost told Cinderella things would be all right, just as her own mother had so many times in the dim alcove darkness that was their refuge against Romain.

It was only when Eve glanced up because one of her girlfriends nudged her that she saw him coming through that crowd of parents and benefactors right toward them. He was coming toward them taking a Kent from a flip-top box, but he was looking right at Eve.

"Any of you girls got a light?"

Eve reached for her purse; she felt slightly nervous.

"Just to let you all know, I could see you swigging on that beer from way, way, way over there."

The girls kind of giggled. Eve handed him her lighter.

"My name's Charlie," he said, giving the others a bare half-look. "What's yours?"

—— Eve.

He lit his cigarette. He had long fingers. He smiled at Eve. There was a wave of girlish jealousy among the others, 'cause they could see Charlie was politely blowing them off for Eve.

One of the girls did the stupid sign, and laughing, asked Eve —— Tell him what your real name is.

Eve flushed up a bit, looked imploringly from them to Charlie.

They knew they had her on the run. Each did the stupid sign like they'd forgotten.

—— Tell him what your real name is.

—— Don't go there, Eve signed.

—— Tell him. Don't be ashamed.

Charlie could see they were gonna ride her down with this. Whatever it was. Then one of them started——Her name is—

Eve grabbed the girl's hands to stop her, but the girl next to her flashed——Jailgirl, Jailgirl.

They were now each signing——Jailgirl. Being demonstrative, flamboyant, dramatic.

Eve came at them angry, humiliated, hurt.——Eat shit and die. Fuck you, fuck you and fuck you.

It was brief and rancorous, and Eve had been seen by a teacher on the school front steps who strode over and came down hard. "What do you think you're doing? There are parents and small children here. What kind of example...? Come with me. Now!" Eve tried to explain. "Now!"

Eve stared at the girls hatefully. As she was led off like some prisoner she averted her eyes so as not to look at Charlie. The girls cooled it till the teacher had Eve in tow, and once Eve looked back they waved, smiling with that touch of innocent viciousness that made her want to slam their heads into the pavement.

Now it was just Charlie and the girls. He stepped between them, reached into one of the purses sitting on the hood of the car, where the beer was hidden. He took an open beer and snuck himself a long swig.

"Don't I know you chicks from somewhere?"

They glanced at each other wondering.

"Yeah, man. I know you. I saw you all in the play." He handed the girl back the beer. "You were those nasty, ugly stepsisters that screwed with Cinderella, right?"

CHAPTER 65

FRAN HAD TO APPEAR at a departmental meeting with the vice-principal and the teacher who'd reprimanded Eve. The school had so far sidestepped Eve's unusual living circumstances. But, as the teacher remarked, "It's bad enough what she said to the girls in plain sight of everyone, but later, when we were alone, what she called them...Well, I don't even want to repeat it."

Eve had told Fran she'd called them 'cunts'.

"We can't have these kinds of outbursts," said the Vice-Principal. "We understand the difficulty of her 'situation.' But consider this a final warning."

Fran had to play facilitator. She listened with conciliatory patience, agreeing that Eve would be reined in, or else.

How the years had transformed lives and conversations. Sitting in the vice-principal's office took Fran back to that alcove of a hospital ward where she lay after the failed escape and the ensuing abortion, watching her parents play facilitator, listening to the police and public health officers with a conciliatory patience, agreeing their daughter would be reined in, or else.

Whatever differences there were between those two situations separated by thirty years, the absolute and mortal feelings were the same. Even down to the way the office and the hospital ward alcove were painted white. The white of a dead and unforgettable past you mean to rail against with all your youth and soul.

Fran drove Eve home in a descending silence, watching the girl's rebellion in her angled pose staring out the car window and how she responded in a bitter and disinterested way to anything said.

"Don't let some idiotic bitches get the best of you."

——Fuck them.

"Yes," said Fran in anger. Then she heard her own mother talking. "But do it silently."

Eve looked at Fran. Eve's eyes were like black vessels. And the truths written on her face spoke of trafficked outrage, and the fire to punish.

· · ·

Eve spent all her free time over the next few days in the darkroom making contact sheets of the photos she'd taken at school, deciding which ones to enlarge, which ones to crop.

It wasn't just a matter of putting what had happened out of her mind, of putting the humiliation of what she'd felt, with him standing there, out of her mind.

There was that row of miniature prints of the little girl in sunglasses on Charlie's shoulders. Eve began to crop away at the sea of heads around her until it was all face, pure and simple.

She made an eight-by-ten contact print and taped it to the wall above the dry bench near another print, that of Cinderella on the stage alone, taken from the wings after her mother's ghost had gone.

There was no denying there in the darkness, as Eve looked at the two photographs side by side, each in its own right was defined and magnified by the visual emotions conveyed through the other.

The contraposition of worlds, of two sets of feelings. The unreal world of a play, the real world of a smiling little girl in sunglasses shouldered with affection above the crowd. The unreal world of a little girl, the real world of Cinderella caught from the shadows in a moment of sadness.

Eve was both girls; she was neither girl. Then as the tissue of each photograph drew her emotional eye to one, as it pulled her toward the other, she imagined a third picture.

This one would be nearer to the vein of self-expression. She'd make one of those contact sheets black and white, the other would be color, they'd be finished enough to just look unfinished. She'd tape them to the dry bench wall, side by side, with some space between them, more than they were now, but not quite lined up right. The positioning should have a sense of roughness and informality, and she'd shoot them from just about where she was standing, maybe a little closer, to capture the split, the separateness, the isolation, yet trying to create some kind of harmony out of disharmony, some kind of—

The door opened so quickly, he was framed by the hallway light with such suddenness. It had all happened in a startled merge of half shadows and there was Romain glaring at Eve with the only space between them the red light hanging from a wire above and masking those two living portraits with a dark and devilish hue.

Romain held out the pictures, every one of them that Eve had kept leaving on his pillow. Each different, each the same.

He'd come home a little jacked on coke and riding a wave of untouchable power, only to find Eve had dropped another snapshot on him.

He wanted to go fullout downstairs and kick the living crap out of her, but he'd checked himself. He had cash in his pocket after all, and was back in the game, so he decided to try and stop his daughter's defiance from working his head a little differently.

He managed a really touched and emotional look. "Thanks. You don't know how much they mean to me." His eyes had a kind of electric glitter as they glanced at the snapshots in his hand. "I know I didn't treat her right. And I'd...I will make it up to her if I ever get the chance." Eve noticed the genesis of a few tears.

From his pocket Romain took a clip of bills. He counted out a hundred dollars and laid the bills on the dry bench. "For clothes, or any other shit you might need."

· · ·

Eve sat in the dark on her bed, leaning against the flag pillow, smoking. She watched the wall shadows shapeshift as headlights from the street flared by.

With every car that passed the collage of photographs and contact sheets she'd taped there became a mural of changing tones and moments. An altering collection of scenes, there then gone. Memories, there then gone. Only to return again highlighted in a swath of bright seconds.

She'd kept the hundred dollars without so much as a word. She already knew how she was gonna put it to her father for that, come the big 18. If only she could capture his face in that red dark, like some weird shade straight out of hell.

She got up and walked the room carrying her pillow in one hand, the cigarette in the other. The moonlight touched the magazine photograph of the Statue of Liberty wreathed in snow. A lunary silver made the paper glisten and gave the girl's face a patina of steeled indominability.

Through the eyes of that statue, Eve could see a great gray sky, and she looked to find herself lurking there as she wondered if her father ever suffered for what he'd done. She wanted him to suffer. She wanted his suffering to be complete, to be vile and hideous. The level of violence she felt made her heart pound and so, frightened her.

She wanted her life to be free of that feeling. She wanted her life to be better, to be happy, to be what she imagined in the quiet of unknowing.

So she began to pray for all that to be. She sat on the floor with her flag pillow snuggled up against her stomach with all its childhood smells and memories and prayed. But it wasn't the fact that she was praying that soon gave her pause, for God had become a remote and innocuous presence. It was the fact she was praying to her mother, who was as close to God as she felt she could ever come.

CHAPTER 66

IT WAS AN ORDINARY SATURDAY evening when Charlie walked into the candy store looking for Eve. Ordinary except for the fact that the counter and stools were being dismantled, the grill and soda fountain broken down into parts, and the ice cream bins and malted milk makers carried away.

Time forces change. It manhandles all that is. There was more money now in stocked goods—bread, milk, cheap lunch meats, and a litany of junk foods packaged with eye-catching colors and stacked into swivel racks that swooned your appetite with one Twinkie-lit word, sugar. Fran called the new look section, Food Stamp Heaven.

The era of soda fountain quaintness was over, the candy store now stood on the border of poverty row.

In between taking care of the customers and dealing with the mess Fran had Eve photograph the change and how some from the neighborhood reacted as they watched, or couldn't watch another little bit of their past be crowbarred away.

The day was a slightly crazed and piecemeal experience and Eve had no idea how long he'd been was standing there at the register giving her a look she felt inside her as sheer confidence. And when he tipped his chin at her everything in her head was effectively silenced.

As she approached him, he said, "Eve, right?"

She nodded. Wanted to ask why he was there. But was too nervous.

"I'm Charlie." He gave her his sign name.

——I remember.

"How are the wicked stepsisters?"

Her face squinched up; she didn't get it. Felt foolish not getting it.

"The chicks by the car fucking with your head. Doing all that yak-yak." He signed for the way they'd talked and he used his face turning them into a serious mock.

——I've been giving them the silent treatment. And Eve took both her hands and turned them into fists.

He grinned at the black humor of it. She hadn't even realized what she'd said, that she made the joke, until it jumped out of her. Now, please, she'd thought, don't let me screw this up and do something stupid.

——What are you doing here?

"I felt like walking forty blocks out of my way for a pack of cigarettes. No.

Only kidding. I went over to the school to check out where you lived. I came over to talk. See if you wanted to go out sometime."

Her mouth got dry. Seriously, seriously dry. Nerve ending dry. Like she'd swallowed about fifty hosts at communion with no wine chaser.

——Would you mind…Just give me…I'll be…back…Okay?

She was gone like that, leaving him standing there like one huge question mark. Fran had been watching the last few minutes from over by the fountain which was being torn loose from its bracings, as Eve went by like everything and everyone in the store had just plain disappeared.

"Where are you—"

——Right back.

• • •

She stood in the darkroom leaning against the closed door feeling tiny pearls of excitement all over inside her at the same time her hands were trembling uncontrollably.

The contact sheets. That's what she'd come in for. She took three or four of the little girl among the dozens taped to the wall. Turning off the light she pitched herself hard——Be cool.

• • •

She was handing him the contact sheets and just as he asked, "What's this?", she saw his face make a turn of surprised discovery.

Charlie went from one to the next thinking how natural and real they were, something done without prompting or vanity. He looked up at her over the rim of the sheets. She was much more comfortable now that she had the photographs in hand. Not so much to hide feelings, but to deflect her own nervousness. As if they were as much the true her, as her.

"How did you get up high enough?"

——Chair.

"In the hall?"

——I dragged it. Got some very weird looks.

She reminded him of Natalie Wood, where everything about her soul seemed to pour out of those huge eyes. A couple of kids swarmed past them to the register. He had to wait while Eve made change. He noticed a woman by the torn down fountain giving him the hawk stare. Adjusting her glasses. He smiled.

He held up one of the contact sheets so Eve could see. "That was some day for Mimi. That's her name."

——You can give those to her. That's why I brought them out.

"She'll go nuts."

——What is she? Sister, cousin, friend?

"It's a long story." And he signed long, running his index finger up his arm like long went all the way to Jersey. Then he said, "But I'll tell you the whole thing when we go out."

——Out?

"Yeah. You want to go out?"

——You mean, like a date?

The way she signed her hands looked like they were weighed down by cement. Fuckin' A, he thought.

He mimicked her——Like a date. Then pausing——Think wonderful.

She got shiny some around the eyes and smiled. She clunked a fist to her forehead. ——A date. I get it.

He remembered. Cinderella and the slipper routine. She was all right.

THE WORLD

CHAPTER 67

FRAN WATCHED THEIR SKITTERISH TALK, with all its imprinted youth. After Charlie was gone Fran said, "Cute."

Eve nodded trying to underplay her self-consciousness. Then, as Eve went back to work, Fran, in a richly flamboyant copy of Charlie signing, told her——Think wonderful, girl.

· · ·

A week later Fran played audience as Eve went about that patience-testing balancing act of trying to be all decked out and funky at the same time. Her hair gone natural, it curled with a touch of the Medusa. And those eyelashes she tweaked, it was almost goddamn indecent to have such beautiful eyelashes and Fran told Eve so and Eve grinned without grinning.

Fran thought Charlie seemed older when they met. He was wearing a dashiki shirt and army boots and he had that edge of something quality.

Fran understood better when Charlie explained how he'd been back from Vietnam only a few weeks. That he hadn't been in active combat, but a supply Jeep he was driving took a pipe bomb hit outside of Saigon. One of the soldiers in the Jeep was killed, two others were badly wounded. He'd escaped with only broken ribs.

The million-dollar wound it was called, since you were still in one piece and it got you home to recuperate, and if you were near the end of your tour there was little to no chance you'd be going back.

There was a full heart of feeling when he talked about how lucky he was, even though he tried to play it like just some cool aside that happened to happen.

Fran snuck a look at the couple from a window as they headed down the street. They were all heart and pulse, thought Fran, and the light they walked in was that drapey blue of dusk you see in movies.

Fran imagined herself in the darkness of a theatre, maybe it was a scene from *Picnic* or *West Side Story*, and Eve was her own daughter making her way into the trafficked world of dreams and possibility.

Her own daughter.

I think of her that way, Fran told Clarissa in her mind. As much almost as an apology as anything else. Fran sat at the dining room table with a drink and settled in for an evening of moody joy and loneliness. She looked at Clarissa's picture on the breakfront——Think wonderful, girl.

• • •

Charlie took Eve on the train up to Mt. Vernon—where in Mt. Vernon was to be a surprise. Eve carried a large shoulder bag, and at the station, Charlie noticed the camera and flash while Eve rummaged through her girl things for a lighter.

He pointed to the Leica, "You take that thing everywhere?"

She made the sign for together and to show just how much, she adlibbed by weaving the fingers of both hands to form one identity.

"I got it, man." He copied her. Then vamped her play on the sign, goofing it all out.

She slapped at his hands and he told her how Mimi had flipped over the photographs and that everywhere she went in the neighborhood she took them along with her to show off.

They were on the train when Eve asked——How is Mimi connected to you?

"Mimi is my foster sister."

——Explain.

"Those folks you saw me with, the Dores, they're my foster parents. They raised me since I was ten."

Charlie went on to tell Eve how the Dores had a son, born deaf, who'd committed suicide when he was eighteen. It totally blew their minds. After they'd gotten it back together they'd started taking in foster kids with hearing problems. There were two before Charlie, both married now. Mimi was the fourth.

"Napoleon, that's my foster father's name, if you can believe it. He runs a small printing business in Harlem. My foster mother is called Queenie. She used to work in the shop. They're pretty righteous people. They saved my ass."

——You can hear. Why did they take you?

He always felt terribly strange telling the story, as if some cloud of disgrace had been passed on down to him.

"My parents were peddlers. Deaf peddlers, you know. Those characters walking around with cards and sign language on them, hustling for donations."

It seemed impossible what he told her. She had seen a peddler once when she was at Grand Central Station with her mother. He was working the crowd. She'd wanted to sign to him, let him know she could talk to him. But she did not. She was too embarrassed. She'd never imagined a person like that even had a family.

"My father was deaf, my mother wasn't. They talked sign, I learned sign. My mother and I both peddled too. They got me peddling when I was little so they could hustle more money. We made a shitload more than most people with straight jobs."

Charlie laughed, but he wasn't happy. Eve tried to feel the history of that boy at that moment.

——Where are they, your parents?

"They busted up. My father disappeared with some chick and went out west. My mother dumped me. I was too much baggage I guess. She's a bum in the city somewhere. Pretty fucked, hunh."

Eve nodded. ——Pretty fucked.

The train had begun to clear the city. The passenger car had those old wicker seats that stick to your skin in the heat. Charlie put his feet up on the seat in front of him. They sat in silence with the white lights outside the windows expanding outwards like stars over the distance. The moment was intimate, yet sprawling, as if vast worlds were being covered by the threads that bind people together.

Charlie went off into his head. Eve tapped him on the shoulder.

——Mimi, is she deaf? I didn't think she was deaf.

"Her hearing's shaky. They had that whole rubella thing a few years back. A German measles run while chicks were pregnant. Fucked up the hearing on lots of the kids. Her too. That's why they're getting her started on lip-reading and sign and learning how to speak. That's why we were at St. Joseph's. In case she loses it all. Her folks were…are…junkies. Headcases. Freakouts. Her old man…I don't think he's twenty yet…is at Rikers for dealing.

"Oh, Mimi wants your picture."

——What picture?

"Yours. A picture of you. You've got one, don't you?"

——Mine?

"Yeah. I told her you were good-looking." His eyes flicked with a bit of the devil. "Of course, she believes anything I say."

CHAPTER 68

THE WORLD THEATRE WAS just a parking lot away from the Mt. Vernon train station. It was a movie house turned concert hall. Hip bands of the day played there, sometimes in an odd collection of pairings, like the Strawberry Alarm Clock being fronted by Country Joe and the Fish. That night the Chambers Brothers were opening for Buffalo Springfield.

In the lobby Eve could already feel the emotional pulse of the music coming up from the belly of the building and straight into her being. She wasn't sure which way to go through that wall of bodies till Charlie took her by the hand, locking his fingers into hers and led the way, and the moment felt absolute and timelessly right.

In one extended rush they were pulled into the undertow of the crowd and pressed on through a smoky archway. Through the haze Eve could see the Chambers Brothers on stage where the movie screen was. The theatre seats had been pulled. You could either stand or dance on the angled floor.

There were bloomlets of strobe being thrown down on the crowd from a machine in the loge. An intense staccato of light then dark that bent the eyes and made the descent through that wave of bodies toward the stage a flash frame sea of disoriented space and seconds. The air was thick with the smell of pot, and kids drank wine caught up in the driving music of those tall, lanky, black men.

She and Charlie danced that night like she never had before, with him sometimes signing to her the lyrics of the songs. What she would never hear, she could feel that night in the floorboards beneath her, as real and close as it was incomprehensible and distant. And it was not just the music she was feeling, but the mood inside you that must come from music.

And in that deafening silence, as she watched the gestures of exaltation from the shadow dancers around her—the boys with their narrowed eyes and wet and salty smell, the girls all superior and fresh, the long-hairs and straights and stoners tripping by with their tinted granny glasses—she experienced for the first time the absolute beauty of shameless youth, at being alive to who she was. As much sheer carnival as it was sheerly carnal.

The dancers stopped and Eve saw the couples converge into tight-knit pairs and she knew the music was turning slow. Charlie came toward her——Alright?

She felt suddenly vulnerable that she would look insipid or foolish and that he'd be ashamed to be with her, but he asked again——Alright? And Eve answered——Just don't let me look foolish.

He nodded and his hand went around her wrist like a bracelet. They glided searchingly toward each other. Self-conscious and graceful, they danced slow, a specter of velvet intimacy in a smoky old movie theatre with its foolishly angled floor. Their hands moved with that first time and forever touch and then in darkened readiness they kissed.

CHAPTER 69

THE LOGE OF THE WORLD had been stripped of seats. It was just a metal and concrete rise of steps where everyone went to get totally stoned or to have a little taste of the physical.

It was also where the strobe machines were and the overhead projectors that flashed images on the movie screen behind the band, images rife with the psychedelic intensity of the day.

Smoke collected down from the rafters, so dense that people were nothing more than rivulets of color balanced in a moment, and the light from the projectors was that sudden incandescence so you felt as if you were being transported to some secret room where the future flashed out at you from an unseen point of darkness.

Charlie and Eve together at the railing looked down at a mirage of bodies as the Buffalo Springfield took the stage. They began with their classic anthem of the day. The crowd swelled up with applause and began to hammer their fists on the loge railing, and that overhang of steel and concrete shook with life.

As they sang, the lyrics of their song were projected onto the movie screen and walls behind them at daring and dramatic angles.

> *There's something happening here*
> *What it is ain't exactly clear*

People began to raise their hands in the peace sign and drive their stiffened arms at the band in cadence to the music.

> *Battle lines being drawn*

Nobody's right, if everybody's wrong

Soon the whole theatre was a surge of arms and it was then, watching, that Eve felt her body tingle as much for the way Charlie held her as for what she saw.

> *Young people speaking their mind*
> *Getting so much resistance from behind*

That sea of arms, like great stalks of wheat rising through the smoke, signing in peace at a riven angle was something Eve's very deafness could touch, could feel, could decipher and translate into a photograph. It was the truest form of language.

> *There's a man with a gun over there*
> *Telling me I've got to beware*

Charlie didn't even get out, "What are you doing?" before Eve had pulled loose from him and rushed into the shoulder bag for her camera. She signed in a swift move for him to hold her as she leaned over the balcony.

Little did she know that what she was experiencing intuitively and capturing in the eyepiece of her camera—that theatre of arms rising through the smoke, signing peace toward the stage where phrases of the song flashed onto the white hot backdrop of a movie screen—would become a seminal moment of chronicled time.

Maybe it was because the moment was seminal in her life, and she felt it in a way the great primitives always did, their senses being there before they are. Maybe it was seminal because the moment created her, carried her, defined her, tempted her with its possibilities.

· · ·

The flesh softens everything about us, and it leaves us susceptible to everything else there is about us. On the train home as Eve and Charlie talked, he noticed a cluster of faces at the far end of the car trying not to look like they were staring at them even when they were.

Charlie signed to Eve——Check out the dudes at the end of the car. Not now, but check them out.

She did. They were Westchester types, all male, wearing tattersall pants and loafers and either tweed sport coats or those pastel-colored Eisenhower windbreakers.

——I'll bet, said Charlie,——they're from Iona College and were up at Manhattanville trying to nab some.

Amidst all those point of view glances, Eve thought that crowd looked rather sad and lonely. The rocking train and bleached out light didn't help, neither did the fact they were passing two flasks between them.

——Are they staying at us, asked Charlie,——'cause we're talking sign? Or because you're white and I'm...Well, my father was white and Puerto Rican. My mother Jamaican and black. Kids used to call me Stu, as in stew. Get the knock?

She found it particularly hurtful, maybe because it brought to mind just another vamp of the Jailgirl nickname.

——You know, said Charlie,——I...He hesitated,——I figured you wouldn't want to go out with me 'cause I wasn't white.

She brushed back her black curly hair.——Whoever said Italians were white?

——I'm serious, man.

——I figured you wouldn't want to go out with me 'cause I was deaf.

Sitting there, touched by such speechless honesty, he felt the infinitesimal pull of her eyes. She was just what he knew she'd be before he even knew her.

Charlie took Eve by the hand and they went and stood on the platform between cars. The city thundered toward them. A castellated skyline of lights where blocks reeled past their eyes stretching on into the night, blocks alive with electric energy and tireless traffic and dark human shapes hustling from dream to dream.

——I went into the army 'cause I didn't want to be like my parents. I wanted to be...one of us...You get it...One of us.

She knew what he meant. The geography of it was traceable in his expression, in his manner, in the way his hands tried to encompass the space that meant "all of us."

There was a wildness to the dark, pierced as it was with wind. She took his hand with a tenderness that meant to try to hold against the worst there is.

CORNUTO

CHAPTER 70

THEY WERE SITTING JUST OFF the street on the apartment stoop, clutched up against each other. Light of mind, still a little stoned, with sparks of feeling aroused by every touch. Charlie's hands caressing the sides of Eve's neck felt soft like a sunflower—that's what she was thinking when she saw him.

He crossed the street through a grime of shadows, stepping into a moulin of harsh slanted light from the broken glass of a street lamp. My fuckin' daughter with a half-baked eggplant, Romain thought. Figures.

He came at them saying nothing. He had a little of that coke edge left and the way he walked filled Eve with dread and Charlie could feel something bad spreading through her body.

As he came up the steps and around them, Eve edged back in the extreme to let her father pass. Charlie watched Romain. Romain was giving Charlie a full dose of that useless piece of shit look, reserved for the likes of him that he'd had to face down more than a few times.

At the door Romain stopped and said to his daughter, "Cornuto," then he gave her the sign of the horns.

Eve turned away hoping her father would just disappear into nowhere, when Romain did the same to Charlie, giving him the horns. Charlie had no idea what the fuck was going down but he stood up, and as he did, Romain slipped a gun out of his pocket.

"You want a piece of it? Do you, eggplant?"

Charlie stared raweyed at the gun while Eve pulled him away and down the alley before something bad happened. When the door closed and Romain was gone Charlie asked, "What was that?"

——My father.

"Your...father?"

Eve looked at the doorway where her father had just stood in disgust. Then, facing sheer humiliation and pain she told Charlie everything.

It was the first time in her life she had confided to anyone, other than Fran, the bare facts of her life, and how they affected the very soul of her.

But she found when she started, that she wanted, no needed to tell him, because she wanted, needed, no it was something more than want or need, to be truly known by him.

· · ·

Fran awoke to hear banging. She staggered off the living room couch stubbing over a cocktail glass on the floor. More pounding, ugly, ugly pounding.

On the landing below Eve kicked and hit at the door to the apartment where her father was holed up. All boots and fists, she was like some angel of supernatural fury unleased and ready to have at it.

• • •

Fran had sent Eve off for a day of errands and she waited, smoking, on the apartment stoop for Romain's ultimate appearance.

When he showed, she stood. Her face had begun to have those wallet lines, the eyes becoming a testament to the darkened edges of anger.

"How does it feel," she asked, "to be nothing? Nothing."

She flung the cigarette in his face before he could answer. She started inside. "I'm not gonna see that girl destroyed. Not by you, or anyone like you. You, prick guinea."

She turned. "And you don't make any comments about who she sees or who her friends are. You're not her father anymore, she's Clarissa's daughter. Get it."

Without so much as losing a beat of time he said, "I need more money."

A JUNKIE SCREAMING
IN THE STREET

CHAPTER 71

EVE WAS SITTING CROSS-LEGGED on her bed, with the flag pillow tucked against her stomach, staring down at her camera.

Fran stepped into the doorway, looked this scene over with a curious silence. "What's with the mood?"

——Charlie's parents invited me over Sunday dinner.

"That is what's causing what I'm looking at?"

——Mimi. She wants me to bring a picture of myself.

"Ahhhhhh."

——I'm embarrassed to do that.

Fran crossed her arms and leaned against the door. Very grave. Eve knew that when Fran went into that mode she was heading toward some venerable comment.

——I see it coming, signed Eve.

"I hate to use religious analogies for anything. Hate it. But here goes. Confession is good for the soul."

· · ·

Charlie lived in Morrisania, just a few blocks from Morris High School. The Dores had one of those old brownstones with a stoop and rounded bay windows.

Charlie and Mimi were in the window watching for Eve when she came up the street checking out addresses. Eve caught sight of their sunned out images waving, and the next thing she knew they were coming down the steps to get her.

Mimi was talking and moving so fast Eve could hardly read the child's lips and since Mimi, as yet, barely knew a word of sign, Charlie had to explain and translate as Mimi took Eve by the hand and led her into the house wanting to know if Eve had brought a picture of herself.

In the doorway waiting was Queenie. She was a tiny thing with bunned, whitish hair, and she signed——Welcome, and put her arm around Eve and ushered her into the kitchen with everyone talking and signing at one time. Napoleon, who stood a head taller than anyone else in the room was wearing a chef's apron and checking a roast in the oven and complaining as he signed——Welcome, then to his wife, "That the damn roast, pardon my English, looks almost done," and just that fast Eve was swept into the breath of that family.

• • •

The picture. Mimi made sure that took top priority with a steady stream of pleadings.

Eve had brought her large shoulder bag, with camera and all. Everyone had seen her last photograph so they expected something good, but what they got exuded hip and intelligence.

Eve had hung a mirror on a blank wall in an empty classroom at St. Joseph's. She had set up a tripod to frame the mirror. Beneath the mirror she had pasted to the wall cutout letters of different sizes, shapes and colors that read: DEAF GIRL, SMILING. Beneath the cutouts were other cutouts of sign to match the words.

She had set the timer, stepped into frame, and the camera caught her smiling in the mirror. Self-portrait and school lesson all rolled into one. As simple as your abc's.

As his parents fawned over the shot, Charlie snuck a kiss on Eve, then said, "I told you she'd come with something right on."

Queenie started to guide Mimi through the words and signs. Eve watched. Remembered way back with her mother and Fran. The memory was pristine on the soul. *The Scarlet Letter*, she thought.

Charlie tugged at the belt above Eve's butt to get her attention. "Why don't you take some pictures of all of us?"

"The girl's here as our guest, and to have dinner," said Napoleon. "And we'll have dinner if your mother can take a minute and tell me, excuse my English, if this goddamn roast is done."

——I don't mind taking pictures. I like to.

"There you have it," said Charlie.

"If she wants to," said Queenie, looking at her husband as if she were against the idea.

"She can do anything she likes." Flustered, he pointed the knife at the roast and silently tried to tell his wife, please, take a goddamn look. Then he turned to Eve, "Take any picture you want. Especially of me."

And that was completely that.

While Eve took pictures Charlie managed to sneak in a little handiwork without his folks noticing. Mimi was wedged into the space between them. Baby sister to the action.

• • •

They were by the breakfront in the hall where the family had its own share of photographs. Eve noticed on one shelf an homage of sorts to a boy. She imagined it the son who'd committed suicide. Tucked into the corner of his high school graduation picture was a mass card from the funeral and the dried petals of some purple flower wrapped in plastic. Every picture is filled with tales, she thought.

Reflected in the breakfront glass, Eve saw Queenie come up behind her.

"That was our son, Nicholas," said Queenie. She took Charlie's hand.

"I told her about Nicholas, Mom."

"We have had our share of sorrows," said the older woman, "and we've had more than our share of joys. And we count them all among our blessings."

As they sat for dinner, everyone began to stretch out their hands. Eve had no idea what was going on, until Charlie explained, "We hold hands and say grace. House rules."

"And a good thing too," Queenie said.

And so they did. Mimi held one of Eve's hands watching her the whole while, while Charlie held her other hand caressing the back of it unnoticed with his thumb.

The light through the window left a certain sheen across the table, the shadows were deep and detailed. And the hands, in that light they seemed to convey a profound sense of family and social unity as they changed color from one to the next.

Eve wished she could remain where she was and at the same time sneak away from the table to catch the moment.

• • •

They hadn't been at dinner long when the screaming started down in the street. Charlie was the first up. Napoleon, a flung aside napkin later. Their moving intensely toward the window grabbed Eve's attention.

Queenie was up too now. And Mimi. Moments like this, fraught with confusion because she could not hear, always took Eve back, threw her back really, to that instant of looking through the camera at the Jerome Swim Club with people running through the frame as her father, behind her, was trying to escape from the police.

CHAPTER 72

EVE JOINED THE CROWD OF FACES in the bay window looking down. On the sidewalk a young Latin woman was screaming. Her face stretched up toward that very window. A visual of agony.

Because of the truncated light and hostile angle of the body Eve could not see well enough what the girl was saying till Charlie, turning, getting ready to follow Napoleon downstairs told her, "Mimi's mother. Fuckin' wacko junkie."

• • •

The girl in the street was junkie to the core. With a burnt-out stare and a face twisted hopeless. The words came out of her mouth half strangled, "I want our daughter, you shits."

By now Mimi had reached the stoop, with Queenie only an arm's length away. The screaming had drawn a crowd. From the stoops and windows people stared in alarm.

The girl lunged toward her daughter only to be grabbed by Charlie and Napoleon.

"You can't do this," said the old man.

"We want our baby back, you fuckin' nigger."

Charlie bear-hugged her. "Don't man, you're acting crazy."

"Fuck you all."

Fighting to free herself of their putrid grasps, the girl tried to bite Napoleon on the arm. It was a hideous display of the erratic and insane. Like watching something undead leap from the grave, ravenous.

It was Charlie who bent her head and pulled it loose before she cut through his father's flesh.

By now Queenie had Mimi in her arms. The child was reaching for her mother and recoiling in shock from what she saw. And her mother, hot-eyed and half breathless, kept shouting the girl's name amidst a flood of guttered obscenities.

Somebody had called the police. A squad car turned the corner at cruise speed. A black and white through the shades of evening moved slowly along then the overhead lights began to flash. Whether it was the car called or not, no one knew.

Things went from anxious and ugly to downright awful. The police came down hard on the girl. Her face at least once got slammed into the hood.

She managed the last of it though as they hauled her handcuffed and dragging into the squad car when she yelled, "Bobby's gonna seriously fuck with you nigger shits for stealing our baby."

. . .

Whatever had prompted or tempted Eve to bring her camera downstairs, she'd listened. From the stoop doorway shadows, embarrassed and excited, but emboldened by both, she'd grabbed shots of that contortion of bones and raped out skin. Childish and old at the same time. Freaked out, crying, rageful. Flesh yellow, but for a fireburst around the eyes.

After the squad car pulled away and things had settled down and Mimi was brought back upstairs Charlie just shook his head and sat on the stoop a minute with Eve.

"This is not even the first time," he said, "the chick is…you should have seen the shape Mimi was in when we got her. Bones. Like something you see in one of those Nazi prison camps."

——I took pictures, Eve told him almost secretively.

"You mean…?"

——Yeah.

He wasn't surprised she'd had the cool and composure to catch that whole warped out scene. He dug her all the more for it, actually. All he asked was, "Did you get a shot of her trying to gnaw off the old man's arm?"

. . .

The day would stand marked in at least half a dozen lives, including Natalie Batchelor, as she watched this wretched aberration of a scene from her folks' house across the street.

The notion each moment is a brief composition, that no matter how far removed by time and place, no matter how disparate the personal circumstances or acts of life, one from the other, there is continuity and connection.

The interconnectedness of things would be the question forever with Natalie as she looked back those years later from her apartment in Co-Op City, writing with a bereaved sense about "the truth of things", as she would be asked.

But today, Natalie was only a brokenhearted twenty-one-year-old, clandestinely watching her ex-boyfriend sitting on a stoop and totally into some girl who was maybe seventeen. And, the girl, as Natalie could now see, was deaf, which meant she'd get the sympathy vote.

CHAPTER 73

THE PHOTOGRAPHS OF MIMI'S MOTHER screaming in the street were bursts of emotion that just soaked up the frame. Not so much photographs as full force impressions just disgorged onto film.

The graspings of a woman child trying to bite an arm, the all too violent warfare between police and citizen, the awled thrust of a junkie mother's arms.

Fran's dining table had become a work station of sorts where Eve would spread out her snapshots for Fran to see and play mentor. These shots reminded Fran of the chaotic years that led to Hitler's climb to power, and she saw now how more and more America, the Bronx, their streets were becoming the battlefield of extremes. A place of daylight dungeons.

Then the world turned. From street shots to those of Charlie's family. Vignettes that stood out because of one simple fact. You could measure the closeness of the people by a gesture, by their physical proximity of joyful contact, by the way someone touched and looked at someone else, how the space between them was not dangerous or foreboding but something shared, a blue-white daylight like a river they all took part in.

And one shot, that of a breakfront shelf with photos of a dead son and caught in the glass door that protected those photographs, the reflection of a mother's face, with pearl eyes, you could read a sermon from those eyes. This, thought Fran, is what the Bible should have been.

As Fran looked from one group of photos to the other, she was left with a sense of dreadful reality that diverging forces were being driven toward each other in conflict.

Of course, in many respects, that was the life she and Eve had lived. But Fran had always felt they were the aberration.

Eve noticed, suddenly, Fran had started ever so slightly to cry.

——— What?

"I had this feeling—"

Fran stopped. Eve came up next to her. Squatted by the side of Fran's chair.

——I don't understand. Explain.

Fran reached for the photos of Charlie's family. Laid them out in a close collage.

"I'm not this. This is a real family. And I could imagine you'd want to be around people like this rather than…me. And this feeling came over me. Struck me. That I could, was going to, lose you. And it made me scared."

The light spidered across Fran's teary face. Eve had never seen her quite so. Not the icon of strength who had always protected her but a portrait of humaneness and frailty, and in that, it made Eve love her all the more. As she put her arms around Fran to console her, the moment spoke to Eve, as her own approaching womanhood spoke to her, of all the dark and barren places Fran had seen and how so many ordinary dreams had been stolen from her.

I - L - Y

CHAPTER 74

EVE AND CHARLIE STRETCHED OUT on a blanket on the roof of her apartment and looked up into the soul of a warm Bronx night. Fran had driven Dr. Frank to Elmira, and would be gone for the weekend. Eve rested her head on Charlie's shoulder. He smoked a Kent and blew tight gray rings into the air which she grabbed at with a finger trying to catch and hold.

When she needed to tell him something she tugged at his shirt and spoke in sign. There was beautiful passion in those long, slender fingers.

She would talk and talk and sometimes he would grab her hand and affectionately bite it to get her to slow down.

She wished she were wearing lipstick when she kissed him. She hoped he'd noticed *and* liked her new perfume. They existed within the simple prose of the human heart. The urgencies of now, the tides of tenderness. Every moment a meaning unto itself.

After all she had suffered and lost, after all she had survived, she'd never expected on God's earth that such happiness could be hers.

From his shirt pocket Charlie took a tissue wrapped present no bigger than the tip of his thumb.

——For you, Eve Leone.

She reached for the present all surprised and excited and he pulled his hand away to tease her. She reached again and he eluded her once more and the two hands moved like butterflies in the darkness, one chasing the other.

He finally relinquished when she put on a look of coy exasperation. He felt a stirring warmth as he watched her pull away the tiny sheets of tissue paper to reveal a necklace. It was a small necklace from which hung letters in silver: I-L-Y.

• • •

They went back down to the apartment barefoot with just a kiss worth of sweat on their skin. Cold beers, constant touching. You could just read desire in the way their shadows moved across the walls.

In Eve's room for the first time, Charlie, upon seeing her flag pillow gave out a salute. She caught on and slapped him hard on the hand.

——Not that.

A little flush took hold in her cheeks and he made the most of it by saluting again.

———You're not hearing me. But instead of using the index finger in front of her mouth to make small continuous circles she used the middle finger for... emphasis.

She went over to a wall of photos and pointed to the snapshot of her as a baby lying asleep on the flag pillow.

The lines of her face had extended dramatically, the eyes becoming deep, dark glassless windows. If that stare were after you, Charlie thought, you could kiss your future goodbye.

"Deaf as a stone," he said, "and twice as strong." He made the sign for her face. "Turn it off. The anger. I didn't mean to hurt your feelings. If there is anyone I don't want to hurt, it's you."

She calmed a bit, but went from photo to photo just so he'd understand. ———This pillow goes back to when my sister was alive, my mother.

She tried to explain how she'd held that pillow to her chest and it had touched everything that was ever buried inside her. It had caught every tear's worth, every dream's worth, every prayer's worth. It carried in that cloth every memory and hope. And that it was as special to her as...she touched the necklace he had given her which she now wore on her neck.

The night around them stilled, the lights of passing cars arched across the ceiling in an instant bit of heaven. The anger slipped away and the seconds became like the pages of an open book, fluttering with the breeze, as Charlie walked to Eve and kissed her.

• • •

You want to be loved. You want to feel the kind of world that never existed. Her hands moved blindly, his moved with a pragmatic grace that answered the question for her, was this his first time?

On the bed their flesh together was like the colors of the earth, their movements rooted in need and passion and by some alchemical linkage that has never been truly understood since time began.

She could feel his body slap against hers in that deep silence, driven as it was with body hunger. She did not realize that he could hear sounds coming up from her chest as she orgasmed and it turned him on all the more.

She would find out from him later, and it would embarrass her as much as delight. As she lay on her flag pillow in the dark with his head against her chest she would think, even sounds you can't hear, can help you.

• • •

They snuck into the candy store naked. Through the windows they could see heat lightning score the rooftops and now and then a passerby, who had no idea.

They got themselves a little something to eat; then snuggled down low with their backs to the counter where they could watch the street without being seen, or at least test the limits of being seen. It was demented and silly and sexy, and just plain fun.

"I'll bet you'd like to get a picture of this."

She grinned, then looked down at him as she ran her hand along his thin muscular legs.——Maybe I will.

There was something utterly and harmlessly bad about what they were doing. She thought about him and her making love right there with the cupcakes and potato chips and cheese doodles for an audience.

——This candy store will never, excuse my English, be the fuckin' same again.

They started to laugh and they kissed each other without caring one shit about where they were or what were the consequences, and they began to slide down low to the floor when Charlie's whole body just bundled up.

He pointed.

It was Romain, walking past the window, slow, lighting a cigarette. He looked in the store, he actually looked in. It was nothing more than a glance taking in space, but still.

He hesitated a moment, looked back over his shoulder. He remained posed, like that, nonchalant but intense, the cigarette smoke rising past his dark watery stare, as if he needed to see what might, might be behind him.

Then he turned and walked on. Charlie could hear him opening the outside door to his apartment and his footsteps climbing the stairs. His door closing. All this he signed to Eve.

They sat there skinned cold in the dark. Charlie put his arm around Eve 'cause he knew what she must be feeling.

"When I think of my own life," he said, "and how fucked it was. How ashamed and angry I was. When I think of Mimi who had it worse yet. And compare them to yours."

He shook his hand, like something burning got that close, that close.

"Yours was the worst. To think that he killed your mother and is walking the street. I mean we live with the fact the army and police get away with it, but—"

"How does it make you feel? How do you get it out of your head?"

There had been dialogues going on inside her head. Full scale screaming matches about this very subject.

More heat lightning. All those Bronx blocks through the shop window became a movie screen of crepuscular light. She had been taught there was such a thing as thunder that came with lightning. And it was described as a loud concussive shock, much like gunfire.

She told Charlie——It's not trying to forget, or to live with it that's the worst part. But it's trying to make sure that he, Eve pointed up toward his apartment furiously,——he, doesn't ever, ever, ever forget.

CHAPTER 75

CHARLIE CAME TO THE CANDY STORE looking for Eve. She was in the darkroom. Charlie had a mood on him, no hiding that, and when she asked if he was alright, he told her——Shaky.

He wanted them to be alone. They walked outside. The street was deep with strangers. "I got to go back," he said. "I just got hit with orders. The fuckers are taking me back."

That blunt statement of fact went right through her.

"I guess it turns out it wasn't a million-dollar wound after all."

They walked to Crotona Park. Just silent restless channels of energy. The sun was already slipping through the gaps in the buildings when Charlie dropped himself down on a bench like something fated and lost.

"It'll be just my luck I go back over there and get my ass wasted."

Eve put her hands up to her ears in that age-old sign of, I don't want to hear it. She meant it not only as a matter of fact, but as a way of heightening matter of fact.

"Got it," Charlie told her. "Know what my father, my real father, used to say? Talk is just a B-version of sign. You know like—"

——A B-movie. Sounds about right to me. She pulled on her ear hard after she signed.

He grinned a bit, played off her play. If for nothing else, it eased the difficulty of the moment. "You're signing in loud and clear."

Eve was frightened and threatened by the fact he was going back, but didn't let on any more than she had to. From the bench where they sat she looked out over the city. It was its own monument to the skyline, and she felt as if she were in some bewitched region where she could lose sight of herself forever.

Charlie ran his hands up her neck, across the side of her face. He tweaked her cheek to get her attention. "You've got beautiful ears, you know that?"

——They're not good for much but decoration. Earrings or billboards.

He leaned over and kissed the ear.

——And that.

"I'm frightened," he said.

She held him and she kissed him and there was not enough sign in this screwed up world to encompass what was inside her.

"Let me tell you," he said, "not being able to hear has its own fucked downsides but, what you lost there..." He touched her ear..."You made up

THE
NOT-SO-MILLION-DOLLAR
WOUND

there." He touched her head. "And there." He touched her heart.

• • •

They said goodbye at Charlie's house. It had rained for hours but the storm had moved inland. A cab waited outside the brownstone. The concrete smelled of afterrain and the tires of passing cars kicked up the last sprinkling of street water.

Charlie was in uniform with one duffel. Just another boy in a string of boys, coming and going. Disappearing into the heart of distance while those behind suffered the wait. There was a certain prose to the moment, the affectionate discourse of the goodbye. The hug and the kiss are the word of support passed on from generation to another generation, of moments just like that.

Eve and Charlie, off to one side, kissed. She wanted to cry, she did cry. He told her, "Get a picture of me as I go."

Eve did not want to, she was afraid it was bad luck. As if fate would allot for her some private doom for stealing this moment.

There were shadows in the sky mapped across the horizon. People passed on the sidewalk watching the blade smooth face of a young man step into a cab.

The moment passed through Eve. All desire and possession. And she understood, between her and the camera, there could be no lies, no restraints. If she was to be real, to be whole, to be complete. For him, for anyone, for herself, she must snap the shutter as one would the trigger of a gun, with remorseless honesty.

CHAPTER 76

EVE LAY ACROSS FRAN'S LAP on the bed, the flag pillow tucked up under her arms. The one Charlie had made such fun of.

Fran knew youth feels and believes unquestionably, whether it be war or peace, hate or love. They want and grieve as if there is no tomorrow.

Eve lay on the scar across Fran's stomach. That scar could have been a child being born. This child-woman. Now it just decorated the flesh, became a statement of existence, like deaf ears.

Youth is armed with such loveliness, even as they suffer, thought Fran. She soothed and stroked the girl's hair, and they remained just so as the light in the room grew tranquil, then dark.

• • •

Between writing letters to Charlie and living her routine, Eve walked the streets with her camera trying to burn off all that emotion. She caught a shot of a Vet outside the Bronx County Courthouse with his prosthetic legs, standing on the sidewalk beside where he sat with a sign that read: TOO PROUD TO BEG. And one of a street evangelist with a mike and a speaker moving like a bantamweight on the Grand Concourse. He was wearing a tuxedo and on the back of the jacket, in star-glittered letters it said: BROTHER THUNDERBOLT—WITH A MESSAGE FOR THE MESS AGE. She got another shot of a movie poster on a wall of Disney's *Sleeping Beauty* out for another run. Only this time someone had graffitied onto the poster Uncle Sam with his cock out and all boned up, getting ready to slip it into Sleeping Beauty's ass.

AN OLD WOMAN
IN A CHURCH PEW

CHAPTER 77

THEY CAME IN THE CANDY STORE wearing that total street swagger. Turks in their early twenties, or just so case hardened they had literally bled away their teens. Eve was making change at the register when one of them asked in slipshod English, "Leone, man…He here…Romain…The pussy here?"

Their eyes were going from spot to spot, fidgeting like the flame on a Zippo lighter. Eve had seen this kind at short range before, when she'd been "a front with a camera" for her father. She understood what was going on in the way that gives you this unnerving intensity.

After making change and nodding goodbye to the customer Eve played mute-stupid giving out with rural homemade sign even a blind brainless shit could understand. ——I can't hear, can't speak.

From the back Fran saw what was going on and came over.

"He lives here, though," one of them said, like Eve should understand anyway.

"Is there a problem?" asked Fran.

Eve warned Fran in sign there was something bad with these guys.

"He lives here…We know…We seen him."

Fran was saying, "I don't understand," when one of the kids got strictly ugly. "We know, cunt…We seen him…Here."

The few customers in the store were now staring. The three talked among themselves in Spanish, one motioned to leave. Nothing more was said. Then, one of the kids came walking back in. He was carrying a newspaper. Something was wrapped up in the newspaper he flung at Fran and Eve. Both women jumped back as the carcass of a dead rat hit the floor with a lifeless thud right at their feet. A mother with a small child gasped when she saw that bloody, dead thing with its gray string tail just lying there on the old dark floorboards.

• • •

You didn't need a roomful of theories to figure out the point they were trying to make. The unnerving intensity Eve felt earlier carried over for both women into the night. It had begun to rain as they sat down for dinner. A slickish gray that spotted the glass. From across the table Eve told Fran ——Throw him out. Do it now.

Fran's fingers tapped on the table nervously as she considered all options and uncertainties. "When you're eighteen. Then he's got no legal hold on you. He's done. Till then—"

Fran got up and went to the window. She looked out into the brick rained dark half expecting to see them out there, and worried Eve would have to pay the price for her father's misdeeds. "These drug sellers like your father…They're the Nazis of our times."

Fran came back to the table and sat. Eve saw Fran's face begin to struggle with some thought. "Maybe we should get a gun?"

The bones of the older woman's face looked to be heaped with worry, and the two just sat and stared at each other in the deep presence of that moment.

——He has a gun. My father. Eve reminded Fran about the gun he'd stolen from the policeman's casket at St. Raymond's Cemetery. The same one he'd flashed on Charlie.——I've seen it downstairs.

Fran watched the front door from the landing while Eve went into Romain's apartment. The place smelled of her father. The search was mercifully quick as Romain had few possessions. She found the gun on the closet floor under a stack of dirty laundry. On the way out Eve passed the bathroom. There was urine in the toilet, and by the sink the telltale sign of needle and spoon. A ghostly chilling went through her. This Eve did not tell Fran about, so as not to worry her any more than she was already.

• • •

Eve was coming up 173rd Street toward the candy store with the shirt sticking to her back when someone or something grabbed her by the arm. Before she realized it was her father he'd pulled her into an alley.

It had been a week since that warning of a dead rat had been flung at her and Fran's feet, and longer yet that her father had put in an appearance.

"Who took the gun?" he asked, shaking his daughter. "You or Fran?"

She signed something he couldn't understand, so she took out a note pad and wrote down: **What did you do, rip them off? So you could shoot some up your arm?**

You'd think by now that Romain would be beyond any form of façade.

"They were gonna rip me off," he said, "so I hit first. And I only chip a little to cut the edge. If it's any of your fuckin' business."

She stared up into the face of the man who'd given her life, of whom she was a very part.

"Now listen. I got a stash that's got to get delivered to a buyer. And I can't deliver it. So you're gonna have to take it."

She wasn't sure she'd read his lips right. She couldn't have. She looked past him for a moment. The alley was dusty with sunlight and tiered windows like sorrowful eyes. A deep shameful hurt went through Eve.

She wrote: **You're a fuckin liar.**

"You do this for me, and I'm gone. You understand? You'll never see me again."

Liar. Eve underlined the word defiantly.

"Hate me, alright. But do this and you're rid of me. I can't do it. You understand."

She kept shaking her head no, telling herself not to listen, that he was a fuckin' factory of lies.

"They'll keep coming back," he warned, "till they're sure I'm outta here. Get it? You want something might happen to Fran? Do you?"

CHAPTER 78

ST. BRENDON'S CHURCH WAS off of Gun Hill Road up by Mosholu Parkway. Your typical ten steps up to a pilloried house of stone prayer.

Eve entered and looked around. There were the usual weekday morning prayer freaks in a few pews. Up by the votive candle rack a man was dropping coins into the money box. The church smelled of waxy smoke that played with her memories.

Walking down the aisle, looking for her contact, she thought about how many times her mother had stopped with her in a church to pray. On their way to work, from work, when they were out shopping. She had a pretty good notion now what her mother had been praying for: please, dear God, let my husband be run over and killed by a bus.

Eve wondered about the secret pleas of the people there that morning. The tired, the needy, the desperate. Fragments from a psalm book of the real world, she thought, as the phrase came to her like a picture.

She felt utterly sinful over what she was doing. As if those statues were silently watching and taking notes on her fall from grace.

She sat in a pew and waited. Noted the prayer books in the pew rack, thought of her mother's missal. Noted a silverfish on the floor by the pew railing. A slithering eyelid of a thing. Wondered if churches are as filthy as a basement apartment. Imagined what Fran would have to say on the subject.

Noted a light coming through a stained glass window and onto an old woman's shoulders, and how those shoulders looked more square and tired in the light. As if the light were leaning on them, weighing down on them, and the shoulders absorbed it all with frayed obstinacy.

She thought about taking out her camera and getting a picture of the old woman. She was amazed she'd had the thought because she was so nervous. Maybe it was because she was so nervous she'd had the thought, maybe she just *was* those thoughts. Maybe that's just how she dealt with life. Escaping from it by escaping into it.

A figure appeared in a sunfilled doorway. Came down the aisle with a sluffing stride. Young, long hair, Christlike till you got a glimpse of the wardrobe. Souped-up Robert Hall all the way, with black hightop sneakers.

Closer, not as young as she thought. A scaly character you'd swear made a life for himself robbing those candy and peanut machines on subway platforms.

He cruised past once, eyeing her. Then he planted himself in a pew a few rows back. She didn't get it. He was the guy, but then—

A kid came in a minute later. Fourteen tops. With a wineglass neck and a head as big as a B-ball. The kid circled. Eve saw the guy with the beard nod his head toward her and the kid circled again, stopped at the holy water trough, blessed himself, came back up the aisle, genuflected with a half dull bow and sat in the pew near her.

He looked at her and nodded. He slipped an envelope from his jean coat pocket. Let her get a sneaking eyeful. It was totally fuckin' extraordinary how it all flashed in her head. She saw his eyes, huge and lifeless as doorknobs. His skin the color of urined plaster. This boy was strictly junked out.

Yeah…he was her, only worse. A junked out front with a sleaze shit for a handler who dealt with her sleaze shit of a father, who was fronting her. The human food chain working on down toward the lowest common denominators.

The kid stared at her like a frozen shadow with leached white lips. He crooked his arm toward the envelope, mouthed, "Let's shitass do it."

She closed her eyes. That moment at the Jerome Beach and Swim Club when her father got busted cut out a deep and wide piece of her courage. But she forced a breath, chucked her fear and just did it.

It all took a few pumped out seconds of heart time. Skag for money. She went her way, they went on toward total oblivion. She didn't look back till she hit Gun Hill Road.

Eve stopped at a luncheonette where her father waited. He sat at one of the four marble tables in the back facing the door. Eve sat and cautiously passed him the envelope. She watched the intense manner he checked it all out while keeping an eye on the door.

"Those fuckers," he said, "who came into the candy store. They won't be back now."

——What about you?

"You did alright. Don't worry."

——What about you?

He got up, walked away. He'd worked it pretty slick he thought, giving those losers a little junk to go in and terrorize Fran and the kid so he could get her to carry.

Alone at the cold and dirty marble table for morose long minutes, Eve then got up and tried to explain to some feckless woman that she needed to use a bathroom. It was a chore and a half 'cause Eve was shaking something fierce.

B.Lo

CHAPTER 79

WHEN HE REAPPEARED A FEW DAYS LATER, Eve knew Romain had screwed her over big time. He challenged his daughter with a stare. She could feel it on some icy wavelength as he walked past her in the hallway and it left a thumbmark on her like a bullet wound.

Eve had never kept a secret from Fran. This was the first time and some ruinish form of guilt went through her that she chalked up to all those masses with her mother.

All those masses with her mother. Eve looked over at a picture of Clarissa sitting on a bench by the old apartment and holding a Fudgsicle. Gail had taken the picture a few years before Eve or her sister were born. Eve tried to effectively read the photograph, to see if she could tell what her mother already felt.

Eve confessed to Fran later that night, but only after Fran had downed a couple of scotches. Fran's shoulders took on the sloping form of a boxer as she listened. Without a word Fran got up, went into the kitchen and began to smash things. Plates, glasses, the bottle of scotch. She flung over a chair walking across the living room, then went to her bedroom and shut the door for the night.

By morning the mess was cleaned.

• • •

Charlie and Eve wrote often. He'd been stationed back in Saigon, at his old supply depot. "'Get out of here in one piece' is my mantra. 'Stay out of Jeeps,' another. He wrote he'd send her a present for her eighteenth, which was coming up fast and that he'd miss.

Eve spent a lot of time at the Dores'. She became a sort of surrogate older sister for Mimi. Of course, since Mimi was only just learning sign and could hardly read, and Eve could not speak, their relationship, early on, demanded a conduit to help them through the rough spots. Queenie was almost always around, and if she wasn't, Mimi ended up at the candy store where Fran was. And a candy store, for a child that age, even with its scarred exterior, takes on breathtaking proportions.

Yet in spite of the early difficulties, Eve and Mimi's connection blossomed because of their achingly real and honest simplicity of affection. And part of that affection had its genesis in loss.

As for Eve, being with Mimi was like redreaming her own life, and parts of her past would just vanish as they sat on the curb and she showed the child how to physically make certain signs, or when they cruised the shops for neat clothes and tried on makeup, or when she wiped Mimi's mouth after it was a mess with food.

A kind of cornucopiate awakening went through Eve on how difficult it would be for a parent and child to connect when one could hear and one could not, and then to, by extension, connect to the world. And from that, a more moving portrait of her own mother emerged, even as the details of her life stayed the same.

This uneducated, parentless, unhappily married woman, cutting terry cloth in a choking warehouse, silently warred past every fear and failing, to find a way for her daughter to escape the trap of her own birth by eliciting help from a stranger who she met for two minutes in a church one Christmas. And then Fran, who after that, after everything, willed her a life.

It made Eve wonder, could she match in any way the dedication of either woman? If love was sacrifice and life selflessness, would she have the character to stand against the daily doses of violence, the emotional vandalisms that steal your spirit, the feelings of being threatened even when you're not while a small set of hands whose survival has your name written all over it, holds yours? Could she do time in an incinerator room, or stand that scar across her belly and still face the long journey afterwards?

. . .

Eve was with Fran one night in a little Italian restaurant on Arthur Avenue. It was one of Eve's favorites 'cause they made these knockout baked clams that were breaded and wrapped in bacon and after dinner a cart was brought to your table with cakes and pastries that turned anything the French could come up with into an eyesore.

Fran was pouring another glass of Chianti from a bottle with a straw handle, when Eve said——I know you don't believe in God. But I wonder, do you think God could be the grand sweep of people who've loved us?

Fran had, to Eve's eye, this wonderful capacity to seem incredibly caring and cynical at the same time. And she wasn't ever quite sure how the woman accomplished it. "I think it's a lovely notion," said Fran. "At least as good as any I've heard." Then, with a crinkle of eyebrow, "Just don't let the fuckin' pope get wind of it."

CHAPTER 80

WATCHING NAPOLEON AND QUEENIE prepare Thanksgiving dinner with their adult children, and those children's children, Fran thought, *they* were the real legal tender of America. Not just symbols, but working reality, pushing the rock of legitimate goodness up that lifelong hill.

Queenie eased Fran away from the others. As they sat alone drinking sherry, Queenie remarked on what a wonderful job Fran had done with Eve and "under such conditions." Then, in a tone that was entirely private Queenie said, "After what her father got away with. And he's still causing hurt."

"What I would like to say about him in English, is unfit for your home."

"Oh, please. We were one of the first black families on this block. We've been called things there is no language for."

"I made some compromises along the way to keep him from getting control of Eve. But on her eighteenth…no matter what…he's out of her life."

"Yes," said Queenie.

Fran noticed a tone of uncertainty in the lady's voice, but did not understand what it was directed at. Queenie glanced across the room. Mimi and her cousins were all over Eve trying their best to embroil her in some exuberance.

Mimi had such a feral brightness, Queenie told Fran, and they were working so hard to get all that bad history out of her system. Get her planted and rooted so she wouldn't end up another piece of fallout with society's stamp of disapproval. "But the girl's parents. You've heard about it. The mother's been in the Tombs since that Sunday."

"I didn't know."

"And her boyfriend. Mimi's father. He's in Correctional." Queenie shook her head in troubled dismay.

Fran put a hand on Queenie's in a show of support.

"Were you ever," Queenie hesitated, "are you ever, afraid? Physically afraid?"

There was a quiet, smoldering intensity to Fran's voice. "I experienced things in Germany, before the war, by the Nazis. They killed off any fear I ever had."

• • •

The kids were starting to swarm around them. Queenie asked Fran would she come outside for a minute?

She led Fran into the hallway, moving through her children and grandchildren with a quiet gravity. She and Napoleon exchanged a look. In the hall, making sure the door was closed, and speaking in a low, low voice, Queenie said, "Something terrible has happened."

"Charlie?"

"No. Dear God, no. Napoleon will tell everyone *after* dinner."

• • •

Throughout dinner Fran kept glancing from Eve to Mimi. Like the windows of apartments across an air shaft, a mirror of lights and darks.

After dessert and coffee, Napoleon cleared the room of his grandchildren, under the eye of Queenie. Then he told the rest.

He'd been notified the day before by phone that Mimi's mother was dead. She had died in the Tombs, where she'd been since she was arrested outside their house.

Mimi's mother, it seemed, had been riding out the dry heaves when she'd lost it and tried to cop another inmate's stash.

"Inmates with stashes, excuse my English, but what the living hell is going on?"

——The cops bring it in and sell it, Eve told them. ——After one of their boys rips off a dealer they put down.

Eve signed so matter-of-factly, like an elementary school teacher explaining to her students the how and why of things. Then, to make it clear signed —— My father is a drug dealer.

The inmate who murdered Mimi's mother had sharpened down a pen she'd conned off the prison chaplain. Mimi's mother had been stabbed. They didn't know how many times.

She was a blood muck of flesh on the concrete cell floor when the jailers got to her. She died two hours later. The coroner removed about two inches of pen casing from her heart.

THE BIRTHDAY PRESENTS

CHAPTER 81

MIMI'S REACTION TO HER MOTHER'S DEATH was a confusion of looks that could barely fathom such an idea. But at the wake, which the Dores paid for, when Mimi saw her mother lying in the casket, with the crucifix on the wall behind it trembling as the elevated went by, so deep was her pain on a primal level the child kicked and shook until she was near senseless.

Of all the people there Eve was the only one she would not allow herself to be separated from. The steady understanding of a touch, an embrace, the way the self is rocked in someone's arms—all this protective affection that Eve had been given by Fran she found herself passing on.

And in that, she looked around the room at that small spectacle of faces, and knowing their personal stories, it came to her, like daylight streaming through the elevated tracks down to the street, in glimpses of shadow and light that elude description, each had their history of hurt and loss and shocking change as emotionally devastating as her own, yet each also had their history of hopes and love and shocking stabilities. In each face she saw a piece of another, and in each she saw a piece of herself, and no longer did she feel quite alone.

Holding Mimi, looking across the room at Fran, who watched her with a matronly stoicism, as the elevated train rumbled overhead so the building shook and the walls rattled, Eve felt a part of that mysterious realm of the human race which suffered the travesties of pain, and loss, and had yet survived.

She kissed Mimi and with her hands signed across the child's back——We'll make it all right.

• • •

Napoleon was having his morning coffee with the first hit of sunlight when a neighbor called. He rushed downstairs in his pajamas with Queenie leaning out the upstairs window to try and see the offense for herself.

Sometime during the night the whole first floor of the Dores' house had been graffitied. The letters, B.Lo, in nasty black acrylic, the period sprayed in a hard red to match the color of blood. Even from jail Mimi's father, Bobby Lopez, was sending the Dores a message he was yet to be dealt with.

Eve came by to see later. It was a pretty imposing sight. They'd run the letters right up the windows, and curved them across the doorway. It was some no holds barred trashing.

Queenie was none too happy as she cleaned the mess away while fielding questions from her neighbors. Strangers happening to pass couldn't take their eyes off the mess and just shook their heads with a "what's the city coming to" look.

There was a girl talking to Queenie who Eve had noticed on the block once or twice before checking her out. Queenie was in the process of bringing her over to Eve. The girl, Natalie Batchelor, didn't look any too excited about the prospect.

It was explained to Eve that Natalie was studying journalism at City College. She wanted to be a reporter, or a magazine writer. Queenie then used sign and told Eve——Natalie is Charlie's old girlfriend.

A neighbor called out to Queenie and unexpectedly the two girls were left there, locked in their private silences.

"I don't speak sign," said Natalie. Which was already plainly obvious.

Eve took out a note pad and wrote: **I don't speak…period. Sorry.**

The moment grew decidedly more uncomfortable. Natalie had an urge to be nasty. She'd sure rehearsed enough little heart daggers to lay on Eve. But it wasn't in her when she got the chance.

"Queenie signed something to you. What was it?"

Eve had a problematic moment, then wrote: **Said you HAD BEEN Charlie's girlfriend.**

The "had been" in capital letters.

Natalie looked painfully hurt over the situation. She started to walk away, decided against it, came out with, "I'm angry at you and jealous. Though I haven't any right to be. Then I get it in my head that you're deaf, and I'm conflicted about being angry and jealous because I'm treating you like someone handicapped instead of just another girl. When I work past that, where am I? I'm back to being angry and jealous. I'm totally fucked and you know what's most fucked of all? You look like a decent person. And even that makes me angry and jealous."

CHAPTER 82

THE MOMENT WAS SUPREMELY SIMPLE. Romain's few possessions from the apartment, a suitcase and box worth, were in the dimly lit hallway at the bottom of the stairwell.

Stepping closer, his eyes slitting together, he saw a note and photograph on top of the open box. He grabbed at them. He hadn't realized they'd been stapled to his nicely folded sport coat.

Riding a coke fever, he tore the note and photograph from the coat. The note read:

> I am eighteen today. Have the legal right to tell you to get the fuck out
> of my life.

He crumpled the note and threw it on the floor. The photograph was another of Clarissa to add to that long lineup of silent assaults.

He tried to stand outside himself for a moment. Not to be Romain, the photograph not to be of his murdered wife, the note not to be from his vengeful, cunt daughter. But inside, where the gun goes off before you even pull the trigger, handfuls of hatred were having their way.

And the coke didn't help either. It only fueled all that brain fire that drove him, in diminishing seconds, to act on sheer impulse and blow off all rational life signals.

He started to scream in the hallway, his voice a white fit. He thrust at the air with his arm, but he was alone in that empty hallway. And it wrenched at him all the more.

Coke fever, like kid fever, fires emotions that need to be answered *now*. Satisfied now. Whether it's hate, hunger, sex, desire, drugs, or just plain vengeance. Damnations came out of him in a torrent as he headed for the darkroom.

He almost tore the door off. Photos on the wall were ripped away. Others in stacks were dumped on the first. He was building a pyre of photographs on the workbench. He'd burn the fucking joint to the ground if that's what it took.

With only a moonslit of light from the hall he moved clumsily. There wasn't enough room for such rage. He knocked over bottles and cans, smashed the enlarger, rolls of film wheeled out everywhere with a swipe of his arm. He flung a timer clock, its black face and white numbers shattering. A developing tray full of liquid spilled on his pants which only infuriated him all the more.

He took out his lighter, thumb-flicked up the flame and put it to the photos.

There was an instantaneous sunburst up his hands.

It happened so fast he felt he'd been sprayed with something cold till he got a smell of incendiaried flesh in his nostrils. The nerve endings inside his brain were suddenly on fire.

His whole body wrenched backwards out the door. From fingertips to wrist he was seared to the bone. His hands were a spectacle of char and smoke as he stumbled out into the dark empty alley. He scrabbled at the air, clutched at the air. He tried for the street, balled up in agony and buckling at the knees.

• • •

In his rage Romain had spilled a highly flammable can of film cleaner. Witnesses on the street had called an ambulance. When Eve and Fran got home they found the apartment door open and the darkroom practically ruined. A neighbor told Fran that the man who lived in her building was taken to the burn center at Columbia Presbyterian. Fran and Eve went to the hospital to find out what the hell had happened, on the chance it could mean trouble for them. At the hospital the doctors informed them Romain would live, but they weren't sure how much use of his hands he would ever get back.

People lined the walls of the hallways waiting for treatment. Some stood, some sat on chairs, some were on gurneys or in cribs, some even lay on the floor. It was like a battlefield hospital for the indigent and the stricken. For any of these, for the least of these, Eve wished for more than she did for her father. And the guilt she felt for that feeling… she fought against it with a vengeance.

Fran was asked by the doctor, "What kind of work does he do?"

"Work?"

"Yes. Does Mr. Leone use his hands a lot?"

"Hands? Sort of," she said. "He robs people's souls. Until tonight, anyway."

• • •

Whatever happened to Romain and his polluted soul after he got out of the hospital, they had no idea. They changed locks, put up an iron grated door; the windows were already barred.

All that nervous expectation that he'd show up again with an arsenal of hate, came to nothing.

Chapter 83

THE PACKAGE CAME TO THE CANDY STORE unannounced, weeks after Eve's birthday. She opened the package with a carefully reckless abandon. Inside was a box with Vietnamese writing on it. Within the box was a card atop newspapers used for stuffing.

The card read:

> *Eve—*
>
> *Know this Vietnamese guy who owns a leather goods shop. He's some artist, really. I think he's a closet Cong but he sucks down American beer like those degenerates in the bar on Bruckner Blvd., the one where they left the guy unconscious in a chair by the front door and put a crown on his head.*
>
> *Anyway, I had him make you something to go with your pillow. Hope you like it. Hell, hope it gets to you on time!!!*
>
> *Remember, the Armed Services are famous for their three levels of efficiency: Fucked—Very Fucked—and Completely Fucked.*
>
> *Everything is bad over here. But I'm sure the news tells you that. The place is starting to remind me of the Bronx.*
>
> *I-L-Y*
>
>   *Charlie*
>
> *P.S.*
>
> *Jailgirl —*
> *Don't know if I love you more than I miss you, or miss you more than I love you.*
>
>   *Stew*

Beneath the newspaper wrapping, Eve discovered a black leather shoulder bag about the same size and design as her own as Charlie had sketched it for the artist from memory.

Inside were slants of leather for storage. Part being for her girl things and part for her camera, flash and film. It was much more organized and practical and sturdy than her own.

But what made it special, what made it hers was the aesthetic facsimile of a flag that had been designed in colored leathers on the front and back of the bag. Not too big, not too small, and shaped like the lens of a camera or the eye on the back of a dollar bill, but instead of a pupil there was a single white star looking out from an eyelet of blue and red striping.

It was a cool night and Eve put on her rummage store blue overcoat and beret, and took the new shoulder bag for a walk.

She checked herself out in passing windows. An image shining back for seconds as a glimpse of the woman she would become.

Tonight, she thought, I even wear the shadows well.

• • •

Eve had taken so many stills for the school that word had spread, and she started getting requests from deaf organizations when they needed someone to photograph an event or gathering.

Eve collected small fees for these gigs, which was a dream hit, but she got more than that out of them. She did the necessary group shots and candids, but she always managed to quietly catch whatever else her eye happened on, and over time she accumulated this rich visual dialectic of the deaf life in the city. Moments signed and sealed with her own unique personality.

• • •

Eve took Mimi to school 'most every day. Who would have guessed, it was like having a kid sister. Someone you got to watch over, run interference for, protect.

And for Mimi, being the runt in her class, and having this guardian angel sister figure with a rep, who you could lock into when you started feeling overwhelmed or exiled from everything, helped keep her seriously grounded after her own mother's death.

Sometimes Eve's classmates would throw her a little shit and they'd salute her, which was their nasty vamp on the sign for 'bastard'. Meaning, of course, that Mimi was her illegitimate daughter.

They had no idea every time they ran that trip past Eve she had this quiet little moment of personal delight.

A DEVIL AND A GHOST

CHAPTER 84

EVE AND MIMI WERE WALKING on 158th Street just a few blocks from the Dores' when a ratted-out old Comet pulled up alongside them doing the slow crawl.

There was a couple of Latins in the car. Young. The boy in the shotgun seat was wearing a slouch hat. The one in the back with his head and shoulders draped out the open window had ringed fingers and was wearing a bandanna.

They had all that bad attitude going for them. Streetwise. Streettough. "Hey…you Mimi Velez? Hey…you Bobby Lopez's daughter?"

There was a lot of sunlight glinting off the car and the way everything was moving, it was tough for Eve to read their lips. She asked Mimi, did she know what they said? When Mimi explained, Eve took the girl's hand and made sure she was between Mimi and the car.

They kept hounding out at Mimi, "You…you. You Mimi Velez? We know you're Mimi Velez."

Eve waved to blow them off, and the one with the bandanna shot back, "What are you, the niggers' maid, or what?"

Mimi yelled out, "Don't call them that."

Eve kissed her fingers and then torched them across her ass and the next thing a wave of bottles were flung at her.

Eve covered Mimi as the bottles shattered on the sidewalk and the wall behind them. A man walking into a barbershop was hit by a starburst of glass. He chased out into the street after the Comet trying to get the plate number as it sped down 158th then burned the light wheeling into Jackson Avenue.

Eve and Mimi were unhurt. The man got half a dozen glass cuts and nothing for his effort.

• • •

Queenie put up a front that everything was all right. After all, she and Napoleon had survived some of the worst that racism had to offer.

But the late night calls. The covert nigger warnings with their Spanish accent. And the Latin kids in that car throwing the bottles. It made her begin to hate Spanish people, all Spanish people, even benign strangers in shop lines and at bus stands.

She talked about it only with Fran. Napoleon wanted to get a gun. The fact they'd come to this, even as a thought, was its own unvoiceable tragedy.

Queenie was afraid. She wasn't sure if it was because she was getting older and felt mortality more—Queenie was well into her fifties. Or because she saw the Bronx itself becoming a breeding ground of violence, already beyond the cusp of getting just plain out bad. A place where a part of you had to always keep an eye out for trouble. There was something inherent and absolute about the feeling.

"He blames us for what happened to Mimi's mother," Queenie said, as she sat at Fran's dining room table.

"'They pride themselves on their ovens and their smokestacks.' That was a phrase of my mother's," said Fran.

"I don't understand."

"My mother meant the Nazis, of course. Drug dealers. They are the same kind of men as the Nazis. Or, as in your own life, the Ku Klux Klan, no different. I saw it in Eve's father.

"The worst part, they are weak men. And weakness in men tends to make them more hateful, more demanding, more treacherous, more in need of power, control, money. It's what makes them more violent. Their weakness insures it, demands it, feeds on it, cannot exist without it."

"He's not getting her back."

"When is he out of prison?"

"I don't know."

Fran pushed her coffee cup aside and stood. She went to the closet, leaving Queenie at the dining room table. Fran came back with a shoe box. From the shoe box she took something wrapped in flannel. She set it on the table. It was the gun Romain had stolen from the casket a lifetime ago.

"They're not nearly as frightening as you think."

Queenie stared at the gun, her eyes under the shadow of all she felt.

CHAPTER 85

ST. JOSEPH'S HAD A HUGE Halloween night costume party at the school for the students, their parents and other invited guests. They set up a haunted house on the playground lot, with tunnels constructed of black tarp, which smoke machines made all the more creepy. It was a hobgoblin's nightmare of spider webs and hung ghoul dummies and teachers done up in hideous masks ready to lurch from hidden corners.

Eve was in a black body stocking, black motorcycle boots and mask. Her only true concession to a costume was the devil's tail she'd made from a frayed whip. Mimi was done up like Tinkerbell. That begged for costume had taken Fran and Queenie untold hours, and they both privately hoped Halloween didn't come around for another five years.

It was a cool night and the lights strung across the school lot blew about vividly. It was a wild array of piecemeal moments that Eve invisibly went about capturing.

A huge ghost rose up among a swirl of small children. It moved with half wicked gesticulating hands and stalked after the costumed little ones. Eve followed the chase when suddenly the ghost turned on Eve and pointed at her while she was photographing.

It was like a moment out of Dickens where the Spirit of Christmas Future points Scrooge toward some fearful unknown.

The ghost began to move through the crowd motioning for Eve to follow. She half smiled a no. At the entrance to the haunted house it beckoned slowly then passed under a sign that read: ENTER AT YOUR OWN RISK. Eve knew she was being worked.

It was like the coal black belly of a snake, with a labyrinth of passageways, some that led to dead ends, some that circled back upon themselves.

Eve made her way along. She swiped at spider webs that blocked her path. Kids with flashlights scooted past her then went down a hazy tunnel where their light beams butterflied along the black walls and then somewhere further on the tunnel turned and all was dark again.

She made her way alone down another passageway that came to a dead end where a bloody human head hung from a noose. She started back up from where she came. There was an ill at ease fun balancing weirdness, being unable to see through the smoke, and when she felt her way along to the spot where the tunnels converged, the ghost leaped out from a drifty gray alcove and grabbed her.

She gasped and tried to get loose. She was slapping at it for scaring the living hell out of her when she saw Charlie's green, green eyes through slits in the sheet.

She grabbed hold of his face to make sure, to get the sheet off and really see for sure. They were pouring out affection, kissing, he was trying to explain he'd gotten out two weeks early and wanted to surprise everyone, but when he'd arrived home no one was there so he went to Natalie's folks who told him about tonight. That's when he got the ghost idea.

——Your folks don't know you're here?

He was grinning.

A wave of costumed gobbledy-gooks squeezed and swarmed past them raising holy hell, when Charlie said, "I never made it with a devil."

She leaned up and bit his ear. ——I never made it with a ghost.

THE RAT AT THE
BREAKFAST TABLE

CHAPTER 86

THOSE FIRST MONTHS CAPTURED were the frosty breadth of something beautiful. Even the slush-wet days of a Bronx winter were every shade of wonderful.

Charlie practically lived downstairs with Eve. And Fran saw the child had a real chance at happiness, at not suffering the same kind of broken loneliness that Fran or Clarissa had.

In January Charlie went back to City College for his master's. His dream was to teach at St. Joseph's. As Eve was graduating in the spring, Fran wanted Eve to go to college and study photography. Eve wasn't having it.

No matter how Fran, or Charlie for that matter, tried to convince and cajole, Eve had that guinea streak of self-determination. She was steadfast in going it her way.

"Is that the real reason you don't want to go to school," Fran asked. "Or is it you feel you wouldn't be accepted because you are deaf?"

——A little of both, Eve admitted honestly.

Inside her, the fact Eve was deaf, made succeeding on her own terms more mandatory. It was as if the outside world had a part of Romain in it.

• • •

The Dores had changed their phone numbers, and since Charlie returned things had gone silent. Even Napoleon's print business wasn't getting any more harassing calls. There was no more spray paint slash and burn defacement, no more slow cruising prowls, no more flung bottles.

The Dores were beginning to feel Lopez had turned all that bad attitude to some other enterprise. Maybe it was because Charlie was back.

Fran wasn't so sure. Romain had done this same kind of about-face with Clarissa. Dropping underground as a matter of personal survival.

Fran and Charlie were alone in her kitchen knocking back a couple of beers. Fran asked Charlie when Bobby Lopez was due for parole. Charlie had heard around the spring. He understood where she was going with this. Maybe B.Lo was just making quiet time while it edged up to his parole hearing. Nothing more was said about Lopez. It was one of those whispers you just tucked away and hoped ground zero never came to be.

Charlie had been around long enough to know about Fran's scar, and what had happened when the ugliness came on. He'd never seen it, it was all just secondhand.

"You don't look too good," he said.

The ugliness *was* coming on. Fran scornfully poured a full glass of scotch.

"Can I do anything?" he asked.

She patted his shoulder as she walked past. He was honest and kind and Fran was goddamn glad Charlie was in Eve's life. Cramped up bad and starting to bleed Fran headed for the back rooms. "Just take care of my girl if I should suddenly drop fuckin' dead."

To Charlie, whatever the flaws and excesses of that woman, you were never unsure who she was.

Fran stopped at the kitchen door, "Anything you need, you know… anything."

• • •

It was a record day for heat when B.Lo stepped back into the world. Two of his boys picked him up in that hulked out mess of a Comet.

The ride back was bad, the air conditioning being strictly DOA. Driving the streets of Spanish Harlem Lopez got caught up on all the recent dirt. Who'd OD'd, who'd been put down by some pig, who was doin' time, which fool was shacked up with what cunt.

Bobby went to his mother's apartment on 116th Street. Seeing her baby, she was borderline histrionic. She couldn't take her hands off him.

While she made dinner, he showered and changed clothes, put on that gold crucifix with the diamond in it that he wore on this thin chain around his neck.

He ate fast then was outta there. Not just 'cause he was hungry to be back out on the street, but because he had all this pent-up rage. He'd had enough of white guards and nigger inmates. He'd had enough of being filed around like some dickless queer. He had his manhood back, and he wanted to start using it.

CHAPTER 87

BOBBY LOPEZ THOUGHT MIMI looked impressionable and eager. She was with a couple of classmates who were circled up around a bench on the school playground. They were half talking, half signing.

When Mimi first saw him, she wasn't sure. He was there at the fence, his fingers hooked into the chain links. Her heart had started to race.

When she got close enough he talked to her in Spanish. Asked if she could hear and understand. She nodded. He was a collection of images, memories. Sightbursts that caused these feelings to come over her that she couldn't understand. She was close enough to the fence so his fingers could reach through and brush the back of her hand.

Something caused her to pull away, but something else drew her back. He asked if he could come see her again. She didn't so much nod either way. He told her, "This is our secret, okay?"

She wasn't sure. That's how it started.

· · ·

It wasn't a lie, Mimi just didn't tell anybody. He showed up a few times at the school fence, then after that when she was walking home. He'd just be there, leaning against the hood of a parked car or cruising up alongside her all studded out and sharp faced.

She didn't understand why she kept the secret. She just felt she had to. Maybe it was because her hearing was getting progressively worse which meant hearing aids or complete deafness. She was scared, and she was angry this was happening. Maybe that's why she didn't tell anyone.

She would lie in bed with the sounds of the world flattening around her and she wanted to fight back. This was fighting back. For some reason, it was.

· · ·

Eve happened on them by accident. They were at the corner where Mimi caught the bus. Eve sensed it was Lopez right away. Something knifed through her with a primal fierceness. Never mind the fact that he and Mimi were wearing the same profile.

Eve watched from up the street, past a through line of pedestrians. She was trying to measure out what was going on. How it happened that it all came to be. She freaked a little seeing the way Lopez moved around his daughter with soft half touches. The little girl in Eve sent out all kinds of signals.

Eve didn't say anything that night. She asked Mimi about the day. No mention of her father. Eve started to check it out. A few days later he showed again as Mimi was leaving school. It confirmed what Eve already knew in her gut. He was making the play.

When Mimi saw Eve weaving her way up through the street traffic she got frightened. Lopez picked up on her stare. Turned. The chick approaching, he'd seen her before when he'd cruised the Dores'. This was the Jew cunt humping the Dores' half-breed.

———What you doing? Eve asked.

"Talking," said Mimi. She could hardly look Eve in the eye.

———You going to introduce me to your friend?

"This is…my father."

"Yeah, I'm Bobby Lopez." He was trying to be casual and cool. He was even thinking of putting his hand out to shake, but Eve blew him off with a stare.

———You sure you should be doing this?

Mimi hesitated.

———Just tell him we have to go home.

Lopez watched all this hand jive shit, looked at his daughter.

———Just tell him we have to go.

"What she telling you?"

———He only wants to fuck with your head.

"What she telling you?"

———He's not supposed to be around. So what does he do? Sneak around. It isn't right, it isn't good.

"Is she badmouthing me?"

———He's a drug dealer. He fucked up your own mother. That's why you were living in a car.

Lopez was staring at Eve. "If you're running me down, run me down to my face."

———He's why she is dead.

"I'm asking you to give me a break here."

———He's playing with your head. He's going to want you to carry drugs for him. So he doesn't go back to jail.

"I'm trying to connect with my daughter, man."

———I'm going home now. You think about it.

Eve started away.

——If he loves you so much, ask him why he has people flinging bottles at us and calling your folks names. Ask him.

CHAPTER 88

EVE SAID NOTHING, MIMI SAID NOTHING. Eve was sitting with her feet up on the card table in her living room. She was smoking, her back was sticky with sweat. Mimi sat across from her. The table had the dinner plates still on it.

Treading lightly, Mimi asked, "Why you so quiet?"

——You know why.

"I never lied."

——No.

"I just never said anything."

——Not a word…not a sign.

Mimi felt that remark all the way down into her shoes. She picked at her plate of half-finished food. "He said he was gonna be cool. You think he could be cool?"

Eve put her cigarette out in her plate, stuffed it right into what was left of the food with angry little turns.

Having Eve mad at her hurt. "Would it be alright, *if* he were cool?"

——Did you ask him what I said?

"No."

——You want to find out if he can be cool? You want to know?

• • •

The Dores filed a complaint with the social worker. Bobby Lopez's parole officer made it clear, dead-on fuckin' clear, that he was to stay as far away from that kid as Shea was from Yankee Stadium.

Bobby was sitting at the breakfast table. The morning sun was already hot along the sill. His mother wanted to make something for him to eat. He preferred a Coke and a cigarette.

She knew the look, when the Bobby Lopez she'd birthed turned into the Bobby Lopez he'd become. She sat across from him. In these moments she talked only in Spanish and asked if he really wanted the girl, wanted to be a father, have all that responsibility.

"How would you feel, man, if something of yours had been taken and was being raised by spades? And who fucked us over but the spades?"

. . .

Bobby Lopez showed up at the Dores' on Sunday when everyone was there having dinner. He picked that time 'cause he had this antagonism in him that had festered like a wound, and he needed to feed that antagonism.

They saw him from the upstairs window. He was pacing the stoop. Napoleon went and got a bat from Charlie's closet, for a little show and tell.

Queenie ordered him to put the damn thing away. Mimi had started crying. Queenie wanted Charlie to go and see what this was about. She didn't ask Napoleon so much as demand that he stay where he was. Eve followed Charlie down to the street.

They all met up on the stoop. In the light of a doorway at dusk. A triangle of faces touched up with tension.

Charlie demanded, "What are you doing here?"

Lopez handed him an envelope. Charlie looked at it like it was covered with poison. "What is it?"

Lopez opened the envelope for him to see. There was money in it. Maybe a few hundred.

"What's that for?"

"For my daughter."

"Keep it."

"What? She could buy shit with it."

"We don't want your money like we don't want you defacing the house, making shitass calls, or throwing fuckin' bottles at my girlfriend and Mimi."

"I didn't do any of that."

"Go away, man, you're not supposed to be here."

"You guys are all working overtime to try and get me off the street."

"We just want you out of our lives."

"You come down on me like I'm nothing."

"We didn't come down on you at all...*yet.*"

"Like I'm not good enough."

"The system said you weren't good enough 'cause they busted you selling. 'Cause you fed your old lady smack and turned her into a junkie with a half starved daughter."

"I didn't turn her into no junkie."

"And it was my folks who picked up the pieces."

"Give me that shit about the system. You were in the army."

"Just go on. I don't want to hear this."

"Who brings junk into the country? I see the news. They ship it in body bags from Vietnam to feed the monster. And how do they get it in stir? It don't come with dinner. It's guards who sell. And where do the guards get it? From cops in the street who pop me so they can score."

While he was talking, Eve had started in signing to Charlie. That hand shit pissed Lopez off. He told Eve, "Why don't you go back to Yonkers? Don't they have some shit for you to do at the synagogue?"

Charlie looked at him like, what did you just say?

Lopez started down the stairs. As he did, he flung the envelope on the stoop.

Charlie kept asking, "What did you say?"

Lopez walked, leaving Charlie to have a private fit right there on the sidewalk.

Then, when he was most of the way down the block Lopez yelled back in Spanish, "You been a nigger for the system too long."

CHAPTER 89

EVE WAS TO MEET CHARLIE over by Fordham University at a coffeehouse with the slick name F-You. Eve was waiting when Natalie showed. They were both always distantly polite, so it didn't take too, too long to discover that Charlie had set it up to meet with them there separately at the same time. They were not exactly smiling when he sat down.

Once he got a little order, he explained. First off, he told Eve, "Natalie's got this editor over at *City Magazine* hyped on a story about the lives of people in a tenement. The down and dirty. It's outlined. But there's no money up front, it's a spec thing. 'Cause Natalie has zero track record, right?"

Natalie grimly agreed.

"Now, what does every article in *City Magazine* have going for it? Kick ass photos. But if they're not gonna pay Natalie, they sure won't pay a photographer.

"Article…photographs. Magazine that's interested. Now, while I go get us all some coffee, why don't you two girls get nice and comfortable and let those creative wheels start turning."

• • •

The building was on the southern tip of Mott Haven by the Harlem River Rail Yard. The place was a statement of brute grim. The building was three stories, the top floor had been abandoned because of fire. Nothing was ever repaired.

Natalie interviewed while Eve photographed. She took shots of families stacked up in rooms twelve foot square, kids brushing their teeth with tub water 'cause the sink was just rotting pipe stems that leaked, a hole so big in one apartment wall you could practically walk through it upright into the neighbor's.

During the whole process the Mott Haven of Eve's past, when Romain and Dominic used her as a front kept surfacing darkly. Her, with that little box camera taking pictures while they dealt their junk. The lamb as part of the never-ending slaughter.

When she looked over the photos taken at the apartment she was not satisfied. They did not convey the same level of exploitation and contradiction she had felt back then, the crucible moment of discovery that hits you with a blast of hot, filthy air like when the express crushes past in a subway tunnel.

Eve told Natalie she was going back. She would take her sleeping bag and camp out up on that third floor till she got something she felt right about. Natalie silently thought Eve was nuts.

Tired, unbathed, and getting plainly angry, Eve was finally called down to one of the apartments. On the kitchen floor lay a huge sewer rat the grandmother had beaten to death with a bat. Its blood had buttoned out into small pools on the ruined linoleum.

But what made the photo was the expressions on the children's faces sitting at the table behind the rat. They had just been served breakfast, and now they looked at either the rat or the camera. This disease-ridden thing on their kitchen floor carried no weight or meaning in their lives. The shock of it, of course, was in how much they'd already lost.

• • •

The photo didn't so much sell the article as make it too tempting to pass up. Eve had a glaring moment of accomplishment. She and Mimi went from newsstand to newsstand scooping up copies like crazed thieves. Every ten minutes she had to look at the magazine and shake her head in disbelief.

The editor of *City Magazine* wanted to meet Eve, as he was always in the market for potential new assignment photographers. Eve pulled a couple of all-nighters and with Fran's help put together a righteous portfolio.

But when the editor discovered she was deaf, he couldn't have been any more uncomfortably polite. He was deferential to the point of being almost demeaning, but no way he'd hire someone deaf. Not with all the fast give-and-go communication in the magazine business.

For a few days Eve had flirted with possibilities, then reality came calling. She felt a deeply resentful anger. Not at being deaf, but at being treated like someone who could not be counted on because they were deaf.

She realized, letting what she felt truly fill her, that some elemental rage at how she had been treated had been with her a long time. Maybe since her mother, maybe since always.

• • •

Eve and Charlie ate dinner at the card table in her living room studio. They ate by lights she'd set up around the room for pure ambiance. She sat in Charlie's lap afterwards, her arm around his shoulder.

He tried to console her, told her they were only just starting to climb the mountain. And she told him she wished, with almost magical intensity, she could sometimes talk so when they lay in the dark, she could tell him how happy he made her and how much she cared.

PLAYLAND

CHAPTER 90

BOBBY LOPEZ MUST HAVE BEEN hard wired in hell, there could be no other way of explaining it. He was not a junkie, so he did not have that junkie desperation. With him it was all the machismo of self-respect, power. A kind of warlock need for identity.

And that day at Playland, he was measuring out destiny. And he meant for Charlie and Eve to know it. It was a living moment for him, like in the movies he saw as a kid, when the Dago emperor stands up in the Coliseum at the end of a fight and signs thumbs-up or thumbs-down, and lives are saved or terminated. It was just that clear in his head, balance was not the key.

• • •

Charlie and Eve drove Mimi up to Playland 'cause Mimi was really down. Playland was an amusement park and boardwalk in Rye. It was pretty far up in Westchester but still attracted bus loads of poor from the city, especially the Bronx.

Mimi had had an eye checkup. It bore out what everyone including Mimi knew. She had to start wearing a hearing aid full time.

Mimi had reached the age of personal identity, when self-knowledge tells you that you are somehow separate from the world. Mimi did not want to be different. She did not want to go deaf.

A hearing aid meant not only were you different, but everyone knew what it was for and they treated you accordingly. Never mind it was not attractive to have those things wedged up in your ears, and she did not care what kind of rap the teachers at St. Joseph's gave her. They were not a turn on.

This was a place Eve knew too well. That moment when she had flung the camera aside and stormed off on her mother and Fran and went to Crotona Park. It was not only was recallable and remembered, it was still as real as it was raw.

Mimi's favorite ride was the Wild Mouse, which was a sort of roller coaster with these small two-seat cars done up like, what else, mice. It had some very nasty turns and dips, and word was a couple of cars had gone off the ratty wooden tracks and dropped two stories. There had been fatalities, but this only made the ride that much more exciting.

Bobby Lopez followed them up from the Bronx. He was watching, waiting for the right moment. Them doing this whole family trip pissed the living shit out of him. Like Mimi was theirs. The only thing that didn't piss him off was Eve's ass. He thought, to get her loaded, then do her like a Cuban. And everyone knew Cuban chicks got off having cock up their ass.

Charlie had gone to the head. Eve and Mimi were sitting on a bench by the Fun House. Eve was checking her camera 'cause she intended to get shots of them all in that maze of mirrors. Eve could see all those turns on the Wild Mouse had not done the trick. Mimi was struggling with a borderline sulk.

——It will be all right.

"I don't want to wear a hearing aid. I don't want to be different. I don't want to be deaf."

This was not a moment Eve was unprepared for. She went into her shoulder bag and took out an old magazine photo she safely kept in a cropped down folder. She had brought it along on purpose. She passed Mimi the photo.

——What is that?

Mimi looked at the photo, then stared at Eve like wasn't it obvious? "It's the Statue of Liberty."

——Is it a boy or a girl?

Mimi's face squinched up at the silliness of the question. "A girl."

——Could be any girl, right?

"Yeah." Then, smiling at her own cleverness, "Any real tall girl."

——Could be a girl who couldn't hear very well. Or a deaf girl, right?

"Yeah."

——It could even be you.

Eve saw Mimi's face momentarily click into the thoughts of possibility. Her head moved slightly as if leaning into notions, or maybe trying to get clear of her own defenses. Then Eve saw it all just shut off and the face slip back into its sulk.

"I'll tell you one thing," said Mimi, handing Eve back the photo. "I don't see her wearing a hearing aid."

Eve tried not to smile at the cut. Mimi pulled her legs up on the bench and crossed them Indian style. She poked at her sandals indifferently.

"I don't want a hearing aid. I don't want to go deaf. I don't want to be different."

——What do you want?

"I want to be able to keep hearing. I want to be like you."

That face, poised as it was toward Eve's, with so many overlapping emotions that Eve could touch, they were *that* palpable. Something went through Eve akin to a welling breath, that is the only way she could describe it. Eve stroked Mimi's hair, then told her:

——I don't know if you've noticed but I am deaf, and I am different. And if I had not been deaf, I would never have met Fran. I would never have been loved by her, taken care of by her. I would never have gone to St. Joseph's. So, I would never have been there with this camera to take your picture. I would have never met Charlie. I would never have been loved, I would never have been able to love you…I'd rather have all this and be deaf.

What she expressed so, with her hands and her heart, reached Mimi. Like some greater truth that pours out of itself, you can taste. It might be too overwhelming to take it all in at one time, but it will be there for you to drink in fits and starts when you are ready.

Mimi watched as Eve put away the photo. She leaned against Eve, and began to tenderly tug at Eve's shirt, to be close, to let her know she was there.

Mimi took to looking at children as they ran ahead of their parents, and squally groups of teenagers as they rushed from ride to ride. She listened hard, concentrating on the clicking wood and metal of the roller coaster cars just across the walkway, and the music from the merry-go-round, the girlish screams coming from the Boomerang, and all those explosions of noise from the arcade games. Sounds everywhere, attached to everything. Everything.

Mimi looked up at Eve, "Sounds…voices. Will I be able to remember them if I go deaf? Will I still be able to hear them in my head?"

The face was desperate for an answer, but Eve had only her honesty. ——I don't know. I never could hear, ever. Remember, I told you. I don't have any idea what sounds and voices are like.

This registered. More than anything Eve had said so far. Because Mimi realized that she'd already had much more than Eve. And it made Mimi hurt for Eve, even though all that beautiful universe of sounds and voices was slipping away from her.

"I'm sorry," said Mimi, "that you never did. It makes me sad. I wish I could give you some of my hearing just so you'd know. So we would know together. So you'd know how much I love you."

What Eve felt right then, this surge of emotion in its purest form, took her from when she was a little girl in that basement apartment to the bench at Playland, connecting all the chapters of her existence so they came together perfectly and spoke with one moment.

Silent, arm in arm, with sunshine and affection, they shared some immaculate and solitary kingdom, when who should come swaggering toward them from out of nowhere with a bandanna around his head and a teddy bear dangling from his hand.

"He's here," said Mimi, sitting up. "My daddy."

CHAPTER 91

BOBBY LOOKED SLEEK and even a little pumped. He was dressed down in that way that costs money. He had a new tattoo on his forearm—B.Lo—made up of all these intertwined black snakes eating their way through and out of a human skull.

"Imagine you here, and me," he said. "That's heavy. I was gonna bring this to you, baby."

He held out the bear. It was sweet and cuddly with big brown button eyes and a T-shirt that had printed on it: I LOVE PLAYLAND.

He handed it to Mimi, and she took it uncomfortably, yet—

He leaned down to kiss his daughter. At the same time, she pulled away, which he dealt with by taking her in his arms and whispering in Spanish what her mother had said to her when Mimi was small.

As he stood Lopez gave Eve a glancing look and he turned his head so Mimi couldn't see him mouth—Fuck you, Jew cunt.

He kind of flexed as he stood. There was a tension to him. Straight, proud, it bordered on the sexual. As if he were relating something personal about himself to be understood, and either feared or desired.

"Hey, maybe you'll let me take my baby on one of the rides. You like that? The Ferris Wheel." He pointed to it. "It's very cool up there. You can see all the way out. And the people..." He motioned with his hands. "They no bigger than dolls, than that bear."

"What's going on here?"

Lopez turned. Charlie stepped between him and the girls. Eve signed fast what had gone down. There was a clumsy interlude of seconds.

"Hey, I happen by. I see my daughter here, thought I could take her on one of the rides."

Charlie motioned for Eve and Mimi to get up. He told Lopez, "We got to get goin'."

"Hey, man. I just want to take my daughter on one of the rides."

Mimi had the bear.

"Yeah, well. That's not happenin'."

Lopez started to talk to Charlie in Spanish. Fast, clipped. There was no nuance to the body language. This was, I'm comin' right atchya, man.

Eve signed to Charlie they were going over to the Fun House.

Charlie nodded. "In a minute."

Lopez saw he was being blown off. He called to his daughter in Spanish. She half looked, half listened, half held the bear, was confused, frightened. Her little heart was beating fast.

"What's this bullshit about you just showing up?"

Lopez went right past the question. "Have her at my mother's house Friday night. We're gonna hang for the weekend."

"What did you do, follow us?"

"You heard me."

"Not happenin'."

"If it's too much for your candy asses, I'll come and pick her up."

"I'm outta here. I don't want trouble for Mimi's sake."

"You see the fuckin' film where that punk Kennedy got wasted?"

Charlie, who'd been walking away, stopped. "It's bad enough the shit you've done, but if you're threatening us—"

"You see the way his head flew outta the car after he got popped?"

• • •

The ride home was quiet. Mimi looked over her shoulder a couple of times thinking her father might be somewhere back in traffic.

"He followed us, didn't he?"

Eve and Charlie tried to remain a pocket of calm, for Mimi's sake.

Charlie was thinking: I enlisted, I ended up in a bullshit war, I survived, I came back with my head on straight, I try to make a normal life for myself, and punks like this get to walk the street and play out their foul-minded dramas. If only the son-of-a-bitch was a junkie and OD'd himself.

Came dusk, they were all up on Fran's roof. Charlie was barbecuing hamburgers and hot dogs while they discussed going to the police, or at least to Lopez's parole officer about the threat. If you could actually press it as a threat. But they weren't sure this wouldn't just make matters worse.

That's the fuck about these things when you're dealing with a suspicious presence, there's no textbooks for it. And even your basic issue street psychology can come up way short in understanding how far someone will go.

When the adults had a moment alone, Fran warned, "It wouldn't matter if he got her back. It's not about Mimi or her mother, anymore. If it ever was. This creature has found his personal enemy. As Eve's mother became a personal enemy for Romain, and like I was after that.

"And people, when they find their personal enemy have a self-absorbed need to keep them enemies. Whether it's a person, an idea, a lifestyle, a sex, a handicap, a city, a race, a religion, or the world.

"My father called it the black art of fulfillment, which is where people who are so devoured by inner emptiness, and so hungry to kill that emptiness, find their personal enemy, create one if they have to, so they can feed, off its insides. And the most frightening part is, the more they feed, the more hungry they grow."

Fran took a drink of scotch, a long Fran-like drink. And in the soft fall of evening, with the smoke of the grill all wind-caught between them, she finished her thought, "Believe me, I know this man. And I have the scars to prove it."

THE MUGGERS EXPRESS

CHAPTER 92

EVE AND FRAN WERE ALONE in the kitchen preparing a tray of plates and condiments so, they could all eat up on the roof.

It had been a long day of emotions that were connected in so many ways. Eve wanted to tell Fran about her conversation with Mimi. To share it with her, since so much of it was about all of them.

Eve watched Fran without her knowing. She saw time was having its way with her more quickly than it had a right to. Fran needed stronger glasses now. She had gotten thinner, had lost some of her strength. She walked sometimes with a slight hitch, thanks to that ruined trail of flesh they'd made of her insides. Even getting up had begun to hurt her more and more. It all spoke so much of giving and mortality.

Eve came up behind Fran as she was neatly arranging condiments on the tray. Eve slipped her arms around Fran and rested her head in the crease of Fran's neck. They remained like that with Fran reaching back and softly petting Eve's arms.

Eve wanted to immerse herself in the moment. To feel it in a way that would outrun anything time might have to say about it. Then Eve moved just a bit so she could sign——Do I tell you enough that I love you? Is there such a thing as enough? And that you are, now don't laugh, heroic to me.

For a few brief seconds, Fran kept arranging condiments, as if they needed it. Then Eve could feel Fran's body clutch a bit and her hands grabbed Eve's arms and held on tightly. And with eyes closed, Eve could feel the older woman beginning to cry ever so slightly. She could feel it coming from that place of soul she so wanted to touch and be touched by.

Then, with her ever caustic sense of humor, Fran signed——No pictures, please.

• • •

A funky dinner adorned by rooftops and skyline. The lantern on the table a single glowing centerpiece. It was the perfect night for heat lightning, but there was none. They all worked to make the evening fun, to get the thought of Bobby Lopez out of their minds.

Lying in the darkness, Eve and Charlie traced their fingers across the other's body. Their knowledge of each other had become a language all its own, something they felt even when the other wasn't there.

Charlie had pangs of jealousy that night because Eve bestowed so much affection on Mimi. At the same time it made him feel that much closer to Eve, and ashamed of being jealous. He imagined them having a baby, a rooftop of their own. He imagined a world where every day took on an elemental calmness that held fast against the dirty dreams around it. Something that made the streets of the Bronx you walked alive with presence and promise.

He told Eve all this later that night and she drew close to his mouth as if to taste every word.

"Your eyes are like rain clouds," he said.

——I'm afraid.

"Of B.Lo—pez!"

——Yes.

"I'll deal with him if it comes to that. I may deal with him before that."

——Don't.

He saw Eve was slightly freaked.

"Alright."

Nothing soothes a conversation like the touch of bodies. Eve wanted Charlie inside her in a way that blinded you with need, that somehow drew you deep into a state of possession, that disregarded thoughts, which would not disappear.

She wanted to make love this way because she felt, and she wouldn't tell this to Charlie directly, that no man could protect Mimi, or her, or Fran or Queenie. That it wasn't right to blame them for this, it wasn't their fault. But in her heart, how do you explain to someone you love, that the strongest person you have ever known is a woman? That it is with her you feel the most safe. How do you reach across a thought like that to this person so they are not hurt or offended, as you did not mean to hurt or offend.

In those hours of sleeplessness Eve wondered if she were different somehow from other girls, that way. Was it the peculiar happenstance of her own life? Or was it something more common than she suspected, something other women knew and felt, but kept silent about.

CHAPTER 93

CHARLIE AND HIS OLD MAN got the name of Bobby's parole officer and paid him a visit. Hit him with all the dirt. Lopez had already seen his parole officer and gave the story a slightly different twist. The parole officer, a meaty Irish son-of-a-bitch, had done this lousy gig long enough to know where the truth lay. For him every day was just another chapter in the crosstown wars. Bullshit heaped on bullshit that he needed to drink through or bang hookers to clear his mind. He wanted to torch the whole place, and every one of those bastards like Lopez. And you could fuck Miranda.

On the way out, the parole officer warned them, "There's a fucked neighborhood inside that kid's head, and you don't want to go in there alone."

Charlie, without telling anyone, did more than that. He went up to Spanish Harlem, to Lopez's house. He was carrying the flag of confrontation that day. But all he got was B.Lo's mother. A poor woman whose face showed fear and despair that some stranger—another stranger in an endless parade of strangers, mostly cops or nose-running junkies—came hunting out her kid. She couldn't hide her pain and anger any faster than she could get the goddamn door closed and bolted with Charlie yelling, "When will he be back?"

• • •

From school Charlie always got off the subway at Westchester and 161st Street. Spent and tired he was walking the platform to get to the stairs up to the street when he heard the name, Charlie, yelled out.

He looked back to see if someone was calling to him. Just the usual flow of bodies making their way home after the four-to-eleven shifts, and none paying particular interest in him.

Someone whistled. It sounded like it came from the uptown platform. Charlie looked across the tracks, scanned the few people waiting. Guess what, he got an eyeful of B.Lo, with his back leaning against a girder column. Extraordinarily calm and punked, Lopez did his hand up, aiming it gun-style.

"Is that meant for me?" Charlie yelled across the tracks. "You threatening me?"

"You come to my turf and shit on my mother. And you say I'm threatening you. That's total dick."

"No, man. That's your gig. I was coming to see you."

Lopez would have liked to put Charlie in the box right there. Do that spic, nigger, Jamaican, whatever he was. Jam every kind of bad business up his ass, stitch it, smoke it, make him cum-crawl like they do at Correctional, licking the shit right off the concrete floor.

"You didn't answer me. Is this another one of your threats?"

Passersby were cheating looks at the two young men, as if expecting something horrible and yet too entranced by the thought they might miss any of it.

"You didn't answer me, is this another of your threats?"

Oh yeah, Charlie was it. The one. The bones of the family. Something the niggers could hang their bullshit pride on, could make them feel less like niggers as they showed his picture around.

"Why don't you answer me, man?"

Lopez played the silent card. The I-know-what-you-want-me-to-say-but-I-ain't-fuckin'-buying-into-it-around-the-livin', especially your fuckin' brothers.

"You followin' me? Come on across and take me head on." Charlie was shouting now.

"Head on," said Lopez. "That's fuckin' A-1 right, boy."

From well back in the darkness of the tunnel an express was thundering toward the station and Charlie could feel its driving metal and rattling wheels.

Charlie wanted to jump the tracks and have at Mr. Prick B.Lo, 'cause he knew now there'd be no end to it otherwise. What Fran had said that night on the roof had hit home. And it made him feel mortal and vulnerable and he was extraordinarily angry that both emotions stuck with him like a low grade fever.

A wall of steel and windows rushed through the station. A strobe of graffiti and fluorescent lit empty stares, and this hot river of wind hurled at him so thick it almost tasted of iron and filth.

Charlie broke for the stairs. He was up and across the walkway halfbacking it to reach the uptown side of the station. He leapt the turnstile and took the stairs two and three at a time.

When he got to the platform Lopez was nowhere to be seen. Charlie walked the length of the platform looking, got halfway up the other stairs. Lopez was nowhere to be seen.

He came back the length of the platform, again looking to see if Lopez was hiding somewhere. A tall dude built like a ballplayer and wearing a janitor's outfit pointed at the tunnel. "The fuckin' Rican went down there."

Charlie looked toward the tunnel. A rush came over him like when he was back in 'Nam after the explosion and he had to drive a Jeep somewhere. A kind of uneasy nervousness you can live with, but who needs it.

"Fuck you," he shouted into the tunnel.

• • •

Charlie went up to the roof and smoked a joint. He wanted to call Eve, and if not tell her, at least burn off all that crackling rage inside him. But, of course, that was one of the few frustrating impossibilities in their relationship.

So, he got stoned and talked to her anyway, as if she were right there beside him. As a matter of birth and personal back story, Charlie had a deep need for connection that he felt at an almost shameful intensity. And his need to be loved…it seemed to ooze to the surface of his skin, he was so filled with it.

But he also wanted to be her protector, someone she could feel safe with.

• • •

Charlie was coming home from City College, riding the D-Train. The Muggers Express, as they called it. A graffitied hellhole where the denizens who threatened your safety rode free and clear and you had to worry if you'd be there when one of them decided to spit cum in the face of the world. Shit, some tagger had spray-painted on one of the subway cars, a shot Eve got…**Even Bonnie and Clyde won't ride this fuckin' train.**

The car Charlie was on that night was a metal netherworld of jive vandalism and tagged with an endless array of identity hunters. It had also been blasted by the slogan freaks…*FUCK ALL POLITICIANS…RAVAGE AND DECAY… AMERICA, THE SUCK QUEEN*…and a smiling poster of one of our city's finest in blue, only he was now sporting the body of a hermaphrodite and the head of his cock had a swastika tattooed on it.

That night on the car, there was the usual array of the dreary, exhausted and those that reeked of trouble. Charlie closed his eyes after doing a spot check of the riders. Whether he closed his eyes for a weary moment or longer, he never knew.

The bullets drove him right out of the seat. He'd been shot through the back of the head and neck from a platform at 125th Street, just as the train was pulling out.

His body landed upside-down in a heap against the empty seat across the aisle, his legs curled up over on top of him. An afterbirth of blood pooled out from his decimated brain while people ran from the car screaming as it gained speed on into the blackness. His textbooks and notes were scattered around him, there was blood and skull matter everywhere.

Two boys were spotted on the platform. Short, dark skinned. One had a slouch hat pulled low over his forehead, the other had a ski cap. The one with the ski cap had "scratch" on his face that approximated a beard.

From the descriptions they could have been high school slackers or street ghouls. They could have been gang punks trying to earn their colors. They could have been anybody from anywhere. Whoever they were, Charlie's murder wasn't about robbery, there hadn't been a confrontation.

PART THREE

A SHADOW ON THE
MAUSOLEUM WALL

CHAPTER 94

WHEN THE PHONE RANG that late at night Fran always felt it first in her heart and then at the front of her closed eyes. Napoleon told her in torn sobs what had happened.

How long Fran stood in the dark at Eve's bedroom door, it would never be long enough. *I was on the other side of that door once*, Fran thought, *watching blood melt in the German snow.*

Fran sat on the edge of the bed carefully and in pain. Her movements awoke Eve. Groggy, she saw Fran's dire hawkish face by the light of the bed stand. There is no hiding that kind of news.

Fran went to speak but her hands, quivering with trepidation, and breaking down word by word, that single image Eve would see in the far reaches of forever.

Eve ran all the way to Charlie's house with the sun coming up over the East River and the smells of night fading against the first waves of bus exhaust and heat.

As Eve ran along the Boston Road, she cried so inconsolably that women stepping into buses on their way to work felt compelled to stop and stare, and men pulling back the iron grating that protected their storefronts were possessed by a need to look and keep looking.

Even though it was something they'd seen before, the fleeting image of someone on the run and suffering, it brought out all the lurking fears people try to arm themselves against with a stubborn will, that the pained human form they were witnessing would never, ever be them.

• • •

Napoleon's house was a hive of relatives and investigators, with friends coming and going, neighbors offering condolences and support. Natalie was there, working the phone, trying to find out about any new leads on the murder.

Bobby Lopez was brought in for questioning. The filthy little bastard had an armload of witnesses for that night 'cause he was with his mother at the Christus Church storefront by Jefferson Park. Seems a little Jesus goes a fuckin' long way at offering up an alibi.

While they prepared for Charlie's wake and the demons that come with death, a composite of the suspects had been put together by eyewitnesses in the subway. When asked if he recognized either, Bobby Lopez was coolly certain he hadn't.

But his mother knew different, one she'd seen a week before by a small bodega where junkies scored. The one with the ski cap and shit for a beard, him.

But even though Bobby had gone against all her beliefs, he was her son and there was a part of her that had never let go of the little boy she'd fed on the fire escape with money gotten from selling herself.

After viewing the drawings and denying she'd seen either one, Bobby's mother looked away, knowing what she'd done was now in God's hands.

· · ·

The wake was packed with friends of the family since Charlie's grade school days. They shared their grief and they shared their shock, they shared their memories and their rage, but most importantly they shared the precious gift of themselves. It was that human quality used to rally against atrocity.

Charlie was laid out in the same room at the Walter B. Cooke Funeral Home as had been Mimi's mother. It was a macabre coincidence the family never once mentioned among themselves.

Above the casket was that crucifix on the wall Eve watched again. It trembled as the train went by on the elevated. The very same train where only stations away a dream had been murdered with unforgiving horror.

When it was Eve's turn to kiss Charlie goodbye before they closed the casket for eternity, she looked down at what had once been him. The wounds to the back of the head had been cosmetically dressed as best they could. The changes to his face were subtle, but dramatic.

In death, people look so false. The mystery of them stolen, their sweetness, the touched stare, the way their mouths reflected in smile. Now gone. The knowledge of that, as it sweeps through, seems to empty you of everything you are and you are certain you will never be again, and you are gripped in a pain that says this moment will last longer than forever could ever hope to be.

She touched his folded hands, then against his chest where his heart had been, she signed I-L-Y.

CHAPTER 95

CHARLIE WAS TO BE BURIED at St. Raymond's Cemetery. It was a short but hard ride up Westchester Avenue. for that cortege of vehicles because the Bronx streets there were alive with memories of a lost one.

Everyone felt it. It was as if they were being spied upon by the past, and at any moment Charlie would just appear on a street corner, or in front of a movie theatre, or coming out of a luncheonette, all the places he'd wandered on the path of growing up.

Like a moment outside the moment, they'd see him in the slatted light coming down through the elevated tracks, ethereal and gritty, and he'd just appear suddenly, delivering that smile of his and they'd see him waving and realize it had all been just an awful mistake and he'd be back with them, in a weightless moment of relief and joy.

The procession had to go past St. Joseph's School, and the inside of that lead car became a somber trap because the silent brick edifice echoed with their lives.

Napoleon broke down crying. "He would have been teaching there in a year or two." His hand pointed ragefully. "He would have been a good teacher." It was too hard for him to bear. He was in the presence of the void as they slowly proceeded on past the school. "God fuckin' damn it." His fist hit against his leg. "Our boy's been murdered."

It took Queenie and Fran to help him out of the car and to the grave site.

• • •

At grave side Eve didn't read the pastor's lips. Words were useless. And God never seemed so far off, so much just hearsay.

Her deafness connected her and distanced her simultaneously. She felt it as a living experience intensified by some heightened level of awareness.

She looked at the breadth of strained faces around her, watched the tears where they left damp traces. This was a true glimpse into the kingdom of our worlds.

She felt Charlie's loss so intensely, a strain of anxiety began to overwhelm her. Something akin to a disease. Her own mother's death loomed suddenly large. And her father, who had robbed the caskets of this cemetery all those years ago, was a haunting and polluted presence in the brittle shadow of summer's trees, watching her.

Eve could not breathe, but she did not move. She began to feel lightheaded, as if there were not a drop of air left in the Bronx sky. It was like suffering some kind of strangling death.

She reached into her shoulder bag, the one she would forever carry. Her hand squeezed around the camera. She wanted to take a photograph, needed to take a photograph. She had refrained at the wake out of respect for the others, but she was compelled to frame this moment so she could somehow deal with it herself. To give herself a chance of surviving it by standing back. To find not only separation and oneness in a decisive moment, but also to somehow transcend that moment in doing so. To make it more than just another death in the annals of time. She wanted to create something that would stand in for time, the time she and Charlie would never have together, and to make it something others could feel and share, and in so doing a little bit of herself and Charlie would be inseparable as art itself.

· · ·

At the end of the service, as people began to collect themselves, Napoleon was alone with Queenie and Fran. A dark exhaustion had settled in. He was staring at the casket in its final hours of a last daylight. He whispered, "If the police don't get him, I should kill him myself. Or have him killed."

His wife grabbed him by the arm to hush him. She looked to see if anyone but Fran had overheard.

"He didn't mean it," she said. "Tell Fran you didn't mean it. It's wrong."

"I meant it."

"There might be other ways," said Fran.

PLEASE, HELP US
FIND A MURDERER

Chapter 96

NATALIE HAD NOTICED the conversation had caused very troubling expressions and a kind of conspiratorial closeness between the three of them. She wondered if Eve, who was standing near her and watching, had read their lips.

"What did they say?"

Eve slipped Mimi her shoulder bag, checked her camera. She gave Natalie the right hand pressed to the palm of the left and pivoting.

Natalie had picked up enough basics along the way. "All right…later."

• • •

Eve slipped back and away from the others until she was seamlessly unnoticed. She watched, moving, trying to discover some essence, some window into that drenched morning of pain.

People had begun to drift back to their cars. Small handheld groupings, the silent black of their clothes against the parched grass of summer, the gray of the headstones.

Eve felt this stress that she would fail herself, fail Charlie, fail the moment. And struggling, it came to her, that somehow Charlie's death was partly her fault, that she should have known more, armed as she was with her own life.

And those years when she was a little girl being used, and failing to understand, to see, and hurting because she believed it could probably not have happened if she had not been deaf reemerged and merged with now. And as life took on this indiscriminate vastness like the streets of the Bronx before she could read and understand, a photograph just appeared.

Napoleon and Queenie had moved off by themselves as if they needed some last minute privacy before the final painful trip home. They had stopped near the road, which fell away out of sight. But something was coming up that road, something coming toward them causing this human shadow to rise up huge across the wall of a mausoleum beside them.

It was something they didn't notice, had no idea was there. They were tucked into each other's arms and blind to anything but their shared grief.

And that shadow, it stilled, as if whoever was on that road had stopped. And so it loomed there high above them, and one could imagine it was the ghost of their departed son sharing this sad and melancholy goodbye. Or it could portray some portent of the future watching with dark and quiet warning.

Eve felt the moment pull her toward it, as if she were helpless against its power.

• • •

In the Dores' dining room that night, Fran's plan was executed. A reward for information leading to the murderers of Charlie Dore was sent to *The Daily News* to be held there. Natalie wrote up a story and presented it to the editors. It spoke of Charlie's life, the neighborhood, the Bronx, and the murder. It included Eve's photograph of him in his uniform that day he got into a cab on the way to serve his country. The composite drawing of the suspects was included.

The story was printed in the Bronx section of *The Daily News*. They loved that kind of emotional and violent tale so they played it up. All the locals reprinted it after that; *The Bronx Press Review, The Islander, The Bronx Times Reporter.*

• • •

They had all worked with a savage haste and dedication to see it done, but just to make sure that on those streets of Spanish Harlem everyone knew, Eve and Natalie took knapsacks of wanted posters that Napoleon had printed up in his shop and got on the subway heading to Manhattan.

And these were not just cheap-ass posters either. These were hardcore, with a composite of the suspects and in blood red blood letters, PLEASE HELP US FIND THE KILLER, in both English and Spanish.

The reward was for fifteen thousand dollars. Half put up by the Dores, half by Fran. Real money if you're broke and down, real money if you're strung out, real money if you're desperate.

Natalie warned them, "The junkies will be on us like roaches. And so will half the city. Every freak—"

"It takes just one," said Fran.

Eve and Natalie started at the subway on 116th Street and worked their way south. They stapled posters up everywhere. Every wall they could find. They hit the groceries and liquor stores, the pool halls and upholsterers, the firehouse. They even had smaller handbills they passed out or stuck in the windshield wipers of parked cars.

All the time they were getting closer and closer to Bobby Lopez's apartment, and then Natalie realized that's where Eve was taking them.

Chapter 97

ON LOPEZ'S BLOCK EVERYONE got a handbill stuffed at them. They closed in on the building that Fran had driven them past days before, so they knew exactly where he lived.

When Eve started up the steps of the building Natalie grabbed hold of her. Natalie was scared and wanted to make sure, 'cause they were already getting some pretty hard-and-fast looks from the locals. But Eve, in her head, she was already inside that building and knocking on B.Lo's door, and all she needed was a handful more steps to catch up.

The inside of the building showed the usual signs of vandalism and decay. Part of one wall had been torn out, and you could see right into the bracings where all kinds of graffiti and lewd drawings had been spray-painted. The first floor was dark, like some gloomy lunar landscape.

Natalie started slipping handbills into the ratted out mailbox slots. Eve noticed a girl at the top of the first floor landing nursing her baby. She couldn't have been more than fourteen.

Eve started going from door to door looking for which one was Lopez's. They knew from the time Charlie went to the Lopezes' apartment that his mother lived on the first floor. A couple of kids came down the stairs. Natalie gave them a handbill. They checked it out and tore ass back where they'd come from.

By then Eve had found it. The apartment door was back at the end of a thin hallway. She pointed. They were getting to it now, and Eve could feel all this rage coming up from her insides.

Without hesitating Eve went down that short hallway and knocked on Lopez's door. Natalie was right behind her. They got no answer. Natalie took a turn at knocking, this time longer and louder. No answer. Natalie went so far as to cup her hand against the door and try to hear if someone was in there.

Nothing. Just that vacant emptiness of space. So Eve slipped a handbill under the door. She even wedged one between the doorknob and wall.

They were just starting back up the hallway, when Bobby cruised through the front door of the building with his hands puffed up in his pockets and a cigarette dangling out of his mouth.

He recognized Eve right away. And there they all were, stopped short in ten square feet of gloom. There was nothing abstract about his stare. He looked ambushed and trying to figure out what it all meant.

He took the cigarette out of his mouth. "The Jew cunt got a soul sister now.

Why you here, man?"

Eve went over and dropped a handbill on him. He took one look at it and you could see the firestorm coming. This was a street ugly punk who knew his territory was being invaded by two skank bitches. And all that self-imposed macho was gonna have to deal.

"What's this supposed to mean?"

——You know.

Lopez swatted at Eve's hands. "I don't understand that deaf shit. Why you here?"

She pointed to the handbill and she pointed at him.

"In the whole city you come to this block. To this building. You trying to put some shit on me?"

He flung the handbill at her and she took another and shoved it at him. He started to scream at her in Spanish. She responded by signing furiously. She was calling him murderer, and to come on and fight her.

——Come on, you gutless shit, kill me right here.

He couldn't underfuckinstand a word, but the hate flying off those fingers came through loud and clear and he pressed toward her.

Eve remembered that night with Fran and her father at the bottom of the stairwell. How Fran had taken Romain's verbal assault straight. Never once backing away or down. Eve had replayed that tape just like a mantra, knowing she might be able to make this moment happen.

Natalie was shouting, "You touch her and you'll end up going to jail." The girl at the top of the stairs had pulled the baby from her breast and run off. The kids had come back and were huddled on the steps, watching through the railing with that hideous excitement something bad was gonna go down and they'd be there to witness it.

People had come out into the hall. Some to get a look, some to complain, before they hid back behind locked doors. One threatened, "I call policia...you don't get out building!" And Natalie yelled back, "Call them, now! Now!!"

Eve kept shoving handbills at Bobby Lopezm and finally he just knocked them away. He got most of the stack, but the rest she flung in his face. That's when he lost it, that's when the need to just obliterate took hold.

He drove into Eve. Lopez wasn't big, he was maybe five foot nine and lean. Eve was almost as tall, but a woman carrying that much hate coming with teeth bared and kicking was about all he could handle.

Natalie just froze and all she could manage was yelling for help, for someone to call the police. She watched the fight from that corner inside herself where you are just utterly incapable of action.

They were on the hallway floor. A caduceus of arms and legs locked in this violent insurrection. And what made the fight more grisly and forbidding was because it was between a man and a woman.

Then it was over. Two men had stormed out of an upstairs apartment. They were Puerto Ricans in their forties. Guys with some weight and heft to them. Who probably didn't need shit cops around or wanted this crap to be settled somewhere away from their own kids.

THE DECISIVE MOMENT

CHAPTER 98

EVE AND NATALIE GOT OUT OF THERE in one piece. The two disagreeable
Puerto Ricans kept B.Lo in check with a few obscene remarks they would fuck
his drug peddling ass proper if he so much as moved. And those two, Lopez
knew them good, there was no safe conduct past that massive wall. They would
turn his prick and balls into a baby slot just as soon as look at him.

• • •

Eve and Natalie took the subway home. They sat shoulder to shoulder on a
corner bench. There were enough people on the train so there was no real sense
of privacy, or aloneness. Everyone seemed close enough to smell.

Natalie touched Eve's hand to get her attention. "Back there in the building.
What did you tell him…Lopez? What were you saying?"

Eve got out her pocket pad and wrote: **I was telling him to come on and
fight me. To come and**…There was hesitation…**try and kill me.**

As Natalie looked at what Eve had written she could see Eve's hands were
shaking so. And Eve, she stared at that note pad as if only now, seeing the words,
she was experiencing the shock of what had just happened.

Natalie touched Eve's hand to get her attention. "I'm not very strong, am I?"

Eve looked away for a moment and into the faces of strangers. She felt angry
that they had so much life ahead of them and Charlie had none. She looked back
at Natalie. What can you do in a situation like this, but accept reality. Otherwise
what's left, veined condemnation. For her, for yourself, the world at large.

Eve wrote: **We get braver as we go along. It's sort of like having a fever.
Fran told me that—I'm not smart enough to make it up.**

"I'm still sorry. I want to be more than…what I am."

In a show of affection and support Eve kissed Natalie on the cheek. Eve put
her head back and closed her eyes while Natalie just absorbed the act. She had an
impulse to say or do something in response. Even just a thank you, but she saw
how Eve's shaking had turned more to shivers. And it wasn't just the hands, but
her whole body, as if Eve had lapsed into a fever chill or was going into shock.

"Eve." Natalie touched her gently. "Eve…are you alright?"

And just like that, without answering, Eve crumpled up in half, starkly pale,
and Natalie had to catch and cradle her in her lap to keep Eve from slipping to
the floor.

• • •

Fran and Natalie got Eve to bed. Fran went into her war chest of pain pills for something that would make Eve sleep. Natalie explained later everything that had happened, and what Eve had written in her pocket note pad.

The girl was emotionally demoralized. The fight with Bobby Lopez being the watershed moment for all her damned-up pain.

Days went by and Eve could do little more than try and deal with her inner turmoil. At that, she managed in a barely tenuous way to keep from being overwhelmed. Most of the time she was like someone alone on a darkened street corner in a city she didn't know.

• • •

The police were getting nowhere closer to having a suspect in hand. The newspaper articles, the composites, the handbills, the posters, all brought out the freaks and junkies, the new wave grifters and resident headcases, the psychics, but not one solid lead you could lock and load on.

The only good thing, so far, the number of thugs, dealers, poorboys, street hustlers, and junkies with a vendetta who came forward with "alleged information" and ended up being questioned by the police, who in no short time had a new phone-books worth of background on Bobby Lopez.

The police started to cruise his block a whole lot more. He was sure he was being followed. He started to get paranoid about who he could trust. And like Romain all those years ago, B.Lo was becoming a dry hole. To his best connections, he was bad news.

Fran had, in effect, with that reward, put the first stake in that vampire heart of his.

CHAPTER 99

EVE STAYED LOCKED UP TIGHT in her apartment. She was in a one-note-down cycle of despair. Totally hope blind. A crash and burn wrapped up around her pillow.

Fran had no intention of letting her stay that way. She stood in Eve's bedroom doorway and said, "You should file assault charges against Bobby Lopez."

Eve pushed herself up from the bed. The sleeping pills had left her flat and dry-looking. They'd helped her sleep through the anxiety, but they'd also cranked up an edge.

——What will that do?

"I talked to a criminal lawyer. If a judge believes his actions violated the terms of his parole, Lopez could be sent back to prison to serve out his term."

——For assault, not Charlie's murder.

"That's right. But we'd have him off the street while we kept looking for evidence."

Eve got up for the first time in a day. Walked groggily to the bathroom. It was the middle of the afternoon. She drank water from the faucet and wiped her mouth on the back of her hand.

Eve didn't want to hear more, so she went to the living room to get away from Fran. But Fran wasn't near done.

"You think I don't know what's going on inside you right now? Right this moment?"

——I don't want to hear it.

"So to speak."

Eve dumped down on the couch. There was an open Coke can on the coffee table. She reached for it and drank. The Coke was flatter than fuckin' curb water, but she didn't care.

"Life is futile, right?"

Eve looked for a cigarette. Found one, signed to Fran that her heart had been torn out, and would Fran mind leaving her the hell alone for a little while anyway, so she could bleed to death.

Oh, yes, Fran thought. *I have been here before and I am the perfect person to be here again. To get it right this time so the scars aren't all that's left.*

Fran came into the room and stood over Eve. "*The Scarlet Letter*, remember."

——Not now, please.

"You think that today, in the midst of it, that despite the calendar, the days and years won't move. That they are, in effect, a casket, efficient at holding you and as deadly. You try to breathe, but there are pounds of weight being shoveled down on you. And those shovelsful of weight are memories."

Eve went to get up and leave but Fran grabbed her by the arm and bent her back down. It was the first time Eve ever felt quite that much force from Fran.

"It never gets easier losing someone. Each time you descend into memory you find new wounds, unexplainably sensed, never seen, wounds that come with the recognition of human pain.

"Like coins from your lost and forgotten past whose value is the years and love and need and joy and friendships and hope they were minted with. And there are tears inside of you that could make you go blind with misery, so you never want to see again."

Fran moved the Coke aside and sat on the edge of the coffee table. Eve would not look at her, so Fran took hold of Eve's face and made her look.

"I'm not letting you die in there." And by in there, she meant Eve's heart, which is where her hand touched.

"There are people who have suffered in ways you can't fathom. There are people from the Holocaust. Soldiers from this country who survived battles and prison camps, places that don't deserve a human name. There are people in this city for whom 'most every joy in life has been stripped away.

"And I know you know this already. But I'll say it. Life is bearing sorrow. Courage is the act of overcoming sorrow."

She let go of Eve's face now. Fran was being given that defiant stare. That, I'm wholly within my right to hold out on any acknowledgment of what you are saying.

"Life is not futile. That is bullshit. And if you ask me what we are struggling for my answer is—another day. Cold-blooded, isn't it? You will not break. I will not allow it. You are going to get up and get yourself together and we are going to get you through if I've got to—"

Eve jerked her arms outward and got free of Fran. She moved around the living room, shaking her hand with a haggard no-no-no look. The last thing Eve wanted to face in the world was Fran being right. It made her so fuckin' angry 'cause it made her feel helpless and weak, like a little girl who didn't know better, and it made her do something stupid, which she regretted as soon as she started to sign...

——You talk. You never went on with your own life. Right?! Max... Germany. You're still out there in the snow. And the only men you go out with are men you sneaked off to meet in…'Cause you didn't have the courage. Did you? Answer me!

Eve saw how badly she'd wounded Fran. And it wasn't what she had said, or how she had said it. It was *that* she had said it. Suddenly Eve felt terribly helpless and weak and childlike. And worse yet, she felt ashamed.

"What you say is true. I did not have the courage to go on in that way. But I have no intention of letting that happen to you. I'm the—cautionary tale—you have to pay strict attention to. My past is the scarlet letter that's going to teach you.

"So if hurting me will help you get well…hurt me. I'm strong enough for it. But what about you? What's the truth of you? That room? Despair?

"The decisive moment with the camera is no different than the decisive moments in your life. You either catch them, or they are gone."

THE HEARING

CHAPTER 100

FRAN WENT BACK DOWN to the store. Eve sat on the window ledge staring out past the disaster of herself, looking at that world of familiar buildings where the light bled through those long streets toward the city beyond. Her heart felt as if it were dangling by a thread, and with the slightest wrong move it would tear away and be lost to her.

• • •

Eve waited till the store was closed to see Fran. Sunset fell across the windows and left blossoms of fire upon the glass. There were only a few feet between the women, but that space felt of enormous and painful emptiness.

As Eve tried to find herself and start, Fran pointed to the windows and said, "Sunset is always so beautiful against the glass. No matter how many times I've seen it, no matter how much the street and neighborhood changes, it's always beautiful."

Eve began to circle her heart with the right hand. Circling it in a slow and plaintive way.

"I know you're sorry. I knew you would be soon as you said it."

Eve pressed her hand to her heart to try and express the pain she felt over what she had said. Then with her hands pouring down from her eyes in the sign for sorrow, Eve broke down crying.

Her head lilting to one side, a human confession, waiting for forgiveness. Fran came forward and took Eve in her arms. She began to wipe at the tears, holding Eve's face toward hers…"Look at me…look…look now."

Fran, in her anger, had blamed her parents for not stopping the forced abortion that killed Max's baby, though they had no earthly power for such an action. She had been cruel to them in ways Eve was nowhere capable of. But through all that anger and pain, her parents had told her one thing…

Fran took Eve's right hand and placed her own right hand around it. And like the teacher showing the child how to speak she shaped Eve's hand so both signed as one, —— Forever.

• • •

The D.A. in Manhattan charged Bobby Lopez with assault. The hearing was set for the fall. Lopez hired himself an attorney out of Bronxville with a serious track record and a Wykagyl Country Club pedigree.

How did B.Lo manage it? The lawyer's wife was a closet junkie. A snorter who ate up charge cards at Lord and Taylor's on White Plains Road, but also had that Catholic-school-girl trash side which needed to be fed. She was Bobby's charity whore, so if and when the time came that he was facing the hole, he had himself a serious gunfighter in her husband.

Bobby appeared in court with his mother and a squad of relatives. They put on a real show of family. And Lopez, he was dressed in a shirt and jacket, for Christ's sake.

The D.A. made a good case of laying out Lopez's character and what went down that day at the apartment. Everyone in the court had a pretty good sense Bobby was going back for some hard time, but the defense threaded the needle on cross.

The prosecution had notified the court to have an interpreter there who Eve could sign to. It didn't take long for Fran or Queenie or Napoleon or even Mimi to realize that the interpreter was either a novice to the court setting and just plainly nervous, or severely inadequate to the task.

CHAPTER 101

"YOU WENT TO SPANISH HARLEM to pass out handbills, did you not?"

The defense attorney had a drooping moustache, so he was almost impossible to lip-read. Eve had to rely on the interpreter to make sure she understood.

——Yes.

"You went because you believed Mr. Lopez was somehow connected to the murder of Charles Dore, correct?"

——Not connected…responsible.

"Responsible. Being that certain, you must have gone there to get him. Isn't that correct?"

The prosecutor was adamant, "Your Honor."

"I withdraw the question."

• • •

"Did you go to Mr. Lopez's apartment to confront him?"

——I wanted him to see the handbills. To know we were not giving up.

Before the interpreter had even finished the defense attorney pressed on hard, "Wouldn't you consider that a provocative action?"

The interpreter wasn't able to keep up, and instead of signing the letters for the word 'provocative' she made the sign for the word 'promiscuous'.

Eve looked somewhat shocked, she didn't understand.——I'm not promiscuous.

Napoleon and Queenie leaned over the railing and tried to explain to the prosecutor the subtle screw-up.

Eve kept looking around, lost.——I'm not promiscuous. You can't call me promiscuous.

The defense saw the flaw and fired right into it. "You went to start a fight, correct?"

The prosecutor stood. "I don't think Miss Leone understands—"

Eve was trying to follow the players, read lips, watch the interpreter.

"You were there to start a fight. Don't you consider that a provocative action? Answer the question, please!"

• • •

"Miss Leone, your father spent time in the Men's Correctional Facility for possession and the selling of narcotics...heroin, I believe, did he not?"

Eve, stunned, looked at Fran, at the judge.

She signed to the interpreter, who answered, "Yes. He spent two years in prison."

"Have you ever possessed or sold narcotics for your father?"

"Your Honor, this is a clear attempt to—"

• • •

The fact Eve Leone had been assaulted by Mr. Lopez had no bearing on the judge's ruling. And from his terse manner and directed stare, the judge was the antithesis of sympathy to Eve's situation.

He ruled that Eve Leone instigated the fight. That she had gone to Spanish Harlem, and Mr. Lopez's apartment with the sole purpose of "provoking" an action that would cause Mr. Lopez to violate his parole.

· · ·

Eve and the others walked out of the courtroom angry and defeated. The prosecution made all the defensible excuses as to why they'd failed. But for Fran it wasn't the facts or the interpreter that had lost them the case. It was the modern twist on the same age-old attitude toward women.

It was just a subtle replay of when Romain and his cousin had explained away Clarissa's disappearance citing her supposed promiscuity and alleged abortion. They'd defamed her character because it played into the policemen's prevailing attitude of what a woman is, and is supposed to be. And if she wasn't—

"You saw the judge," said Fran. "We lost in there today because a young woman, and a deaf young woman at that, taking the action she did, violated the judge's sensibilities as to what women should be in his world."

The prosecutors tried to talk her down from this idea. Even Queenie wasn't sure that Fran was right, but Fran, she saw the world as man's invention.

"Even if the interpreter got it wrong," Fran declared, "why do you think Lopez's attorney used the word 'provocative'?"

CHAPTER 102

BOBBY LOPEZ WAS FULLY AWARE of the danger around him, and so after the hearing, he disappeared from their lives.

He sat at his mother's kitchen table in a sleeveless silk shirt, where she'd fed him, taken care of him, absorbed his anger. Moody and self-possessed, he couldn't help but think how they'd worked the system to run him down, rat him out, and almost ruin him. He was hurting for money which meant he was hurting for prestige.

"No more," his mother said to him in Spanish as she set food on the table. "Please, no more. Alive is better than anything else. Be alive."

He nodded, as if dwelling on things more important and distant.

Time can be like gunpowder you keep filling bullets with, so when you fire the gun, whoever is hit feels all that waiting.

    If you do it right.

• • •

Life, which only *is*, moved on with its endless power. The first holiday season after Charlie's death—as we are creatures of emotion and creatures of reflection—brought with it some of the loneliest moments they had to endure, and some of the loveliest they were blessed to share.

    In the Christmas pageant, Mimi got to play one of the shepherds in the nativity scene. They had two live baby lambs on stage. Mimi was holding one by a leash. The highlight of the play came when her lamb got loose and she had to chase it into the audience. Mimi offered to become Eve's personal slave for whatever amount of time was necessary if she'd burn the photos. These, of course, made the school yearbook.

• • •

At the end of winter Mimi was confirmed at St. Joseph's. The chapel window was tinted with a lovely late morning sunlight as Mimi took "Eve" as her confirmation name.

    It had not come as a surprise, Eve had known weeks before. And yet, there was not only a feeling of wonder when Mimi said the name Eve, there was a kind of magic timelessness to the moment. So much so that Eve, standing off from the pews to get photographs, momentarily stopped, because she had begun to feel her mother's presence more intimately than she had in years.

    It was as if Clarissa was beside her. As vivid and tactile as anything she had ever experienced. Eve seemed to be able to smell her mother's toilet water again, and feel the touch of her hand, where all that terry cloth had rubbed the skin shiny smooth.

    Eve made a quick glance at Fran. Maybe it was just all those years so closely spent together, or the fact the day carried for both women such shared memories. But Fran nodded to her, and unobtrusively mouthed, "I wish she were here too."

• • •

That night Eve sat on her living room floor with only lit candles around her and looked at every picture she had of her mother. The moments spread out on the floor, softly intangible, a small mural of sorts, placed so in time. She looked closely at the photos of Fran and Clarissa on the roof holding that wounded dove.

Eve realized, sitting there, that she was not much younger than her mother had been the day she'd been confirmed.

And she realized too, how soon after that her mother would be dead.

THE MISSAL

CHAPTER 103

"IS THIS FRAN KUHL?"

Fran looked at the clock. It was very, very late.

"Fran Kuhl?"

The man had a Russian accent, spoke with a gravelly, uncomfortable pitch.

"Who is this?"

"Romain Leone asked me to call."

Fran, after a cautious silence, "Why?"

"He wants to see his daughter."

"I'm going to hang up on you now, and don't call here."

"Wait. He told me to say...he wants to give his daughter her mother's checkbook and missal."

All those years ago, back, in one chilling sentence.

• • •

The address was in Castle Hill, at a bar along Westchester Creek just off Zarega Avenue. The creek fed into the East River by the Whitestone Bridge. This was the kind of neighborhood that if a woman went there at night alone she'd have to be considered suicidal.

Fran drove. It was chilly. They had the heat on in the car. She hadn't wanted Eve to do this.

They made their way down a nondescript street with nondescript pilings of junk that filtered out into nondescript fields of high weeds that ran damp and frosty to the water's edge. They passed an oil drum with a burning fire where they watched shadows that drank and shot dope.

Their headlights plucked the bar out of the darkness ahead. It was a rat hole of boards partly edged over the water on pilings. Burning neon in a tiny window was all there was to mark the place.

They sat in the car as it idled, watching. Even with the windows closed the smell of bilge water was all about them. Fran tapped on Eve's shoulder. She turned.

"Shall I go with you?"

——You can't.

There was nothing more to add or ask or say. Eve got out of the car. She did not know that Fran had brought the gun.

• • •

The bar had a low ceiling. There was a jukebox and a few tables. Along the bar were strung Christmas lights. Half were burned out, the rest looked to have been there for a thousand years.

Eve stood in the doorway with the collar up on her old blue coat, the bag slung over her shoulder. She was met with half-burned stares from the barely able end of the life chain.

The bartender came forward and a few of the colored lights illuminated his profile. It was the Cossack. She recognized that burly face with its puttied corners, only now the colored lights gave him a macabre glow.

He recognized her too. "I haven't seen you since—" He was trying to get his hand to the right height.

If Eve could have talked she would have cut him down fast with…since my father was running heroin for you out of Flushing.

She walked to the bar, felt the eyes on her. She took a small note pad from her shoulder bag and wrote: **Where is he?**

The Cossack led her to a side door. He stepped outside and pointed. There were boats docked along the creek and you could get to them through the high weeds by a trail of rotting slats.

"That first boat."

• • •

The door closed behind her and with it went a part of her breath. She made her way through the brittle weeds. Across the creek, she could see headlights moving north and south on the Hutch. And beyond, she could just make out the Whitestone Drive-In. She could see, at a crooked angle, scenes flashing against the night, huge and brilliantly colored.

It was there he'd given her the box camera, the one from the pawnshop window. A deep sense of time came over her, and feelings drenched with the past. Looking at the screen was like watching her memory projected onto the sky. And for a moment she felt the real meaning of the word "forever."

CHAPTER 104

HE WAS BELOW DECK when he felt the boat rock slightly as someone came aboard. He sat at a small dinette. He reached across the table for a flashlight.

Eve saw the beam flood up the stairwell and it began to wave sluggishly, calling her in. The very bones of the boat felt of hollow cold, and it was like stepping down into a grave.

Those first moments he could see her, she could not see him. The dissipation of time had done little to alter one fact. The ghost of his wife, now fully grown and more defiant, was staring past the light and toward the darkness he hid in.

He heard the word "damn" slip through his lips. Then he turned off the light.

The boat rocked slightly in the dark, the damp clung to Eve like a straitjacket. She did not move, she refused to move. *We are not afraid*, she told herself. *We are not. Not Fran. Not Mama. Not me.*

A butane lamp on the wall over the dinette table began to burn up brightly, shadows ebbed back toward the walls. And there he was.

It had been years, but not enough years to cause what she saw before her. He was eaten down to bare bone. The wavy hair was thinning, though the sharp lines of the widow's peak remained. The meanness hadn't gone, but there wasn't enough flesh to really carry it very far.

And his hands. They moved with deformed slowness, the fingers looking at best to be just wired in place. On someone else it would have been an unfair tragedy, on Romain it was hard-earned.

"I passed the 'sell by' date, haven't I?"

——Where is the missal?

"It's been a long time since I read that finger shit, but I know what you're asking."

He reached into his coat pocket. He held the missal near the butane lamp. The light printed the hand and missal's image huge against the far wall.

Eve stood there in angry belief and disbelief. Just like that, he had so much as admitted he'd murdered her mother. As he held out to her this personal, unverified version of the truth, Eve wondered if she could kill him if she got the chance.

She went to grab the missal away, but he pulled it back surprisingly fast, and put up a hand for her to "hold on."

"Did you bring your camera?"

Her eyes flinched a bit. Had she heard him right?

He demanded now, "Did you bring your camera? You never went anywhere without your fuckin' camera."

She touched her shoulder bag, took it out for him to see.

He slid off his coat. She did not understand. He rolled up his sleeves. It was a shunted and cumbersome task. He put out his arms for her to see. There were track marks and veins so broken down you'd swear they couldn't hold one drop of dark blood.

"First it was just a taste to forget, seeing her dead like that. Then it was just a little coke when I had to be on top of my game. Do you have the courage?"

He moved away from the dinette. He was holding the missal. "Don't you want to get a picture of a murderer?" He opened the missal and showed her the checkbook. Still there. "What better way to prove what I done than having a picture? Get one of the dead man, before he's dead."

She stepped toward him and he stepped back assuming she was trying to grab for the missal, but she was only raising the light level in the cabin by stepping up the butane lamp.

For a moment Romain saw himself, his old self, staring back at him. Till she brought the camera up to her eyes.

She aimed it like a gun, like someone getting ready to test a force, to demand a logical end, even if it would in some way engulf her.

And so he began to tell her how that night had gone down. From a disfigurement of expressions to a profile in darkness, condensed by the light around it. Frightening in its naked weight of physical gestures showing how he'd first hit her mother, how he'd crushed her throat, how he'd wrapped her in a tarp and dumped her in the back of the truck like so much garbage, how he'd put her in a swamp and weighed her chest down with stones so she'd sink. It was the veil of darkened life exposing itself, the mad blackness of a man tied to his secrets.

Eve was shooting photos and crying and she shot even though she couldn't see any more through the tears, and she wasn't even sure what she got but she kept on till her father staggered into silence, bereft of everything except his own wasted emptiness.

And when the camera shutter had stopped clicking, when he knew it was over, Romain did his junkie turn. The emaciated gamble, the ground zero ploy. "What you want most, I'll bet, is to know where she's buried."

The camera dropped down from Eve's face. She was sobbing.

"That way you can bury her proper."

What she felt, as those words formed out of his mouth, she didn't know. *This* was some unmarked voyage. Some place she couldn't really be experiencing, not really experiencing.

He reached out to her. "I need money."

She felt as if she'd been hit in the throat and couldn't breathe.

He stood up. "I need a lot of money. You bring it tomorrow night and I'll give you the missal and I'll tell you—"

She started back-pedaling toward the galley stairs and didn't even realize it.

"—where I buried her. Then you can go to the police."

She was reaching backwards trying to find the cold air that would lead her up and out of this place.

"After you give me the money. You'll have the pictures. But don't go to the police till you give me the money."

She ran through the weeds toward the idling car, stumbling over mounds of junk, and what she couldn't hear, what she had been spared by her deafness was him still yelling into the night, "If you go to the police I'll never tell you where I buried her."

CHAPTER 105

EVE MADE FRAN GET THE HELL OUT OF THERE as fast as they could. It wasn't till Eve calmed down enough that Fran pulled into a gas station up on Westchester Avenue.

Eve had Fran give her a cigarette. They sat in the car with the windows rolled up and the doors locked and she told Fran everything.

To know the hard and fast of it all, to know your closest and dearest friend in life had been taken and left—

I should have killed him, Fran thought. *All those years back. I should have. It's like the Nazis. Everyone waited just a little too long.*

"I'll be right back," said Fran.

She got out of the car. A bodega across the street was still open. She had the gun in her pocket and she understood why people, innocents, get suddenly shot. Her hands were still trembling when she gave the shopkeeper the money for a six-pack of beer. They were all carrying guns now, these shopkeepers.

She and Eve drank in the car, right there under the station light. Thinking, thinking.

"How much does he want?"

The car was smokey. Eve cracked down the window just a bit. ——He gets nothing. Zero.

"We're going to the police."

——We are not.

"I don't understand."

——The police go down there, he'll have tossed the missal in the creek. They'll never find it. Wherever he put my mother's body, she's buried. The rest of her, the real her, is here. Eve touched a hand to her chest. ——Inside us. You and me. And she'd want us to put it to him. Not to lay down. Giving him money is laying down. It's letting him work what he views as our weakness.

Fran let everything Eve just settle in. "What about the pictures?"

Eve finished her beer and put the empty back in the bag with the other beers. She looked at the camera on the seat between them.

——They were meant to hurt me. He knew I'd have to live with them. He's getting back at me for…for everything, I guess.

"Throw them away. The pictures."

——I can't.

Fran reached for the camera. "Then I'll throw them away."

Eve grabbed Fran by the wrist. The grip meant, let go. Fran let go.

——I can't meant, I won't. Those pictures are part of my new life. They are part of…the record.

——Remember what you told me after Charlie? Remember? I will not break. Whatever I got back there on that boat is an honest fragment of the real world. And if I can't face it, if I can't look at it, I can't get beyond it.

"So what do we do? Anything?"

——One favor. Please.

"Yes."

——Call the Cossack tomorrow and tell him, Eve slammed her fist on the dashboard, ——to give my father this message. She slammed her fist down again on the dashboard. She was beginning to cry. ——Tell him Clarissa said to go fuck yourself.

BEST OF SHOW

Chapter 106

THROUGH HIS DEGRADATIONS and vileness, Romain had, in effect, bestowed upon his daughter two gifts, neither of which he would ever know about.

First, he'd steeled Eve's inner resolve so she was capable of grappling with Bobby Lopez after he had tried to kill Fran and her.

And second, for years Fran had been sending copies of Eve's photographs to juried exhibitions, without Eve's knowledge.

One night Fran asked Eve to get dressed up and come with her to City College. The art department had sponsored a juried exhibition, open to all photographers living in the five boroughs, and Fran wanted to view the works.

Walking the walls of photographs, Eve felt so much the ugly duckling, the most unartistic of artists, unworthy somehow of even the most dubious of moments. Then, she spotted Mimi, the Dores and Natalie at the end of the wall where the award-winning exhibitions were hung.

It must have been a minute, or so it seemed to Fran, with Eve asking how they all ended up here, before she realized the BEST OF SHOW photographs were hers.

That look, when reality hit, was priceless, followed by a delicious shock where Eve just had to make sure, make certain sure, that the photographs *were* hers, and then the spontaneous burst of elation when she actually touched the ribbon by her name—her name.

Eve was trying to get back down to earth and understand how all this had happened when a man came walking over to them. He had longish graying hair and a moustache. He was tall. And politely speaking, a gritty looking thirtyish with a dab of nice features.

"Excuse me," he said.

Fran tugged at Eve's arm to get her attention.

He pointed. "By the way you're handling that ribbon you must be the photographer. Eve Leone?"

She nodded, touched the ribbon again.

"My name is Dean Harlan. I'm one of the judges."

Eve nodded, signed to Fran, and Dean realized.

"She wanted to know if you voted for her."

He smiled. "I did. Twice."

Eve grabbed him and kissed him. The energy was just pouring out of her. She made Mimi kiss him, Queenie, Fran, Natalie. Napoleon said he'd take a rain

check.

Dean Harlan was slightly embarrassed. And to top it off, he couldn't quite take his eyes off Eve, and it wasn't because she didn't fill the stereotype of what he'd expected the photographer of those pictures would look like.

The photographs—most of her best were there. The hands making the peace sign through the smoke at the World Theatre, the shadow on the mausoleum wall like some black chess piece looking down on Queenie and Napoleon. And her father, in all his emaciated horror. He was there too.

"I want to tell you," said Dean, "your work has none of that calling card look, that how-hip-and-talented-I-am-flair. None of that flash and trash disco style. None of that art world preoccupation.

"These are just real. As if you had spied on something eminently important. And those," he was pointing now to the ones of her father. "They're like combat photographs. And that's something I know about firsthand.

"That man." He meant her father. "The photos. They have no redeeming quality about them whatsoever. Nothing to uplift the human spirit. They are not stylistically self-serving. They just, pure and simple, make you feel like you're looking straight into the barrel of hell. That's how fuckin' good they are."

Somewhat nervously he took out a business card. "I lecture at NYU, when I'm not on assignment. I'm a photographer too. Maybe we could get together sometime and—"

He cut himself off from saying the word. But Eve took out her note pad and wrote down: **Talk?**

Embarrassed, hands trying to gesture, he managed, "Yeah."

She went to a clean page in her note pad, wrote the capital letter **A**, and beneath it, *The Scarlet Letter*. She handed him the paper.

"What's this mean?"

She reached out and took his hand. He wasn't sure what she was up to. "You're not gonna read my palm, are you?"

She shaped his hand in the sign for the letter *A*. She then pointed to the *A* she had written down, and back to his hand.

"Got it," he said.

A PHONE CALL FROM
BOBBY LOPEZ'S MOTHER

CHAPTER 107

BOBBY LOPEZ WATCHED EVE lock up the candy store as Fran pulled around the corner in their car. While they drove to St. Joseph's, Lopez crossed onto Fran's roof from the adjoining building and with pathetic ease crowbarred loose the door lock.

Natalie had taken Mimi's class on a field trip to the *Daily News*, so they could see how a newspaper was made. While they were all driving down to the Dores' for dinner, Lopez had broken into the candy store and was dousing the walls with gasoline.

Just days before, Eve had taken portrait shots of Natalie's parents for their fortieth wedding anniversary. It was a present from Natalie to them. Lopez had located the fuse box and was just chopping away the wood around it when Natalie asked Eve if she had brought along the proofs.

He was wadding strips of gasoline-soaked rags into the joist openings by the time Fran was driving back up Bruckner. Since the Batchelors were going to be at the Dores' for dinner they thought it would be fun for everyone to see the proofs.

It was well past dark when Fran pulled up to the candy store. Lopez was just coming up from the basement when he heard the apartment building door open. He shrunk back out of sight.

The proofs were in the darkroom so Eve had to pass the hall entrance to the candy store. She was moving so quickly, her mind on tonight and what it meant, it being the first anniversary of Charlie's death, when all the way down in her bloodstream she felt something bad.

With one eye against a slit of basement door, Lopez could see a shadow stop and turn. It stood like that, without moving. He had the crowbar in one hand and with the other he eased the ski cap down over his face so only the eyes and a round bit of open mouth showed through.

It took Eve a moment to get through the vague wariness and know what the something was that wasn't right. A smell…heavy and pungent. Eve squinted as if somehow that would help her place it. It couldn't be…gasoline?

Lopez could see whoever it was move toward the hall door into the candy store. It had to be the girl or the old woman. Whichever it was, were they alone? He heard a doorknob turn. Was it the candy store door, or another door? He was gonna have to make a move, man. Something fast. Something so they had no fuckin' chance of identifying him.

As soon as the door opened and she saw the cracked wood along the lock, the flesh on Eve's arms rose in a black chill all the way to the back of her skull. The moment she shoved the door open a nether image swept across the wall from back down the hallway.

The figure charged her wildly. She threw up her arms in defense. The robber's mask was all she saw: the eyes, the mouth wet and hideously pink.

She staggered back to avoid being hit. She managed to get into the candy store and instinctively slammed the door at this masked thing coming at her. But the door slammed back and in a thin river of streetlight coming through the window, she saw the crowbar.

Eve ran to the front of the store. Mimi sat with her arms draped across the open window of the car door, her chin resting on her hands, waiting out those few boring minutes till they were out of there.

She was the first one to see Eve in the window signing frantically ——— Trouble, trouble, come quick.

The women were no sooner out of the car and ordering Mimi to stay where she was when they saw this shapeless face come soundlessly up through a black row of aisles and swing a crowbar at Eve.

And in that ghastly instant, Fran, unable to stop the blow, saw her whole life derail.

CHAPTER 108

THE FIRE TRUCK HAD ARRIVED just after the paramedics. The policemen not long after that. Whoever had planned to set the fire and attacked Eve had escaped up the stairs and across the roof, the same way they'd broken in.

Eve had been lucky. The crowbar had raked the top of the shelf, which deflected the blow. It had left a two-inch gouge in the wood and metal. But for that, Eve would be dead. The blow had caught her on the back of the shoulder and the side of the neck leaving a foot-long red welt of broken veins.

The paramedics wanted to bring her into the hospital overnight to check for concussion or broken bones, but Eve wasn't having it.

She told Fran ——— Tell them I'm one of those hard-headed Italians.

Fran was too shaky to oblige. She just paced the hallway where Eve was being checked over. Fran was so terribly pale she looked to have only pinlets of blood in her body. The paramedics tried to get her to sit down; instead, Natalie was sent upstairs to make her a drink.

• • •

Natalie had called the Dores to tell them what happened. They arrived when Fran was in full torrent at the investigators.

"Bobby Lopez. You don't have to go any further than that to know who did this."

"None of you can positively identify him."

"I should have just lied," said Fran, "and told you I knew it was him."

"Better you didn't."

She'd already sketched for the officers all their dark histories with Mr. B.-fuckin'-Lo. "You know what today is? It's one year to the day he murdered Charlie Dore. One year to the day. That's the boy's parents right there. They'll tell you. We were going to their house for a memorial dinner. You think it's a goddamn coincidence that tonight of all nights—"

For the one-dozenth time, the lead investigator said, "We need hard evidence."

A fire marshal came up from the basement. "The gas line's been tampered with. Wiring padded with soaked rags. Whoever did this knows something about torching buildings."

The lead investigator told the man with him, "See if this Lopez has any history of arson."

The fire investigator had one more point to make. "The building. It would have gone up fast the way it was rigged."

• • •

After the others left, everyone went up to Fran's apartment trying to figure out ways to handle this insanity they were caught up in.

Eve had gone back down to her apartment to get more ice to put on her neck and shoulder. Mimi had quietly followed after her.

Standing in the kitchen doorway, the girl said, "It's my fault, isn't it?"

——What?

"This."

——Say again.

"All this. It's my fault."

It was the same kind of dread and confusion that had gone through Eve like a rumor when she was a girl, leaving its poisoned innuendo in her head as she tried to deal with not only what her father had done, but with what Lopez had done to Charlie.

Eve ached where she put the ice. She had Mimi get her some aspirin from the medicine chest. She took a handful to kill the pain, then she sat at the kitchen table and had Mimi come over. This had all given Eve time to think.

When Eve put her arm around the child it was like the way her own mother had put an arm around her. And when she explained, Eve could feel Fran over her shoulder, helping her through the thoughts. It was strange and beautiful at the same time. Eve—she felt stronger and more together because of it. As if no matter what happened, the two women would be there to guide her.

——You think it's your fault for the same reason I did when I was your age and I had to deal with my father. Who wasn't much different than yours.

——See, if it isn't your fault, whose fault is it? Is it just that the world is crazy, that it's totally unsafe? And how can I survive in such an insane world? Who will protect me? How do I protect myself?

"The world *is* crazy."

——I'm not. Fran's not. Queenie and Napoleon aren't. Your older brother and sister aren't.

"If it's not my fault, I wish it were."

——Why?

"Then maybe I could make everything stop."

CHAPTER 109

THE NEXT MORNING MIMI TOLD Napoleon that she was going to see some friends, then head to Eve's. When Queenie called Fran around noon, she discovered that Mimi had never arrived.

They didn't want to panic, but after Queenie called Mimi's friends and none of them had seen her the face of the day decidedly darkened.

• • •

Mimi had, on her own, taken the train to Spanish Harlem. She stood at the front of the first car looking out the window. There was a turbulence inside her as she watched the train shudder and drive on through the darkness. No train she had ever ridden felt this fast.

She remembered sleeping with her mother in a wrecked car under the Major Deegen, and the night the police came with some kind of huge lights and took her away.

• • •

For a few moments Bobby Lopez's mother did not recognize the girl standing before her in the darkish hallway. But when she did, she began to mumble to herself in Spanish. Shocked, she looked out into the hallway to see if the girl was alone.

"It's just me."

The woman noticed the hearing aids. "Are you deaf?"

"Mostly."

Speaking louder, "Come in."

Once inside, with the door closed, the woman actually hugged the girl. Mimi let her, though she did not hug the woman back.

"What you want?"

Mimi leaned back against the wall. The apartment, she thought, smelled funny, strange. "I'll stay if you make him leave them alone."

The woman was not sure she understood, she had Mimi repeat herself.

"Make him stop hurting them…my father. And I'll stay. I don't want to. But I will."

Bobby Lopez's mother felt ashamed that a child could come to ask this of her, that a child *had* come to ask this of her.

How many times had she wondered if there was a way to salvage her life after lying to the police as she had.

That pretty girl standing there, so polite, so well-spoken. Her hands crossed one over the other. She was like a dream waiting there just for you.

"Anyone know you here?"

"No."

• • •

Eve had been sent out into the street to try and find Mimi while Fran manned
the phones calling hospital after hospital. The anguish of remembering what
had happened to Clarissa—how she and Eve had walked the night from her
apartment to Romain's—made her pace that living room like some thievish
figure waiting for a stay of execution.

When the phone rang, she had no idea who the woman was with the heavy
Spanish accent.

"This is Maria Lopez."

Fran assumed she was a nurse or a clerk from one of the hospitals she'd
called. But the name didn't correlate to any on her list. "What hospital are you
calling from?"

There was a confused pause. "No hospital...no. I have Mimi here. This is
Maria Lopez."

· · ·

Fran and Eve drove to Spanish Harlem together. The East River drive was a
bumper-to-bumper hellspace. Fran rode the horn like a cabdriver the whole way
cursing every goddamn pothole and nothing Eve could do would calm her.

Maria Lopez invited the women in. Knowing what her boy had done, it was
a dreadful feeling just to look at them. Mimi was sitting at a Formica table in
the kitchen drinking a Coke. One broken table leg had been taped in place with
wads of thick gray masking. Maria Lopez explained what happened.

"Take her home," said Maria Lopez. "She should no be here." Then, to
Mimi, reluctantly, as if she could make up for all that was terrible with this one
act, Maria said, "No come back. No change who my son is. But he my son."

· · ·

In the car Fran was beside herself and it looked like her heartbeat was sweating
right through her body. She came down hard on Mimi, not only for what she'd
put them all through but for even thinking that she could, or would, be allowed
to go off with her father.

Mimi sat in the back, wan and dejected, but also quietly defiant. As if she
had understood what she'd done and was not sorry for it.

All this made Fran all the more emphatic about getting her anger across. Eve
told Fran, —— Enough. But Fran kept on with repetitive mercilessness till Eve
finally slapped at the steering wheel, —— Enough.

Fran quieted and began to mumble to herself in German, as if agreeing to be quiet, but quiet on her own goddamn terms.

Eve bent around in the seat toward Mimi——She's just scared, like all of us, that's why she's so angry.

CHAPTER 110

"YOU KNOW WHY she didn't want the girl," said Fran. "The honest secret reason."

——Because she knows what he is.

"Yes, and I'll bet she has firsthand knowledge of what he's done."

Eve was with Fran in the candy store, scrubbing walls, trying to Lysol away that gasoline stench. The shop was closed and would be till Monday. If that wasn't bad enough the foodstuffs and magazines, comics and packaged goods, anything that had been dowsed had to be thrown out. The iron grating across the front of the store was in place, but doors were open and fans were blowing.

"We're going to find Lopez ourselves."

The investigator from the night before had talked with Bobby's mother. She had not seen him in weeks, which is exactly what she swore to them. Truth or not. And since he had served out his parole, Lopez was free to disappear for stretches of time.

——I wouldn't know how to find him.

"Well, think of a way."

——Why?

Fran took the rag she had been cleaning the walls with and flung it into a pail of Lysol and water. "Because I'm going to kill him when we do."

Eve looked at Fran to see if this was just some lurking thought that would come to nothing. Like when Napoleon and Queenie talked. A moment born of emotional exhaustion and frustration, but taken no further. Fran pulled off her rubber gloves and flung them on the floor beside the pail.

She walked past Eve and the more Eve looked at Fran the more her face seemed to encompass the outrage of all those years. Or maybe Fran had been at that place since almost always, and events just finally came to find her.

"You think I'm gonna let that 'thing' burn our home down? Burn this store down? This is yours after I'm gone. It's all we have. No, no, no. If we'd come home last night and gone straight to sleep, if Mimi had stayed over where would we be today? Why do you think I was so goddamn mad at the child?"

Fran walked into the storeroom and took a cigarette from an open pack on a shelf. Eve followed her.

"Find him."

Fran lit the cigarette. She walked on out into the hall.

——You could go to jail and, it's wrong.

Fran snuffed out the match with her fingertips then licked the tip to make sure. She put the match in her pocket. She went and sat on the stairs. After days like she'd been through—the work, the stress—sitting was an uglied process, conceived as more like torture.

"I could go to jail, girl. But it isn't wrong. The tragedies we've lived through, those are wrong. That's what the word wrong was invented for.

"The names and the faces of the vile change. Romain…Bobby Lopez. But their deeds are the same. Max…Clarissa…Charlie."

Fran looked up that long stairwell. "I'm going to have to start keeping a bottle of scotch down here on the first floor."

——I'll get you a drink.

Eve went to climb past Fran but Fran grabbed her by the arm.

"No. Listen to me. You've had too much catechism class. This is the same argument I had with your mother. It was the huge difference between us.

"You know, I read a lot when I was your age. I read how your religion tossed out lots of gospels, books, canons, to make up their kind of Bible. I got into reading all that instead of staring at the hole where my womb used to be. So maybe I could better understand. Well, I understand better now.

"In one of those gospels they threw out, Eve…Eve was made superior to Adam and God. It was Eve who created God. Who gave Adam his soul. It was she who cast the dark angels out of heaven. And it was she who eventually judged the God she'd created, found him guilty of injustice, and destroyed him.

"I find what I see around me unjust and just too dangerous to live with."

THE TENEMENT ON
CYPRUS AND THIRD

Chapter III

How do you find someone in a city with so many brick alleyways and squalid tenements, with its endless miles of windows and tiny apartments tucked down oblique and dim corridors?

Eve sat on the darkroom floor smoking. The red light trained down on her concentrated features. How do you find Bobby Lopez when he has the black comfort of darkness going for him?

She closed her mind to everything but that one command. And like she would when working a photograph, to get just the right composition, the right degree of shading and contrast, she went through possibility after possibility like some crafty pawn, failing, failing, failing, until the artful hand of fate reached out, just like any mother would with a child, to help her.

• • •

Eve wore filthy jeans and Charlie's old fatigue jacket and took up watching Bobby's mother. Eve made herself as skanked out as possible, and being dark-skinned she could pass for third world. As far as anyone was concerned, she was just another piece of local color.

Eve followed the woman, took photographs of everywhere she went, everything she did, everyone she saw. Eve knew that one day Bobby would need her, need to exploit her, or to use her, just as Eve had been used by her father, and that Bobby's mother might be the perfect fodder for manipulation. Unknowingly or otherwise.

But the days of emotional promise gave way to weeks of essential despair. The woman was thick-bodied and heavy-legged. She walked with a bowed gait and there were terrible channels of dark under her eyes. Her life was a descending cycle of the mundane and lonely.

Then once, while she was in a bodega over on Second Aveenue a black pimp pulled up in his convertible. A couple of Spanish kids wanted touch money for watching his car. The pimp threatened their little asses, and while he was inside, one ran to the alley and got a can of gasoline. As the other knocked on the window to get the pimp's attention, the first doused the inside of the car, then lit a match. The one at the window gave the pimp the finger and the other tossed the match.

The interior went up in a wash of flames just as the woman was coming out of the bodega. Watching, Eve thought back to the night her father had burned himself down. And, man, watching the pimp trying desperately to put out the fire with his hat, and then Bobby's mother moving down the street in a state of beaten reticence, as if this was a surreal hallucination, a voice inside Eve told her with a kind of omniscient assurance that all the time spent was nothing more than a formality.

That dicks like her father and Bobby Lopez and that pimp fuck themselves up in ways they don't even get. They think they got it all in hand, then the whole thing blows, just as the hood of that pimp's car exploded into the air spinning like some metal playing card, while everyone on the block ran every which way for cover, except the old woman.

Yeah, this time spent was nothing more than a formality. They would connect, her and fuckin' B.Lo, just like she and her father had connected on that boat in the cold dark of night. She felt it, saw it; time was calling to her.

CHAPTER 112

BOBBY'S MOTHER LEFT HER APARTMENT near dusk walking with a shopping bag toward Lennox Avenue. There she got on the train heading north. The queer thing was the woman never went out after dusk, not far, anyway.

They crossed under the river into the Bronx, Eve watching from between cars. Her face was angled into the glass just enough. The woman was holding the shopping bag in her lap, her arms crowded around it.

The train was crunching through the dark. The air smelled of filth and humidity. At the Grand Concourse the woman changed trains. She got off at Fordham Road and started walking east. By now it was late and they were deep in the Bronx and closing in on those blocks where Eve grew up.

The woman walked like she had a distance to go and not a lot of time. Eve didn't know what to make of it, when the woman walked into St. Barnabas Hospital.

Visiting hours were still on, so the lobby had a steady flow of people. Bobby's mother went and sat in a chair under a giant mural of St. Barnabas as he walked towards his martyrdom in Cyprus. Her arms again crowded around the shopping bag.

She sat there just that way for five, ten, fifteen minutes, like some nervous soul looking strangely pale beneath the long ceiling of fluorescents.

It was all wrong. Then Eve became keenly aware of how the woman kept glancing from person to person as if she were being watched for her reaction. A bristling chill went up Eve's back.

It was that day in the church all over again. In that bag the woman was carrying drugs, just like she had. Smack or coke or whatever else B.Lo was putting on the street. Eve just knew. It was her street past talking to her.

Something caught the woman's eye and she got up. Eve looked across the lobby to see what it was. The woman was heading toward the ladies' room. Eve watched from the dark edge of the street and considered following the woman in, then second-guessed herself if that was a good idea. She waited, hopelessly torn about what to do.

Whatever was going down took a long time. The hospital doors jerked open and closed relentlessly, sending out blasts of cold air. The light atop an ambulance flashed across the hospital windows as it rushed toward the emergency room. Eve was sweating.

And just like that, the woman came out of the bathroom and started toward the doors where Eve was. But not before a girl had come out of the bathroom and Lopez's mother, for an instant, glanced at her.

The girl was Jamaican, moving quickly down another corridor. Eve followed the girl with her eyes. She was making for the far exit when a guy at the food stand swept in alongside her. He had skrag for a beard and wore a ski cap.

Eve could follow the street trash, or Bobby's mother. A decision had to be made, and quickly. Everything inside her was stumbling toward screwing this up. The street trash or the woman. Eve stood there, like gravity had locked her in place. She couldn't bring to bear one faculty to make the right decision.

It was all tumult and vacillation. Then her eyes picked up on something so fuckin' obvious—Bobby's mother was no longer carrying the shopping bag.

• • •

Eve caught a piece of them heading up Third. She had to run to keep close. They moved with the skill of street dealers who had survived working the shadows.

When they reached Cyrus Place they stopped. There was a four-story apartment on the corner. Against the moonlight Eve could see it was abandoned and windowless. The shop on the main floor looked like it had been taken out with hand grenades. Half its frontage had crumbled onto the sidewalk.

They gave one serious look up and down the street. Eve kept walking along slow, playing just another jerk-off they didn't need to pay any real mind to. A passing bus lit all around them. And as the light flooded on, they slipped into the blunt darkness of an alleyway alongside the building.

· · ·

Yes, all that time was just a formality. Eve watched for nights from the roof of a building across the street. Business came and business went. During all those long hours with the moon she saw Lopez from time to time through the partly boarded up window of a top floor apartment where he could see both streets and the alley.

Sometimes late at night, once it all quieted down, she would notice he had his lighter on for long stretches of time and it looked to her as if he were branding something into the wall with strict precision.

Every time Eve came home Fran would ask had she found him? Eve lied and said she had not. She lied because she was struggling with the first traces of a decision that was making its way across the borders of consciousness. She herself was going to kill Bobby Lopez.

CHAPTER 113

EVE SAT UP IN THE DARK with all those long shadows and the secret thing inside her. If he was to be killed, her best chance was to kill him in that building. If that's where it was to be done, she would have to know the inside of that building because she would have to kill him at night, in the dark, after all that junkie traffic was gone, and he was alone. Killing him there at night, she thought, would give her the best chance of getting away.

From her living room couch Eve turned a flashlight to the darkness. That thread of grainy light searched the walls of photographs for faces, moments, memories. It framed too well that fateful turn of years.

Transformed from all their sorrow, those faces. Ghosts, now part of Eve's personal history and art, reclaiming their smallest moments. Near that first picture of Mimi on Charlie's shoulders Eve had taken, was one she'd taken when she was with Natalie, of a black woman giving birth on a tenement floor.

In my house, are many mansions. Eve turned off the flashlight and began to plan.

Eve crept into the building on Third and Cyprus under the cover of daylight. A wino slept it off in a cardboard box in the alley, his filthy bare feet stretched out across garbage.

Eve brought camera and film. She photographed every step of the way up to that third floor apartment. She photographed heaps of board and trash she'd have to manage in the dark, hallways with their broken doors and torn out walls, chinked stairwells and railings that leaned ominously.

She would have to know that place like a blind person, to be able to walk in silence knowing that he might hear her, but she would not hear him.

There was a hole in the roof where the sunlight came through dream-white and she opened the door to the apartment that Lopez hid in. She moved as only the frightened can.

There were empty food boxes on the floor that now belonged to the rats and roaches. There were needles and beer cans and Coke bottles. There was a mattress by the window that had stains which were the color of rust and could have been anything once, including blood.

Then she saw it on the wall by the window where he had used his lighter—B. Lo. It had been burned into the cracked and battered plaster. It was clear as any photograph, pointed as any shot. He was telling the world, Here I am, I exist.

Even that she got a picture of.

• • •

Eve took the gun from the shoebox without Fran knowing. There were five bullets in the chamber. Eve went up to Woodlawn Cemetery at night. She knew a place where the fence had been pried and bullied apart from her high school stoner days, when she and her friends would get loaded and checked out graves of the famous like La Guardia and Pulitzer, Melville and R.H. Macy.

She had to fire the gun to at least *know* what it was like. She walked the rows of headstones trying to get a feel for the weight and grip of the weapon. Gangs cruised the cemetery now at night. She'd be some fuckin' surprise if they stumbled on her. She tried to embrace a cold fearlessness.

One shot is all she could afford, two at the very, very most. She had no intention of being remembered buying bullets, and a deaf chick going into a gun store to shop for bullets had too good a shot at being remembered.

Far off the street Eve found a place where the graves dipped down into a swale of cool dark. She aimed the gun at the black distance. A wall of city lights flickered beautifully far beyond.

Once at the Cossack's in Flushing, she'd watched her father and some other men play cowboy, firing a gun at a mountain of chrome wreckage. The men had handled the weapon as if it were their inalienable right, as though they had been trained in this kind of sortilege since birth.

Eve took a breath…waited…and pulled the trigger. A burst of flame scorched out from the barrel. She felt the concussion up her arm. But that was it, that was all. It was not what she'd expected; it was much, much less.

Maybe the sound makes it different, she didn't know. But suddenly she understood, with far-reaching simplicity, how it was people got killed.

THE MOTTO ON
THE BRONX FLAG:
NE CEDE MALIS
(YIELD NOT TO EVIL)

CHAPTER 114

EVE PICKED MIMI UP AFTER CLASS. On the bus home they talked quizzes and speech, and all those other spiderwebs of personal reality that make up a day at school.

But as they talked, Eve was wrestling with a question she wanted to ask, needed to ask. Most of the morning and all that afternoon Eve's mind had latched onto the day at Playland when Lopez just showed up. Him with that stuffed bear swaggering from out of nowhere over to his daughter. Doing a complete Romain, and trying to brain fuck Mimi into wanting to be with him. And how that night Mimi had cried and ached so for a life that never was.

Eve lightly tweaked Mimi's ear to get her attention. ——I want to ask you something.

The bus was packed. People standing all around them. Even though Eve was signing, she felt nervous that some set of eyes would understand.

——If your father died, how would you feel about it?

Mimi stared up at Eve trying to see what lurked behind such a question. "Is he going to die?"

What she'd asked just hung there.

——If he died.

There was a shape and power to how Eve signed, to the moment itself, and Mimi could feel it, just like she could feel all that sunlight coming off the bus window and the people pressed against her. And the way Eve looked at her with such utter completeness and urgency, Mimi knew the answer was very, very important.

The child rested her chin on the schoolbooks stacked up in her lap. She thought a long time before answering.

"Will we be alright…after, I mean. Will we be all right?"

• • •

Eve sat on the window ledge. It was midnight and damp. She was looking at the photo she had taken at the World Theatre, those hands reaching through clouds of smoke as the band sang, and above them on the movie screen, the lyrics of their song:

> *There's a man with a gun over there*
> *Telling me I've got to beware*

In the light of right now that photo took on other meanings. Beyond the personal about Charlie. The moment itself seemed as ephemeral and temporary as the times. And it was only 1975.

And she understood how a photograph could say one thing to a generation, and something quite different to the next. From the oppositions of time to the enigma of appearances. From dreams reached for, to dreams that got away or were killed or lost, to dreams yet to be. Even down to the fact that something, which had been so intense, was now just a piece of quaint irrelevance.

The shoebox landed right in Eve's lap and startled her, then fell to the floor. She looked up. There was Fran.

"Where is the gun?"

Eve gathered herself. She put the photo aside. She picked up the empty shoebox, put the flannel the gun had been wrapped in back in the box, put the top back on the box.

"Where is the gun?"

Eve stood. She handed the shoebox to Fran. Fran would not take it.

"What are you doing?"

——You can hardly walk up a flight of stairs without being in pain. How would you do it?

"You find him, and I'll show you."

CHAPTER 115

DAYLIGHT CAME IN DRIZZLED GRAYS. The weather report called for rain. Eve decided then, tonight would be the night.

By her bed stand were three photos, reprinted small enough to fit folded in her jeans pocket. One was her mother, one was of Charlie, and the last was of her father, in the crowning moment of his personal immolation.

She would take them with her. She would wear her old, long, blue coat. She would leave her bag behind. In one coat pocket would be the gun, in the other her camera.

She drank coffee in her darkroom and went over the rough shots of the building on Cyprus and Third. She passed Fran on the stairs. There was still a bit of a hangover from their conversation the night before. Nothing irreparable, just unfinished.

The day moved through Eve like sand in the hour glass. By afternoon she began to "unbelieve," as the exact nature of how dangerous and difficult this would be came upon her.

She walked the blocks around the candy store to push mind and body past the sinking fear she would fail her heart. When Eve returned, Natalie was in the darkroom glancing at the photos. At the rough shots of where she would kill Bobby Lopez.

"Fran told me you were in here."

——I went walking. Eve took off her wet coat. ——To think.

Natalie put the prints she'd been looking at down on the dry bench. She took a note from her purse and handed it to Eve.

"It's from Dean Harlan. I bumped into him outside the *News* building. He's been away on assignment. He made me wait while he wrote it. I think he's got a thing for you."

Eve put the note aside without so much as a show of interest. There was, in fact, no reaction whatsoever, which Natalie thought curious. Eve nonchalantly went about collecting up the photos.

"What are those about?"

Eve jiggled her fingers by the side of her head, which when dealing with photos, always meant they were experiments. They may lead to something, they may not.

· · ·

The afternoon gave way to dusk. The rain was the color of slate. The streets ran deep, crowded with traffic. It would be a dark planet that night in the Bronx.

The alleyways and window blinds deepened the mood, and lit storefronts, incandescent and neon, looked to be branded onto darkening time.

Where Eve walked, little moments spoke to her. A newspaper stand where the soaked and fluttered pages of newspapers were like the wings of trapped birds. Tomorrow the papers would have another story to tell. She passed the storefront church where in the window by her reflection was a hand-painted sign:

DRINK OF YOUR TEARS WITH FAITH
AND YOU SHALL BE REPLENISHED

On the street, people tried to hide against buildings from the rain. How many of that still life jury noticed her?

• • •

Just walk with your head down and be as anonymous as the rain. Eve watched from the roof for Lopez. Stoic in her drawn up collar, searching every inch of abandoned stillness with her eyes.

It would be a long night waiting within herself, facing the whispers that this act was against the law of man, the law of God. Whatever the final verdict, she accepted one fact, she would unrepentantly carry the outcome with her from world to world.

She noticed a flinty shadow walk past a window. For better or worse, it was him. A lifetime would now be distilled into minutes.

She took the photos from her back pocket. The rain beaded down on their time-caught faces. She didn't so much as look at the picture of her father as absorb it. The face was as ruined as the building across the way.

There was more than a piece of her in that picture. And more than just their past.

Chapter 116

BOBBY LOPEZ WAS LIGHTING A CIGARETTE and getting ready to blow that rat hole when Eve entered the building. By then Fran had discovered that Eve had left her shoulder bag behind.

It was something Eve had never, would never do. An empty sound came up out of Fran's throat. She now understood the night before and why the gun was missing.

• • •

The first steps through the blacked-out and broken doorway, the moment crossing into the desperate and unchangeable, with the gun close to her side.

The open stairwell rose to where the night came through the caved in ceiling. Rain intact with gray damp. The loose and hanging support beams like eyebrows floating above dead space. A face awaiting.

Every photograph Eve had taken meant nothing. Each step was endless distance through that scarred ruin of pitch black. Rain ran down the walls she clung to, step after step.

There was a blue volt of lightning in the open sky at the top of the stairwell and that's when she saw him against the charged background. A human form that just tasted of darkness.

Her face was soaked. She tried to get back, get out of his line of sight. In doing so she stumbled over a skeleton of torn out floorboards.

Always on the aware Bobby Lopez slipped up to another level. He listened after the sound. A night like this no telling what might try to get itself out of the rain. Just as long as it wasn't some warrior-crazy trying to score.

He picked a brick up out of the rubble. "Hey," he shouted above the rain. "I see ya, man. You hear me, shit." He started in Spanish.

Eve squeezed beside a doorway and made herself into as small a bundle as she could. Lopez came to the edge of the open stairwell where the rain funneled down all grainy. He listened but nothing came back so he flung the brick into the darkness.

Eve saw something hurtle through that rainy path of open sky and away from her, where it was lost.

Lopez kept listening as he reached for a shank of water pipe laying in the rubble. Using it like a war club against the railing he started down the stairs, one violent smash after another signaling his approach.

But for the shaking and the gun, Eve felt almost substanceless. Uncertain, she waited. She looked hard into the abandoned space before her.

And where the steps rose up from the landing, where the wall had been gouged apart for anything valuable inside it, where the rain poured slick off the stairwell down that void of floors, she began to make out something shapeshift the dark, and that something became a tableau of vague movements, and that tableau of vague movements became Bobby Lopez with a shaft of piping that he hammered down on the stair rail so violently every few feet or so that it snapped back up in his arm.

From where she hunched down he would end up maybe a dozen feet away when, and if, he started down the stairs to the floor below. She would be off to one side of his back. He'd be close, and it would give her a chance to rush at him and get closer. That is when it would be done.

She prepared herself, made sure of herself. There could be no second thoughts, no questions, no hesitation. She went into a hypertense state. Her matchtip eyes focusing on him, on the moment.

She didn't realize her breathing had gotten louder and louder as her body constricted around the gun. But the rain, falling through those wounds in the roof, spilling down floor by floor, trickling from the stairs and ledges, tapping into spreading pools of water, created this ambience of sound that disguised the fact someone was there.

As he crossed the landing with his pipe shank hammering out the feet between them he looked her way. He tried to see into that rubble of oblique shapes and opaque corners. And just as he turned to start down the stairs, Eve rose up.

CHAPTER 117

MAYBE HE HEARD HER THEN, or maybe in the corner of his eye he caught some movement. He came around just in time to see this wraithlike figure emerge from nowhere.

For a moment it was as if he did not trust what he saw. Eve hadn't rushed at him, she hadn't fired. She had ordered her body to do both, but the flesh had disobeyed. Then there she was, staring into a surreal suspension of seconds, and suddenly there was no choice at all.

He was coming straight at her, backdropped by rain, pipe extended. A sinew of quick dark intentions.

She fired when he was less than ten feet away. An acetylene flash lit the space between them into a pure form of iron yellow and blue. Turning it into something alive and burning. She saw his body thrown back against the wall where it hung there frozen in space before it fell.

She thought he'd be dead, but he came up staggering almost as quick as he'd fallen, holding the pipe in both hands. He tottered a few steps and flung it sidearmed. The pipe sheared the darkness and batoned up from the floor just in front of her.

He should be dead. He should be. She fired again and that black stretch of hallway flared with the explosion. It could be seen out the empty windows all the way down that rain soaked street.

Lopez was gasping as he managed to throw himself into Eve. Blood covered the front of his shirt from breastbone to belt buckle.

She could feel his face next to hers as she was driven back into the door frame. They hit it sidelong. They went tumbling into what had once been the foyer of an apartment. She tried to get back and up enough to shoot him but he hit her flat on. His face smashed up into her jaw. The inside of her head burst white and the whole world tilted. She could taste blood in her mouth. She thought she was going to pass out.

He beat at her with what was left of himself. It was only the adrenaline that kept her conscious so she could kick and hit her way loose enough to shoot.

He was trying to claw her life out as she crabbed over a landscape of refuse and piled trash, shrapneled wall plaster, of food packing, of beer cans, of broken glass, of mattress springs, of magazine pages used as toilet paper.

For one harrowing moment Bobby Lopez got his hand on her throat. His fingers locked into the top of her coat. Her neck was being bent around. The gun…she managed to press it against what she thought was him. Something began to cut into the flesh along her throat when she fired.

That tiny pitch black alcove of space looked like it had been blasted with sunlight. For a heartbeat Eve could see the walls were desecrated with graffiti. And there was Bobby Lopez, sitting, back to the wall, legs spread apart. He was a profile of agony with sparse seconds between himself and whatever eternity was. His eyes were open, and they spoke with terror about what was coming.

Watching him, Eve crawled upright. The gun, she got it back into her pocket. Her hands, they had on them his blood. The camera, she reached into her other pocket for it.

It was as if she were there, and not there. As if she were seeing this from some far distant time, deep, deep within herself. She watched him trying to fight death. His features contorted, the mouth flexed and jerked, the throat looked like it was trying to spit out whatever was killing it.

But for her what was most powerful was the silence. Bobby Lopez looked to be gasping out word parts, or at least sounds. She wondered, were the sounds anywhere near as powerful as what she was witnessing.

She took her camera, she raised it up. She wanted one more thing from Bobby Lopez, even though it might be as ungraspable as his very soul.

A CONVERSATION
WITH CHRIST

CHAPTER 118

EVE CAME OUT OF THE BUILDING on the alley side where the brick around a
window had been kicked clean through the size of a garage door. Huge, stuffed
trash dumpsters were docked along the wall like boats. A river of rain ran down
the cobbled passageway to where a man stood on the sidewalk looking at the
building and pointing.

Eve turned and went the other way. She used the wall and the trash bins to
slip into the fading distance. She kept glancing over her shoulder. The man must
have seen her because now someone else had joined him and he was pointing
down the alley toward her.

Eve had no intention of being caught there. She would just keep on till they
dragged her down. The man was shouting for her to stop.

She walked on with naked determination, her stare almost hypnotic. Under
a boarded up doorway, a burned out stare wrapped in a blanket, caught her eye.
As the man looked up and focused Eve bent her face into the collar of her coat.

• • •

Fran had smoked an ashtray worth of cigarettes watching every silhouette that
came along the street. By the time she spotted Eve, the police had arrived at the
building on Third and Cyprus and the man on that sidewalk was showing them
the alley where someone in a dark coat escaped after he'd heard the shots.

Fran was already at the building door when Eve came up the steps. Her hair
was matted flat, her coat was soaked and covered with muck. She could barely
make it up to the door. Eve took her hands out of her pockets. Fran saw there
was blood on them.

——I found him. In an abandoned building. I killed him. I got away...I
think.

Fran bundled Eve up in her arms and got her inside fast.

As one team of officers searched the building, another walked the alley behind
a wave of dusky light. They discovered a derelict in a boarded up doorway. As
he described with alcoholic malaise a woman in a dark coat, and maybe a hat,
a dark hat, that had passed along the alley, Fran sat a played out Eve on a chair
in her kitchen.

Fran started to unbutton that wet and filthy blue coat. She had it partway
off the shoulders when Eve stopped her and took from one pocket a rag bundle.

The black of Eve's eyes followed that bundle into Fran's hands.

——The gun.

Fran took the bundle and placed it by the sink. She wet and soaped a towel. As she cleaned Eve's hands, the officers in the building looked over the corpse of Bobby Lopez.

The front of his shirt was a mass of gluey blood where dirt and bits of trash had begun to coagulate.

Fran told Eve, "I didn't mean for you to do this."

As Eve signed——You were too old, an officer shined a light on what he thought to be awfully strange, but telling.

Bobby Lopez had a gold crucifix with a diamond in it around his neck. This was not shaping up to be your typical low-end, dealer versus junkie homicide.

Eve signed out as best she could, in exhausted spurts, the confrontation in that rain black hallway, while Fran undressed her and readied a shower. She wanted Eve to clean away any and all traces of tonight.

Eve sat slumped on the bed—what had happened, it took what, maybe a minute, two minutes. In her head the details were like extended moments of time, freeze-framed on film. They had that slight blur to them, all except his face.

As she led Eve to the bathroom, Fran noticed the necklace Charlie had given her was missing.

Eve stared into the sink mirror. Fran's face was tight next to hers. The steam made both women appear as if they were looking out from some otherworldly place. Eve ran her fingers along her throat where the skin had been cut.

"Did you lose it back there?"

Eve's head tilted a bit. ——I don't know. I must have.

Eve lay on Fran's bed. There was lightning against the windows. Fran sat beside Eve.

——I'm not afraid, you know.

Fran knew. She stroked the girl's hair. They stayed like that together in the dark as Fran began to plan out for tomorrow.

CHAPTER 119

WHEN THE EDITOR for the Bronx section of the *Daily News* saw Bobby Lopez's name he remembered a story they'd run about a year after the murder. He called Natalie first thing to see if this was the same Lopez. If it was, they might have a hot follow up.

Natalie got to Third and Cyprus just as they were removing the body. The streets were still rain slick, but the sky was making a valiant effort at clearing up. Natalie made her way around a gaping crowd of bystanders that acts of violence or death generally attract.

As she started to collect up the facts, Natalie couldn't understand why she began to feel this kind of free floating anxiety. At first she put it down to the thought that this might be the same Bobby Lopez and it brought back everything they'd all been through.

But it wasn't that. She stood back in the street and stared at the building, with all that blown out debris on the sidewalk. And the more she stared, the more she was gripped by this frightening deja-vu.

• • •

Fran was in the candy store helping to stock shelves when Natalie arrived. Fran thought her quite duressed.

"I need to tell you and Eve something."

"Eve is lying down."

"It's very important, Fran."

Fran had Natalie wait on the landing on the first floor which was odd. The women came down to the landing, Eve remaining a few steps up.

"Bobby Lopez was shot to death last night."

The two women reacted with surprise. At least it had all the physical attributes of surprise.

"Do they know how it happened?"

"He was shot in an abandoned building not far from here. They don't know the motive. It wasn't robbery. He had drugs and cash on him." Natalie glanced from one woman to the other, as if they were all dealing with some secret matter. "A woman was seen in the alley not long after the shooting. They said she was wearing a dark coat, and maybe a dark hat. I don't know what other kind of description they have of the 'woman.'"

Natalie waited now, as if something more should happen, or be said. But both Fran and Eve were curiously silent.

After a time Fran asked, "Do the Dores know?"

"Not yet."

"I'll call them now. Mimi will have to be told."

Fran started back up the stairs to make the call, and Natalie said to Eve, "The pictures you took of that building I saw. I could swear it was the same building where Bobby Lopez was killed."

• • •

As much as the Dores wanted Bobby Lopez punished for what he had done, as much as they were privately satisfied he was dead, they made everyone sit around the dining room table, hold hands, and pray God have mercy on his soul.

Fran would have none of it.

Later, Fran overheard Mimi ask Eve, "We'll be all right now, won't we?"

CHAPTER 120

WHEN EVE WALKED INTO Fran's kitchen that night, Fran was wrapping the gun that killed Bobby Lopez back up in its bloodied rags. Fran slipped the bundle into a small brown paper bag.

"I didn't mean for you to have been the one to do this."

Eve's old blue coat was draped over a kitchen table chair. Fran worked the paper bag into one of the coat pockets.

——What are you doing?

Fran was not wearing her glasses which caused her to squint, and even though she couldn't see well, her eyes had a piercing sharpness to them.

"In the morning I intend to go to the police and tell them I shot him."

——What?

Fran reached for a lit cigarette in an ashtray on the sink. Eve came over and shook Fran's arm, ——Explain.

Smoke blew out of Fran's nostrils in thick gray lines. "I never had any intention of walking away from the act. I always planned to turn myself in for killing that shit."

Fran walked around Eve whose eyes followed in stunned disbelief.

"I should have killed the bastards that came after Max and me. I should have killed Romain before he took your mother. I believe killing Mr. B-fuckin-Lo was right. I believe the act was right. Just as I believe what I'm going to ask you is right."

Fran opened a cabinet. As usual, she filled a glass with scotch leaving room for only the barest amount of ice.

——Are you doing this because you think they'll find out it's me?

Fran drank down some scotch. She touched her mouth. "Didn't you understand?"

——I just didn't believe it.

"Believe me."

——I'm not afraid. I'd go turn myself in rather—

Fran swiped at Eve's hands. "You're twenty-four goddamnit. You have a whole life ahead of you. I have a whole life behind me."

——That's not an answer.

"Mimi wants you, she needs you. She'll need you more as time goes on. More than she'll need the Dores. And the Dores, they're not young either. They'll come to rely on you. I'm fifty-four. I wouldn't have the strength or the years for all that. These are the practical reasons, but they are not the most profound reasons."

Eve put out her arms, as if pleading to understand.

Fran looked into her glass, she drank. She put the glass down, she put the cigarette down. She leaned back against the stove. Her face was tense. She was reaching into herself to find the most direct way to explain the territory of her soul.

"When my mother was dying, years after my father had passed on, she came to lay in my bed beside me. She thought she would pass on that night, and she wanted to…" Fran's head shook a bit, as if to keep from being overwhelmed by the moment. "…She wanted to die in my arms. She wanted me holding her when the end came. It was an act of love you have to experience to understand completely. That moment—"

Fran needed more scotch, because she needed more time really, to let the memory settle into that place where you can explain it. "We lay in the dark and she told me the only other experience in life that felt of such intimacy and love and meaning was when you give someone life."

The word "life" was just barely, gently, formed on her lips. "That," said Fran, "I haven't had. The chance for that experience was stolen from me, taken against my will, against my hopes, my dreams, my needs."

Fran reached for her cigarette again. In those small pauses, with their uneven fragments of expression and naked look of wear, Fran held fast to one idea.

"Let me do this, because in its own way…it would let me give you life."

Eve now saw, she now understood.

"It's something I can take with me. That would be a form of completion." Fran's mouth began to draw in, she fought back crying. "I could get a chance now to be, truly, a mother. To be…your mother."

Eve could only grasp the front of Fran's dress to shake her till she saw, and knew.

——What do you mean? You're as much my mother—

Fran grabbed Eve's hands. "Don't say it. Not now. Just let me do it."

——You want me to let you go to prison for something I've done?

"I've never really asked you for anything that would hurt to give."

——No. And sometimes I wish you had. Because I would have given and given and—

Fran made the sign for——Forever. "I'm asking you now."

Eve buried her face in her hands, shaking her head. She did not want this, she did not want this. Fran came over and pulled those hands away.

"Even if they don't know…now. Even if we got away with it…now. We could be looking over our shoulders for years. It would then be like the years we compromised with Romain, the years we had to deal with Bobby Lopez. We don't need that. We're strong enough to fight this. And defiant enough to survive it."

CHAPTER 121

ON THE LANDING IS where they said goodbye. Fran had Eve's old blue coat folded over one arm. Eve held Fran's face in her hands. She ran her fingers along Fran's cheeks down to her mouth. All those years of lines from taking care.

Eve brushed away strands of hair from the corner of Fran's glasses. She was looking for any little thing to keep them together a little while longer.

"Take photographs of all of it. Me in court. Me leaving. All of it."

Fran reached down. Eve's camera was in her other hand, the one the coat had been covering.

"All of it," Fran repeated. "Remember in the car with your father."

It was, Eve understood, Fran's way of saying no matter what, keep on. Use this, to keep on. Make something of this to know you're keeping on.

When Fran got down to the landing, she turned back to look at Eve. The light, coming through the opaque front door glass left a white-gauze square on the hallway floor by Fran's feet, broken only by the shadow of the iron bars across the window. Mute testimony, that Eve captured, of what lay ahead.

• • •

Fran was going to turn herself in at the 48th, which was just under the shadow of the Cross Bronx Expressway, the road that had cut the Bronx in half and altered, for good, the lives of untold neighborhoods. It was also the precinct house they'd come to when Clarissa went missing.

Within sight of the precinct house on Washington, there was a church. Fran had no idea if it was Catholic, Protestant, or whatever else was going around at the time, but she found herself pausing there on the sidewalk, and not out of reluctance at turning herself in.

The church was empty but for her. It had that closed and candled oppressiveness that reminded her of the gothic mausoleums she's been weaned on in Germany.

At the altar she stood looking up at the crucifix on the back wall, with one private thought. She began to put on Eve's coat. It was a little too loose and long. She rolled the sleeves back up just a bit.

And while looking into that scourged and dying icon, and all it was supposed to mean, Fran said, "At the very least...*I'm real.*"

• • •

Inside the 48th it looked like rush hour on the subway. Every officer booked up with some kind of headache. Fran wasn't the type of person anyone paid much attention to in a precinct house, so she had to corral some young beat cop who was shuttling by.

"Excuse me. I...I'm here to turn myself in for the murder of Bobby

Lopez."

The officer's face drew up into that cynical Bronxy stare. Then Fran, very matter of fact, took the paper bag from her pocket. She opened the bag and slid out into the palm of her hand the gun wrapped in its bloodied rags.

. . .

A 54-year-old Bronx resident and shopkeeper guns down drug dealer—that was the lead story on all the news stations.

Investigators searched the candy store and apartments and came away with a few boxes of superficial or meaningless evidence. Eve was questioned through an interpreter. These were long and clumsy sessions with answers Eve had rehearsed in her mind. Never once did the investigators assume a deaf girl, handicapped as she was, could have had an active part in such a homicide.

And the incident where she was attacked by Bobby Lopez in the hallway of his mother's apartment, that "provocative" incident, in investigators' minds, only added further motive as to why Fran Kuhl took it upon herself to commit murder. But in the end, it was the gun and Fran's confession that were the lock.

There was a revolving door of reporters and news stories. Life laid bare. Fran Kuhl, who was she and how did she come to commit this violent act. All except for Natalie, who was in the throes of a deeply personal and ethical conflict, as she was certain, in *her* mind, it was Eve who had killed Bobby Lopez.

As Fran waited with calm perseverance for her trial she began to receive letters—many, many letters—from people all over the Bronx, and later the country, who had read about her case.

They were not mere letters of support. They were a human document of the victimized, of those who had to deal with the shapeless anxieties of their times, whose needs went far past prayer. They lived in tenements and decent homes, they were mothers and seamstresses who cut cloth in grimy basement spaces and waitressed in luncheonettes. They worked in beauty parlors, in supermarkets, and even at the courthouse itself.

And what those letters had in common, the through line of connected emotion, was that the writers had been living with a sense of hopeless unfairness about the world. But when they read of Fran's life, leading up to the moment she walked into the 48th Precinct, they felt an energy moving through them, something that might transform their sorrows, annul the discrepancies of the past. How her defiant struggle through actual sorrow gave them faith as they fought to create a democratic change in the landscape of their own lives.

Words such as mercy and leniency, phrases such as mitigating circumstances, began to move like chess pieces upon the legal battlefield in the state's prosecution of Fran Kuhl.

· · ·

Days before the trial Natalie came to see Fran. Separated by a glass wall, they talked on the phone.

"It wasn't you," Natalie whispered. "I have an ethical responsibility to the truth."

Fran was wearing a plain blue smock. She took off her glasses. Her face was firm, though tired.

"You're only twenty-six, you'll find there's an awful lot of truth left to go."

With that Fran hung up the phone, kissed her fingers to the glass, and went back to her cell.

· · ·

In February of 1976 a jury settled on convicting Fran Kuhl of second degree-manslaughter. She was sentenced to the State Correctional Facility for a term of no longer than five years.

Though the prosecution had been defeated in their demand for a much harsher sentence, there was a silent breath of relief at the judge's ruling as the tide of public favor was against them.

When Fran was asked if she had final words to say to the court, she turned and signed to Eve, ——— I-L-Y.

THE HEADSTONE

Chapter 122

Fran faced her time in prison with an almost monastic nobility. Because of all she'd been through—her raising the child of a drug dealer, the scars on her stomach, her age, the notoriety of her case—she was granted a certain status among the prisoners. She became the respected icon who approached every day with dignity, the mother whose self was still intact, the matriarch of compassion and defiance who younger women could go to, to deal with their inner demons, their cries of despair, their rage, and the need to readdress their lives.

Because of her years growing up in a school for the deaf and living through a time when the disabled were disregarded, if not utterly destroyed by the state, Fran, better than most understood the problems of inmates who were handicapped, disabled, infirm and aged.

She began to make suggestions to the authorities; these, in turn, begat more complete outlines, and these begat letters to local editors, and these begat, in time, the backbone of published articles in respected journals which became the groundwork for her life after prison.

The artful hand of fate, along with the inner strength of her character, had turned Fran's punishment into something of profound value.

In 1979, a little over three years after she had been imprisoned at the Bayview Correctional Facility, Fran Kuhl was paroled.

• • •

Coming home. The day the locked door closed on her for the last time, the first breath of sunlight that was hers and hers alone, the ride home with the people she loved, holding Eve's hand for as long as she wanted—through all this, Fran recalled part of a letter the father of an inmate had sent his only child. In it he wrote:

The simple majesty of life is bearing sorrow, with an eye toward forever.

They had a coming home party in Fran's apartment, which was exactly the same as the day she'd left it.

Napoleon, holding up a bottle of scotch, asked Fran, "Drink?"

"Oh, yes," said Fran.

"How much do I fill the glass?"

With a grin that bordered on the devilish Fran answered, "About three years and four months' worth."

• • •

For the next ten years Fran lived to see Eve's career and life flourish. Unlike Fran, Eve had moved on from the past. She and Dean Harlan had a long-term relationship, though Eve's sense of independence, and aloneness, precluded marriage, or even living with someone.

Fran was there to see the changing relationship of the deaf and the world around them, and how technology enhanced the landscape of their choices.

She was there as the Bronx went through a rebirth. Razed buildings were replaced, blocks taken back. Places of history and elegance that had fallen into disrepute were cared for back into new usefulness.

Fran was there when Mimi graduated from Gallaudet University, and when she moved in with Eve and began her teaching career at Lexington.

Oh…the future is forever busy.

• • •

In 1989 Fran Kuhl was diagnosed with cancer. After all possible treatments failed to stop the ravaging of her flesh, she was sent home to die. She asked Eve, one night, if she might sleep beside her.

As they lay in bed Eve asked,——I know you don't believe in God. But, do you ever wonder what it was that brought you to that particular mass on Christmas Sunday when a little deaf girl walked up to the altar?

Without hesitation, as if the answer were a matter of public record Fran said, "That, I leave to everyone else."

——Do you know what I think?

"Tell me."

——I think on that particular day, as Mother believed and would say, God was watching.

Fran kissed her child and said no more.

As they lay in the warm dark with the windows open, with Fran resting her head on Eve's shoulder, Eve knew. The frail body against hers, the flesh little more than dried-out paper, the labored breathing, Fran had come to die in her arms.

Eve took Fran's hand, and as Fran slipped toward the ephemeral darkness that shuts all human eyes, Eve wrapped her hand around Fran's so they formed one sign——Forever.

Eve could feel, lying there through the hours, Fran's breathing begin to slow. Moonlight fell about her bed in gentle evidence of time and Eve watched the face that had been so beautiful to her, slip on, the hand within the hand, soften to nothingness.

Eve's heart began to fill with mortal longing that someone who she had loved so much, who had been so much of her life, was no more. She began to whimper into her pillow, but at the same time, at the very same time, there was within her a measured peace, somehow profound and imperishable, she could not imagine words for.

• • •

Fran was buried at St. Raymond's Cemetery in a plot she had bought years before. In her will she had given specific orders that she wanted Clarissa's name, her date of birth and death, to be carved into the stone beside her own. Below both was to be written:

WOMEN, SISTERS, FRIENDS

Eve did this but added one thing not in the will, but in her heart. The headstone was to read:

WOMEN, SISTERS, FRIENDS, MOTHERS

CREATOR,
PRESERVER,
DESTROYER

CHAPTER 123

FOR THE FIRST TIME SINCE she'd murdered Bobby Lopez, Eve took out the photograph of him dying that she had kept hidden away.

Using her TTY, she called Natalie to come over.

Eve had moved up to Fran's apartment. Her old apartment on the floor below was still her studio. It had always been Spartan, no furniture really. But now, there were photographs everywhere, stacked, spread out on the floor, thousands of them from when Eve first began with a camera.

"What is all this?"

——We're going to do a book. You tell the story in words. I with pictures.

"About what?"

Eve walked over to a card table in the corner of the room by a window where she would sit and smoke and think. On the table was a folder. From it she took a photo she then handed to Natalie.

Though it had been fifteen years, time had not conquered the power of the photograph at capturing the ferocious and violent moments before B.Lo was taken.

Natalie looked up from the photo, shocked, but not so shocked. After all this time she finally knew the truth, though she had been sure of it all the while.

She understood the repercussions this could have on Eve's life and was going to tell her so. But then, she also knew Eve.

• • •

The book and photographs were to encompass the story of their lives. And in her mind Eve had one photograph that would close the book, that would in a sense be a summation, a declaration, and a confession.

The months Natalie wrote, Eve emptied the living room studio. The wall across from the three huge windows was stripped and sanded till it shined, and then painted a sharp and flat white. It would be, so to speak, the canvas for her mural of photographs.

Eve set her camera on a tripod where the shot would be taken from. She began bit by bit placing one photo near another, arranging and rearranging, adding, subtracting photos. Some were vastly enlarged, others cropped dramatically. She took her American flag pillow, emptied it, then sheeted the casing to the wall.

At the far right of the mural, when you were looking at it from the camera's point of view, she had placed the photograph of Bobby Lopez. It had been reproduced on high-contrast paper to make it more striking, then cropped in a non-conforming way to draw the eye.

Natalie would often come by and discuss the book. The mural was about six feet high and fifteen feet long. From the camera's point of view, at the far left, there was a three-foot-wide space from floor to ceiling that had been curiously untouched.

Natalie had often asked what was to go there, but Eve would not tell her.

Eve collected up dumped license plates and junked signs. She used a metal cutter to excise letters of different shapes and backgrounds. And along the border of that empty space—almost framing it up one side, across the top, and down the other—she hammered the letters into the wall to make three words:

CREATOR
PRESERVER
DESTROYER

Eve stepped into the empty space and placed a photograph of Clarissa and Fran in spots she'd marked that were just higher than where her own shoulders would be. With night against the window, she sat at her table smoking and looking over the final workups. To her eye, she was ready.

Eve watched the sun move upon the windows. She took light meter readings off her arm along the length of the mural. She checked her camera, set the timer, then started to undress.

Before she began, Eve had read through book after book of murals, from Picasso's *Guernica* to the tiled walls of Asiatic temples, and found that in ancient times from Greece to India, God was sometimes represented as a holy trinity of women. One the Creator, one the Preserver, and one the Destroyer.

Eve stepped into that open space of mural and turned to the camera, with Clarissa and Fran's spirit portraits placed just above her shoulders.

As the timer clicked off, Eve let her arms extend down to her sides, palms outward. One hand signed the scarlet letter A. She bowed her head just enough to let the hair fall across her face.

This was her way of telling the world in a modern sense, in a real sense, in an honest sense, to her, Clarissa had been the creator by giving her life, Fran had been the preserver by caring for and protecting her against Romain, and now she was taking her rightful place as the destroyer, by admitting to the world she had murdered Bobby Lopez and that she could, as Clarissa and Fran had, stand naked before whatever fate may bring.